# Ben & the
# MOUNTAINS

Ben and the Mountains © 2024 Stephen Brown

Printed in Australia

Cover and internal design by Shawline Publishing Group Pty Ltd

First printing: August 2024

Shawline Publishing Group Pty Ltd

www.shawlinepublishing.com.au

Paperback ISBN 978-1-9231-7195-4

eBook ISBN 978-1-9231-7213-5

Hardback ISBN 978-1-9231-7224-1

Distributed by Shawline Distribution and Lightning Source Global

*Shawline Publishing Group acknowledges the traditional owners of the land and pays respects to Elders, past, present and future.*

A catalogue record for this work is available from the National Library of Australia

# Ben & the
# MOUNTAINS

## STEPHEN BROWN

# CHAPTER ONE

*Lost*

It was getting dark and colder, the wind was picking up, the light fading and light snow was beginning to fall. The temperature was plummeting, forcing Karen to admit to herself that she was lost and in real trouble. Needing time out for a few hours from her year twelve studies, she had walked into the steep wooded country, which she thought she knew, having ridden her horse in that area before. Becoming disorientated, Karen found that time and daylight had beaten her so she knew wasn't going to make it home tonight. Fortunately, she was wearing clothing for the walk, including cold-weather boots, windproof trousers, and a windproof jacket. She wore a woollen hat that she could pull down around her eyes for extra warmth.

The priority was to find shelter out of the weather. There were several small caves and rock overhangs in the area so she started to head for where she thought they were. She cursed herself for not carrying any matches with her as she normally did when out walking; she fought the panic rising within her as she tried to remain focused.

Just when she was out of control, a figure stepped out of the shadows, giving her a huge fright.

'You'd better come with me.' Karen immediately recognised the person as Ben from her same year at school. The introvert from school was wearing his familiar mid-length severe weather coat over the top of heavy woollen trousers, boots, foul weather gaiters and a broad-brimmed felt hat. It was not entirely unexpected to meet him out here as he was seldom seen around the town, only arriving or leaving town with a large rucksack on his back but she was still not happy to see him.

'Why would I want to go anywhere with you?' she said, none too pleased to see him.

'Because you are lost; it's getting dark and you need a place to spend the night. My guess is you were looking for the caves over there. If you come with me, you get a warm place, a warm meal and scalding black tea to wash it down with or you can do it alone.'

'What makes you think I'm lost?'

'Okay, you're not lost; my mistake. Have a good night,' Ben said as he turned away.

'Okay, I'm lost. You're right.'

'Righty-o then, you'd better follow me.'

'How do you know I was here? Were you watching me? If you were, what would you be up to? Have you planned this?'

'Pull your ego. Did I invite you here? I saw you are few hours ago and I thought you were okay. I was set up for the night and saw you a little while ago. Now I know you need my help so here I am, you lucked out big time. You got me, not James Dean. Are you coming or not?'

Karen followed him to a deep rock overhang, which was well sheltered from weather. When she sat down, she took in her surroundings; there was a small fire burning in a hole behind a stone wind barrier, a billy simmering on the edge, a covered pan settled on a small stand of rocks, the smell of which made her mouth water.

'Is there anyone else here?' she asked hopefully.

'No, and I'm not expecting anyone either. It is just you and me, I'm afraid,' Ben replied as she placed the pan back on the flames.

'So, what do we do now?'

'Now we eat and have a cuppa before the weather closes in properly.'

'Then what do we do?'

'Then we get some sleep and assess the situation and the weather in the morning. If the weather breaks, I'll walk you out.'

'And if it doesn't?'

'We'll cross that bridge in the morning.'

'Why can't we go now?'

'Because it is going to snow; this place will be in white out in a couple of hours and the track will be icy. As I said to you, it's going to get very cold in the next few hours. It will be far too cold and dangerous to attempt to walk out. Do you want some of this?' he asked, holding the pan up to her.

'Yes please, if you have some to spare,' Karen replied.

'There is plenty,' Ben replied, beginning to scoop half into a second pan.

'Were you expecting company?' Karen questioned.

'No, but I always carry and cook plenty, just in case. Here, take this,' Ben told her, handing her the second pan.

'Thank you. This smells great,' Karen replied even though the stew didn't look the best.

'It's okay. It tastes better than it looks.'

'I'm sure it does. What were you doing out here if you weren't out here spying on me?'

'I live out here. This is where I spend most of my time when I'm not at school or taking care of the animals at my place,' Ben replied as he sat down with his plate.

'You live here?' Karen asked before tasting the stew.

'That's what I said, didn't I?'

'But why live out here alone? This is great, by the way.'

'It's where I belong.'

'But that's just it. Out here you belong to no one and nothing.'

'I belong to people like you, who get lost wandering around out here.'

'So, all the stories about you really are true?'

'What stories?'

'About you living and knowing this country.'

'They're just stories.' He shrugged.

'Well, they'll pale into insignificance when it gets out that we spent the night together.'

'And how is anyone going to know?' Ben questioned.

'When you walk me out.'

'Still doesn't answer my question; I'm only taking you as far as familiar country. You will be on your own after that. No one is going to see me with you and I'm certainly not going to tell anyone.'

'Then how do I explain how I survived the night?'

Ben threw her a box of waterproof matches. 'You never go anywhere without them,' he told her.

'So that it? I just tell them I found a cave, lit a fire and settled down for the night?'

'Exactly.'

'And what if they ask about you? Isn't anyone going to be looking for you?'

'Why would anyone be looking for me? I'm not missing,' he questioned.

'So, you are out on your own and no one knows or cares?'

'Your words, not mine,' Ben replied, which killed the conversation, the two of them contenting themselves with eating tea.

'Where do we sleep?' Karen asked, breaking the silence.

'You take the back, where it's warmest. I'll stay here and keep the fire going.'

'You aren't going to try anything, are you? I'd rather you be honest and we deal with it now than have to fight it out later.'

'You have nothing to fear from me, now or ever but you are free to leave any time you want or I will leave. I can find another place if it really bothers you.'

'No, it's okay. So, what drives you out here? And don't tell me it's where you belong. At school, you are so elusive and cut off from everyone. What is it that creates such distance?' Karen challenged.

'That is best left unknown. In the morning, you will be back with your family and all this will be is a distant memory.'

'So, I spend the night alone with you and all it is to you is a distant memory. What happens at school?'

'Nothing happens at school, it's just another day, and you don't even have to acknowledge my existence,' Ben told her.

'But you want me to though, don't you, given this little secret of ours?'

'I don't want anything from you or anyone else; is that so hard? I just want to be left alone and be allowed to fade in the background. My only ambition is to be invisible for a few months and then we don't ever have to see each other ever again. Please, give me that much,' he begged her.

'You not just talking about me, are you? Is that how it is with you; being invisible?' she questioned.

'I just said so, didn't I?'

'Yes, you did. You really want to be alone.'

'I am alone; let's just leave it at that, shall we?' Ben told her.

Later, she slept under Ben's blanket, staring out at the snow falling in the moonlight. She watched Ben sitting in front of the fire, leaning his back against the rock wall, looking into the night.

'Do want me to take a turn watching the fire?' Karen asked at one point.

'No, you sleep. You have a big day in the morning,' he said without turning to look at her, his shoulders huddled beneath a heavy coat. He dozed; he was in his element.

\*

In the morning, Karen woke to the smell of breakfast cooking in the first light of the morning. 'Good, you're awake. We'll grab some breakfast and get you out of here before it snows again,' Ben told her.

Karen folded the blanket before joining him, grateful for the coffee and bacon and beans.

'So, what's the plan this morning?'

'The same as yesterday: to get you to a point where you can get home. I'll head you in the direction that I expect any search party to come from to improve the odds of intercepting them.'

'You are not going down to meet them then?'

'No reason to. They will be looking for you, not me,' Ben told her.

'So, you want me to lie for you?'

'I'm not asking you to do anything. It does not phase me what you tell them, but given your concerns last night, I can't see why you would want anyone to know I was with you.'

'You're right. Will they believe me, do you think?'

'They have no reason not to; you are a very resourceful, intelligent person. I can't see why they wouldn't. Come on, it's time we got going,' he told her.

When they had packed up, Ben led her through the bush, apparently without direction, for almost an hour before anything even vaguely looked familiar. Then, without warning, he stopped beside a big rock on the edge of the track at the top of a low ridge.

'You can take it from here; Daly's hut is at the bottom of the gully.

Any search team will be moving out of there from there shortly. All you have to do is walk down to them and you're home.'

'So, that's it? You are just going to walk away?'

'That's the idea,' Ben replied before turning his back on her and walking away without a backward glance.

There was nothing she could do but walk down towards the hut where she met a small group of searchers moving up the hill towards her. She was greeted with great enthusiasm by a team who expressed immediate confidence that she would be okay. Being well-dressed for the weather her story of finding shelter and lighting a fire to keep her warm was accepted without question. If some of the older bushmen back at the hut were a little sceptical, they kept it to themselves. As Ben had said, no one asked after him as they concentrated on recovering Karen and returning her to her parents.

\*

Returning to school, her reputation for self-reliance and initiative was only enhanced, her friends welcoming her back from her overnight adventure with great enthusiasm. It was a story that made the school magazine one of survival of being self-reliant, a lesson for everyone. Karen was embarrassed by the attention but knew she had to keep her word to Ben not to tell of his part in her survival.

Almost unnoticed, Ben slipped quietly into school just as the first bell went. He was wearing an old mid-length oil skin coat and polished walking boots with course grey school trousers. His head bowed; his eyes, when they were visible, were sad. During the excited conversation, Karen heard comments questioning Ben's real ability to survive under similar circumstances despite apparently heading into the hills most weekends. Karen hated the talk and looked to Ben, who refused to make eye contact with her, preferring to keep his head bowed and remain as invisible as possible.

During the days and weeks that followed, Karen looked out for Ben. While everyone had some place in the social sphere of the small year twelve group, Ben remained isolated from everyone. He talked to no one unless spoken to first and then his replies were always very short if not abrupt.

In class, he sat alone in the back of the room, known by everyone as Ben's corner. At lunchtime, he ate in a quiet corner of a classroom before finding an even quieter corner of the library. He attended none of the social functions and got by the compulsory ones by engaging in menial tasks. For the most part, he was silent and lost in the background; he was, as he said, invisible. When questioned in class, his ideas were far from backward but often showed great insight into the world about him. He became slightly animated his when asked to express a view and his answers spoke of a hidden intelligence and understanding that few could match. It was not seen as a positive by others in the class but a sign of arrogance as he kept his knowledge and views to himself. It was his eyes that haunted her; she saw them whenever she thought of him or on the rare occasions he made the briefest eye contact with her. As she watched, Karen realised that few took any notice of him, not wanting to know the person behind the mask.

# CHAPTER TWO

## *Mountain rescue*

That winter was as cold as anyone could remember with icy winds bringing snow showers down from the mountains. When it wasn't snowing, moisture-laden air swept the valley in the form of drizzle or showers saturating the ground and chilling the air making for low to freezing wind chill. Sporting events were cancelled or moved to locations closer to the coast where the weather was not as harsh. The schools struggled with continuous wet weather timetables and extra measures had to be put in place to conduct any outdoor event.

The school cross-country run had to be shortened and SES personnel lined the course with a number of students succumbing to the conditions. Ben was called aside with the recovery team headed up by Mountain Rescue. They patrolled the course on horseback in the bush, each capable of stabilising a patient while the other members joined them to complete the recovery. Seeing Ben on horseback with his long Driza-Bone coat and brimmed hat gave most a sense of security knowing he was there but others were cautious and did not want to be rescued by him because they did not want to be physically close to him.

'How's it going?' Karen asked when he pulled up at one of the checkpoints.

'Good from our point of view but a lot of them are doing it tough out there. Keep an eye out for Bell, she is really doing tough but she is determined to finish. Deb is walking because of the weather rather than injury but we are keeping an eye on her.'

'How are the guys going?'

'Good so far; two are out so far but the rest are hanging in there. Rob is riding with Nick but he's okay for now. I'm about to head back to the bank to see the last of the group off that then I'll follow them in. I'll see you back at the finish.'

'Okay, take care out there,' Karen told him as he headed back into the bush.

They all got through what was one of the toughest cross-country events in years. While everyone huddled around the heaters at the finish, Ben rode in behind the last runner ever vigilant over his charge. Gary was applauded as he ran the last few meters to the finish while Ben watched then turned his horse back to the SES rooms where he would join the others for some food and an immediate debrief. As much as he was part of the community, he was part of the adult world in ways that others could only aspire to.

Everyone else went about their jobs as best they could with road maintenance teams kept busy with minor flooding and clearing landslips from roads and drains. Again, his skills were called upon to check some of the more isolated assets such as bridges for which he was paid bringing in some income for himself. Few of the students did not understand why he was asked and not them but everyone also knew that he could be relied on and he could survive out there so few others were going to get a look at the job.

Of those who did notice Ben's absence, they joked of it being too cold for him, but Karen suspected otherwise. It was not unusual for Ben to be missing from school from time to time and while his teachers showed no concern, they offered no explanation to the rest of his class. As it turned out they usually knew where he was. He would either call in or those he was with would do the same. Ben was often gone for a couple of days before he was noticed missing and could be back a day before his return was equally unnoticed.

While the snowfields enjoyed an early and plentiful snowfall, the lower mountains were no place to be wandering. Despite that, Ben was missing at the same time as a bushwalking group from one of the universities became lost to the north-west of the town when attempting to walk from the snowline. The conditions were so bad that local SES and police were restricted in their ability to operate, leaving the searching to the most experienced bushmen in the form of Mountain Rescue led by a legendary figure of the high-country, Jack Carmodia. The ability of Mountain Rescue to remain in the field independent of outside assistance and to operate in the worst of conditions was well-known but reputation counted for little in this weather.

Ben had been out with the search teams a couple of times and had returned to town to collect a pack horse with fresh food and foul weather gear as conditions continued to deteriorate. Once he was set up, he went to the rescue centre to be on standby when he was needed. While he was waiting, he listened intently to the radio traffic and monitored the movement of the searchers on his own maps. After listening for some time, he asked and gained permission to talk to Jack on the radio, suggesting that they search a ridge and gully line outside the search area. There was some argument over the airways until Jack got on the radio and told everyone to shut up so that he could listen to Ben. Over the airways, they listened to Ben state his reasons.

'What are you going to do, Ben?' Jack came back.

'I'm going to get my gear together and head there now. I should be in the area around last light so if they are there, I can hopefully make contact.'

'You're that sure of that location?' Jack questioned.

'Well, we know they aren't in the current area and the last description they gave of their surrounds sounds like only one other place and that's where I'm heading now,' Ben replied.

Not everyone agreed and there were further arguments over the airwaves but Jack overruled them.

'We go with Ben's plan; he may just be right and right now, we have little to lose,' Jack told everyone.

'And how do you figure that, Jack? This kid gets a hunch and you follow it. Do you follow the hunch that every tea-reading kid gives you?' a police sergeant asked him.

'I've known Ben for a few years now. He is one of the most observant and knowledgeable people I know when comes to this stuff and I've learnt to trust his instincts in the same way he has. Right now, his hunch, his instincts are all we have. That's the end of it,' Jack replied and gave a rally point for where they were to meet. It took five hours in the worst possible conditions to find the group where Ben met them. It was a long way from the best estimates of their last known position and well outside the expected search area.

Hours later, the first radio reports reached base.

'We've found them; Ben has dropped us right on top of them,' Ed Wild called back from the teams' new camp.

Ben jumped to assist with those in most need of assistance. He got a fire going immediately to generate some warmth for the victims as the teams assisted in drying them off and getting them into emergency dry clothing. He heated some stones, put them inside a rescue bear and gave it to a young woman who was struggling to beat the cold that had entered every part of her body. The young woman was suffering from severe hypothermia and Ben knew they had to get her out tonight if she was to survive.

'Hold this close; it will help get you warm quicker,' Ben told her as he pressed into her hands and then folded them under the thick emergency blanket.

'What's your name?' the woman asked through chattering teeth.

'Ben,' he replied as worked to secure her to a cradle as she was incapable of walking and would have to be carried out.

'You got a last name?' she stammered.

'I'm just Ben,' he replied as he secured the harness straps over the waterproof sheet he had draped over.

'Okay, Just Ben, thank you. I might just make it out of here tonight.' She blinked, fighting back tears.

'No might about it, you will make it. You'll be in a safe warm hospital bed in a couple of hours,' Ben assured her.

'You believe that, don't you?'

'We've spent a lot of time trying to find you; we are not going to let you down now,' he assured her.

'It is us who has let you down; we are not where we told you we were?' she questioned.

'That is of no consequence now,' Ben assured.

'How did you find us?' she questioned, holding out her hand to him.

'We got real lucky tonight,' Ben replied as he grabbed the covers over her in preparation to move her.

*

It was well after dark before they could stabilise them enough to start walking them out.

He indicated that many in the group were in the final stages of hypothermia, forcing Mountain Rescue to carry them out. The SES had set up a reception centre at the closest point in the forest that they could get vehicles into given the conditions. When they got into the reception centre, the group received further treatment to further stabilise them before they could be transported to hospital.

When the ambulance left, the rescue team themselves had to be treated for cold and fatigue, and everyone changed into dry coats. They were all then given some hot food before the teams were then able to begin the long ride back to town with their horses. They were soaked through for a second time by the time they made their way to town.

It had been a tiring and lengthy rescue by any standard, pushing the entire emergency services to their limit, which gained national attention from the media. It was not the attention that Jack sort or welcomed so it suited him to return to town in the middle of the night through misty rain and fog the riders hidden beneath broad-brimmed hats and long riding coats. A lot of people came out to meet them and assist them in their own recovery at SES headquarters where various axillaries waited with hot food, showers and warm clothing for the riders while others attended to the needs of their horses including two vets who donated their time to the team.

Karen worked with her mother on auxiliary, preparing for their arrival, ensuring that every rider was processed as quickly as possible. She watched Jack as he inevitably waited for the last rider to secure their horse and gear before following them into the hall.

'Well done, Ben. Those people owe their lives to you. We all owe you a great deal of thanks,' Jack told him as he helped him with his horse.

'Just doing my job, boss,' Ben replied weakly.

'If only everyone did their job as well as you, Ben, we would all be in a better place. Make sure you make it to the debrief on Wednesday and write down your reasons for looking in that location,' Jack told him.

'Will do, Jack,' Ben replied.

It was only then that Karen noticed that Ben was among them, the last rider in; his face drawn with cold and fatigue after hours in the cold. He looked up as he accepted a blanket from her and let her lead him to a chair by the open fire.

'Thank you,' he offered weakly as he slumped in the chair, steam soon rising from his sodden clothing.

SES members soon assisted Ben and the rest of the team in stripping and showering in order to warm up before returning to the main room dressed in orange overalls and wrapped in blankets where Karen and other members of the auxiliary served them hot soup. Ben looked up at Karen with sunken eyes when she placed the soup in front of him, too tired to eat so she sat with him and began to feed him.

'Thank you,' he offered.

'I thought you might have been with Jack. It must have been rough out there.'

'It was unbelievable. Another few hours we would have been bringing out bodies, not bushwalkers,' he said with a voice etched with sheer exhaustion.

'Listen, I'm really sorry about my attitude from the other week. I apologise.'

'Thank you but you don't have to apologise. I understand the concerns you had at the time.'

'Still, I should have trusted you.'

'It's alright. You did in the end and you know you can now,' Ben told her.

'Yes, I can, thank you. Your father must be so proud of the work you do with the team,' Karen offered.

'He doesn't know; I haven't seen him for over a year and certainly not expecting to see him any time soon,' Ben told her in an unguarded moment.

Karen was shaken by the comment because it meant he was living alone as some had suspected and possibly for some time.

'Ben, I am so sorry. Is there anything I can do?'

'You can keep that information to yourself. No one needs to know.'

'If that's what you want, I won't tell anyone. Is there anything else at all I can do? I had no idea you were doing it so tough.'

'You can stop feeling sorry for me for starters; I'm doing okay.'

'But that's just it; you're not.'

'Not by anyone else's standards, perhaps, but I'm okay. I've been doing this for a long time,' Ben replied.

'How long?'

'Years but it doesn't matter. You are not to tell anyone,' he said, grabbing her arm to make sure she understood.

'I won't. You can trust me,' Karen told him, meeting his gaze and gently placing her own hand over his.

'I know I can. Thank you.' He nodded, offering a faint smile – the first time she had ever seen him smile.

Just then, Jack's wife tapped her on the shoulder. 'It's okay. We'll take care of him; you see to the others,' Maureen told her gently.

Karen left him to assist other team members who were all equally in need of comfort. While she was working, she realised so much made sense to her about Ben and why he kept everyone at a distance. While everyone struggled with parents and siblings, Ben was doing it alone. His self-reliance and arrogance were his own way of coping with the isolation of his home life.

Another thing that occurred to her was that if he rode with Jack Carmodia in such conditions, it was because he was accepted by a unique group of people to whom hardship was a way of life. Jack was a man who often lived as the men who settled the country, spending many weeks of the year living in isolated mountain huts tending cattle. He was a hard man but his friends were loyal and loyalty ran deep. There was a toughness about Ben, every bit as hard as Jack, yet there was a fragility about him too that was hidden, deeply hidden, she thought.

The following day, Ben was back at school looking more tired and drawn than usual but few knew that he had been part of the rescue team. His un-ironed shirt and worn jumper made him look more drab than usual. The warm room and the effort of the last few days caught up with him and he began to lose concentration and doze off. At one stage, he fell asleep at his desk.

'Hey, Ben is so boring he's put himself to sleep,' someone called, which brought laughter to the room, waking Ben with a start.

'Don't wake up on our account,' Rick said, which brought more laughter.

'That is enough,' their teacher, Emma Dennison, snapped at the class. 'Ben, go home and get some rest. Don't come back until you have recovered,' she told him.

Ben didn't need to be told twice and almost tripped himself up as he fled the classroom to the snickers of others in the room.

Emma turned to the rest of the class. 'Right, the rest of you can sit down and be quiet. You all judge him but he puts a lot into this community. While you were in here complaining about the cold and joking about it being too cold for Ben to be at school, he was out there with Jack's group in the worst of it, rescuing people he doesn't even know. You all think about that and show him a little respect. More than most of you, he has earned it,' she told them.

A few days later, everyone stopped at the café on the way home. Everyone was sitting around having a snack and talking when Jack Carmodia walked to buy some tobacco. Rodney Steiner saw the moment to gain a few points with his classmates at Ben's expense.

'Hey, Jack, I heard Templeton was your horse boy. Now, if you ever need more than a horse boy, I'm your man,' he called.

At first, Jack did not respond but turned slowly to look at him.

'Is that a fact?' he said, looking at him with complete contempt. 'Two things; only my friends call me Jack and you are not one of them. Second, only the very best lead my pack horses and that is why Ben leads them and you never will. He has a place at my campfire any day of the week. Now, if I ever need a circus act, I'll be sure to give you a call but if I want real work done, I will call Ben, not you,' Jack said, sentencing Rodney for life because in Jack's world, there was no room for compromise. The room fell silent and remained that way after Jack left. Rodney's challenge had backfired in a big way and everyone was embarrassed for him and about him.

For Karen, who observed the encounter from a corner of the room, it helped her understand that many men longed to be counted in Jack's company but Ben was one of the few that did. For the rest of the year twelves, it just proved that Ben belonged to another time and era and was certainly not one of their own. It was like Ben was in a time warp, living rough with the horses rather than mixing with the others and planning a life away from country.

# Chapter Three

*The past catches up*

Later in the year, there was a social studies excursion to one of the mountains, working camps where timber mills and road gangs operated in the mountains. Ben sat alone on the minibus on the way up to the camp, watching the country go by, much as everyone expected but that was where expectation ran into reality and Ben ran into his past.

When they arrived at the camp, they were met by a Department of Natural and Resources Officer who spoke to them about the origins and function of the camp. He then handed out some maps of the camp and went through the safety procedures for the area.

'You should not go beyond the limits of the camp without a guide' – he indicated to the two DNRE rangers – 'or with Eric. He used to live in this camp and knows this area better than almost anyone.' He then gave them the opportunity to ask some questions. There was a little interest until with fairly predictable questions by students trying to be more interested, they were. When someone asked about some of the specifics of the social life of the camp, the head rangers passed the question to Ben, indicating that he had lived in the camp shortly before it closed. Ben had reluctantly replied with some great insights into camp life. It was all going so well until some asked about one low brick building not marked on the map.

'That was a cool room for the kitchen, I think,' one of the rangers said.

'But it's too far from the main kitchen and at the bottom of the hill,' someone indicated.

'Our records indicated that it was a cool room, that's all. It may have been of more general use.'

'It was used as a general cool room but it was also as the camp morgue,' Ben replied.

'How could you possibly know that? Did you ever see inside it?' someone asked.

'Yes, it was where they took my mother when she was killed in a car accident on the way here. That was the last place I saw her,' Ben replied and suddenly there were no more questions, everyone shuffling away in embarrassed silence. Left to stare down at the place he had seen her, he turned away and walked to a rise above the camp where he sat with his thoughts.

'I thought I'd find you here,' Karen said as she walked up to him.

'Yes, so you have,' Ben replied without looking up at her.

'This was the last place your family was last together, wasn't it? It must be tough being here.'

'Yes, it was. I have a lot of memories in this place; it was the last place I belonged.'

'And it was here that you started a different life with your father?'

'Yes.'

'It must hurt?'

'It was all a long time ago.'

'That's the problem though isn't it; it's like it was yesterday, isn't it?'

'Yes, but I'm okay.'

'But that's just it; you're not okay.'

'I'm doing alright. You'd better go before anyone catches you talking to me.'

'Okay, Ben, but I am not the enemy,' she said before she turned away.

'I know, Karen, I know,' Ben replied, knowing Karen could not hear him.

Later, he walked around the camp and through the old dining hall.

'What was it like eating dinner in this hall?' Ellen asked.

'It was an amazing sense of community; we spent many a night here singing songs over the piano.'

'You miss those days?' Ellen questioned.

'Yes, I do very much.'

'Were there any other children in the camp?' Ellen asked.

'No, no families were not supposed to live in the camp; we were only allowed because both my parents worked here. We should have lived away, probably at my current home but we had a house in the camp instead.'

'Weren't you lonely having no other children of your own age?' Ellen asked.

'No, I had younger siblings and had any amount of friends among the men and older women of the camp.'

'It sounds like you had some good times.'

'They were but that was then this is now.'

'And today is hard, isn't it?' Ellen asked.

Ben did not answer for a moment but just looked at her before he replied. 'Yes, it is, much harder than anyone could know.'

'You do have friends today if you need to talk. I'm here and so is Karen from what I've seen.'

'Thank you,' Ben replied and like Karen, saw for the first time deep pain in her eyes.

On the trip home, Ben was more distant than ever, haunted by the memories of that place. Nobody joked but nobody wanted to talk to him either. After observing Ben for a while, Karen was tempted to go and sit with him but knew enough of him to leave him alone rather than embarrass him with any sort of attention. Other students looked at him in a new light on the trip home as he struggled with his memories of a number, wondering if they would not be like Ben had they lost his family in the way he had. Despite knowing a little more of his past Ben remained isolated from the rest of the group. The reality was that while they knew a little of his past they did not want to know more because they had seen a glimpse of the sadness of his past they did not want to know more.

*

'What do you know of Ben Templeton?' Karen asked her mother that night.

'Not a real lot. He works for your father from time to time. In fact, he helped your brother and Ian mend and replace fences after last summer's bush fire burnt through our northern boundary fences. Why do you ask?'

'Just curious. There is a sadness about him that keeps everyone out of his life.'

'I know what you mean; there is a sadness about him. He has had a tough life since his mother's death. I suspect he spends a lot of time at home alone.'

'Can I ask why Ben doesn't come to the house when he is working on the farm? Has Dad banned him or something?'

'That's the odd bit; we have invited Ben to the house on many occasions but he always had reasons for not coming. It was Ben who made the rule about meeting Ian on the job, not your father. Ian speaks highly of him actually; he says that Ben is the hardest working and most reliable person he has ever had work for him.'

'I wondered about that.'

'You're not getting a thing for him, are you?'

'No point. He's not going to ever let anyone close enough. I also suspect that he will leave when this year is over and head up into the hills somewhere and then no one will find him.'

'You may well be right. There is not a lot keeping him here.'

'No and that is the sad part – he will leave and no one will really miss him because nobody knows him.'

'Others may not know him but he will be missed. He's put a lot into the community over the years. A lot of the older folk and those on the fringes have come to rely on him,' her mother said.

'That's true. He does relate to those on the fringes; it's just a pity that he cannot connect with people in the mainstream as well.'

'Well, that is his choice,' her mother replied.

'I know I just wish that someone had been able to connect with him,' Karen replied.

# Chapter Four

## *Challenged*

Spring brought with it warmer weather and renewed optimism. It also brought with it the realisation that their time at secondary school would shortly end. With employment extremely limited in the area, their time together and in the town was also limited. A few would work locally on farms or in family businesses but even that was limited without education. Perhaps because of this, there was a greater sense of unity in the group embracing everyone except Ben who remained isolated showing no interest in engaging anyone.

All the girls were sitting around talking when the conversation turned to the guys in their year. They talked about each of them with different intensities as some were admired for their look, sporting prowess and their looks. Ben was not exempt and Karen was interested to hear what the other girls thought of him.

'The thing that I don't like about Ben is that he pretends not to look at me but I know he does. He looks at me, they all do,' Carol said.

'Yes, we all know how irresistible you are,' Joy scoffed.

'If you've got it.' Carol smiled.

'Will you listen to yourself? Ben is not interested in you. He's not interested in anyone for that matter,' Ella said.

'Oh, he's interested alright, he just hides it better than the rest.'

'The problem is you think that way but he knows that you don't want him and he is not going to give you the satisfaction of looking or asking,' Ella told her, which was quite a statement from Ella who normally said very little.

'I think he has far too much on his mind to worry about any of us or what we think of him,' Tess said.

'What makes you say that?' Petra asked.

'My parents suspect that he has been living alone for years. They were talking to a logging contractor up north who apparently knows his father. He said that Ben's father works six days a week and only goes home a couple of times a year. Apparently, he sends money home to pay the bills but keeps to himself most of the time.'

'That certainly explains why he's so weird,' Petra said.

'He's not weird, just very lonely I would say,' Ella said.

'And since when did anyone listen to what you had to say anyway?' Carol snapped.

'Do you have to be a bitch all your life?' Ella snapped back her. Carol stood up to react physically to her but Ella stood her ground.

'Carol; sit down,' Petra warned.

'So, Mr Nobody has one fan, does he?' Carol said as she sat, knowing that Petra was not someone to be messed with.

'I think you'll find he has more than one,' Ella said before walking away.

\*

Most thought Carol would have left it at that but she challenged Ben a week before the dance. She approached him in the main corridor just before class so that she had a maximum audience.

'I've just come to tell you that if you were for going to ask me to the dance you were wrong. I wouldn't go with you if you were the only guy left,' she challenged.

'Good on you. One, I was never going to the dance in the first place. Second, why on Earth would you think I would ever ask you if I was? I don't like you. I don't like anything about you,' he told her.

'But that's where you're wrong. You want me.'

'Oh, obviously; how could anyone possibly resist you? Whatever was I thinking? And you think I have issues. You need to seriously get over yourself,' Ben told her before walking away, leaving her standing in the corridor.

'Bastard,' Carol yelled at him as a parting gesture.

'Ouch,' Ben replied grabbing his backside, which brought wails of laughter from the hall and a chorus of 'Hooray for Carol, hooray at last, hooray for Carol, she's a horse's ass.' This again brought more laughter.

'You deserved that, you stupid cow,' Petra snapped as she passed.

\*

Naturally, a huge amount of work had gone into the night and the hall was looking great because of that hard work. Sadly, no one worked harder than Ben, checking and repairing every table and chair before laying them out in the hall ready for it to be set up. He washed every inch of the hall and stage setting up the gear with the band. When it was ready and everyone went home to change, Ben simply went home.

'What are you doing?' Ella asked when she saw him mopping the stairs at the side of the stage.

'Helping out.' He shrugged.

'But you of all people don't have to do this, not if you aren't coming to the dance.'

'I know but you need a hand so I'm here.'

'Well, your help is much appreciated,' Ella told him, trying to catch his gaze but he did not raise his eyes to her.

'You're welcome,' Ben replied.

On the night of the dance, everyone dressed up in their finest to spend one great final night together. Naturally, the girls were to outdo each other, buying, creating and making the best outfits they could get together. Most of the guys didn't scrub up too bad escorting many of the girls but Ben was not one of them, going nowhere near the hall.

The ball was a great success for most. Carol arrived without a date and left the same way. Karen went with a group of girls and had a great time dancing with the girls and accepted a couple of dances with some of the guys. She missed Ben but was not sure why. Having spent a lot of time designing and then making her own gown, she wanted people to admire her but Ben did not even get to see it. A few of the students coupled up without giving them much of a chance of making it long term but they were happy enough at the time. Karen left with some of the others to have an after-ball party at her place where a few of the girls shared her room for the night, sleeping through most of the morning before returning to the hall to clean up that afternoon.

The next morning, Ben was back working to clean the mess that others had enjoyed making, getting a lot done before the others arrived. He cleared most of the tables and had already emptied most of the bins by the time the first of the other students arrived to clean up.

'Hey, Ben, what are you doing here? This is not your mess to clean up,' Petra said when she entered the hall.

'I know but it's got to be done, so I'm here.'

'But you don't have to be here,' she added.

'Yeah, but you know I can't be here for the dance so I'm here now.'

'I won't pretend to understand but thank you for your help. I appreciate it,' she told him.

'Not a problem,' Ben replied.

It was something that Karen could not understand about Ben was why he would contribute to an event he would not be part of.

'Why do you do it, Ben?' Karen asked in frustration when they stopped for coffee.'

'I contribute.'

'Contribute to what? To something you're not part of?' she questioned.

'But that is how I am part of it.'

'But you don't get to dance with anyone and no one is going to thank you.'

'But you're thanking me.'

'Yes, and only me and Petra. No one else cares.'

'Hey, don't worry about it. I'm not.'

'But you missed the dance.'

'Yes, I did. Mission accomplished,' Ben told her before walking away.

*

Carol could not let go after such a public humiliation of going to the dance without a partner, no one asking her after such a public display. She began to circulate damaging claims that she believed Ben was looking at her through her bedroom window at night. No one believed her but she hoped seeds of doubt were being sown nonetheless. Sometime later in the same café, she was telling the same story when Hans Muddle was at the counter buying his usual pouch of tobacco when he heard her talking.

He turned to her angrily and stood at the table where she was sitting with some of the other girls and slammed his fist on the table.

'You! Why you say such things? You say he looking through your window at night? When you say he look through you window?'

'Last Tuesday night, as a matter of fact. I saw him,' Carol snapped back.

'You lie,' Hans snapped, stabbing his finger at her. 'Last Tuesday, he my place. My goats, they escape onto road and police and ranger they call. I call but no one come, you know who come? Ben, he come. He not come to watch and laugh at Hans try to get back goats. No, he out in rain all night and not finish till all goats back in pen. He climbs into creek; he walks through bush and he help find everyone. He then stays and fix fence.

'I say to him thank you, I alone in this country. He says to me I not alone, you call and Ben come. He is a good man, a friend. He got no time to sit in café and look at you across the room at you like them,' he said, indicating the guys in the corner. 'Or look through window at you at night. There no one at home for him; mama dead, brother, sister dead. His father he away work timber all time. He lives alone. When I say to him Ben, please help, he not says he too busy he helps all night and morning go home, do his work then go to school.

'He got no time look through your window, he just trying to get through one more day. I say to him, you hungry you come my place any time, I give you to eat. I say to him, you tired I give you bed to sleep but he too busy, he goes home alone and he work so no one take him away because Papa neglect him,' Han said with a tear in his eye.

'You not like him because he not like you, he not sits here with milkshake or nice coffee and look at you. He needs nice girl like Ella or Karen, not you. When you cook him meal and talk to him, when hang clothes on line for him, cut grass or cut wood for him on weekend.' He asked everyone, 'When any of you say, friend, I help? No, you laugh at him and you call him name just like you call me name. You think you so grown up but Ben already a man. He lives alone. No more lies,' Hans said again, stabbing his finger at Carol. The room was deathly silent after he left and slowly everyone left the café. No one said anything, even Carol said nothing being the last to leave. Her friends who owned the café refused to even offer a goodbye. Ben was left alone after that.

\*

Before the year ended, Karen rode out to one of the back paddocks to catch up with Ben while he was working for her father. When Karen arrived, Ian left them to it, driving back to the shed to pick up some more star pickets, having no concern about leaving them alone together.

'Are you coming to the end-of-year party?' she asked.

'No. I haven't been to anything before this; I don't see the sense in starting now,' Ben replied.

'You should come. It may be the last time to see everyone and say goodbye.'

'There is nobody I want to see or say goodbye to and I assume the feeling is mutual.'

'I think you might be surprised. Aren't you going to at least be there to say goodbye to me?'

'No, because we'll see each other again. We are practically neighbours and I'm sure you'll be home from time to time.'

'Doesn't it bother you that this part of your life is about to end and that you may not see the people you lived it with again?'

'I can't wait for this part of my life to end and believe me, no one has lived this part of my life with me, I have lived it very much alone.'

'Point taken. I feel sorry for you, Ben, you're letting the best years of your life slip by. There are so many occasions and friendships slip past you. If you let people in, they could help and be a real part of your life.'

'I tried and almost got crushed by people who thought they knew what was best for my life. You should also never feel sorry for me; I regret nothing,' he said with a voice etched with bitterness.

'What will you do when after you finish school?' Karen asked.

'I'll leave for a while and then I'll come back and see if I can make a go of this place if my father doesn't want to return.'

'And if he does want it, what will you do then?' Karen asked.

'I'll leave him to it and leave the district for good,' Ben replied.

'Where would you go?'

'Into the New South Wales Southern Highlands. There is plenty of mountain country where a man can live alone.'

'Let's hope that doesn't happen then. Will you share it with anyone, do you think?'

'I doubt there will be ever enough work for two people to take on anyone.'

'No, I meant a wife and a family maybe one day.'

'Get serious, no one is ever going to love me. You have a good life, Karen,' Ben said before abruptly turning back to his work on the fence he was pinning down.

She walked away for some distance and turned to look at him as he continued to work, having already blocked her from his thoughts. Not once did he look up at her. It never occurred to her that no one would love him. Apart from being disconnected, he was a decent person who cared enough to put his life on the line for strangers whenever he was needed. It broke her heart to think that someone would never look upon him and return that caring that he had in his heart and not love him.

＊

When the formal school year did end, everyone went wild and danced about the school. Students embraced each other and shook hands with their teachers. Few noticed Ben pick up his bag and walk away without a backwards glance.

'Doesn't he ever stop to say goodbye?' Joe said to Karen as they disappeared down the end of the street.

'No, I don't think he can,' Karen replied.

'How do you mean?'

'I think Ben was cut adrift from the world you and I know when his mother died and his father left him. I think he's already said goodbye to too many people in his life,' Karen replied.

'Do you really think he's been doing that hard?'

'I'm afraid so and I think none of us have the courage to ask, in case I'm right.'

'You may be closer than any of us think. He's missing out but then, so are we,' Joe said before turning away. The two girls stayed and talked for a while reflecting on what had been and what yet lay ahead.

＊

Everyone returned in casual clothes for the English exam. In the short time that elapsed since formal classes had ended, some had changed but none more so than Ben. Arriving on horseback, his hair was longer and his face unshaven. He wore heavy jeans, a rough shirt and a broad-brimmed hat over his eyes until he took it off and left it on his saddle bag. Making eye contact with no one, he walked back into the school, showing little interest in anyone. It was not that he was trying to impress anyone; he had just moved on, living out of the mountains somewhere.

'How's study going, Ben?' Ella asked as he passed.

'Good, thanks. There's no distractions where I am at the moment.'

'You're not at home then?' she asked.

'No, Devon's Hut,' Ben replied, which the locals knew as a dusty stockman's hut a good few hour's hard ride into the hills with only candles and an old log fire for light and a long drop toilet some distance away in the trees; certainly not a place anyone would like to stay.

'Did you ride down from there this morning? You must have left early.'

'Yeah, about five but it's great riding out into the sunrise at that hour of the morning,' he replied, Ella seeing a sparkle in his eyes before heading into the classroom she had not seen before. It occurred to her then that he had already moved on.

It was the same with all his other exams arriving with indifference, making only fleeting eye contact with the students he passed already so distant from everyone.

On the final days of exams, he rolled up with a pack horse in addition to his main ride. He left the horses hobbled in the paddock behind the school oval, taking time to ensure they were settled before securing his saddle and packs along the fence line.

'Going somewhere tonight, are you?' Tim asked as they were about to enter the hall.

'Looks that way.'

'You're not staying for the bonfire then?'

'Doesn't look that way, does it?' Ben replied.

'Why not? Everyone else is,' Tim questioned.

'Got places to go,' Ben replied then walked away.

When the last exam was over, Ben walked out to the paddock, loaded the horses and secured his saddle before taking a last look at the school that had been part of life for so many years. He then walked the horses out of the back gate before climbing into the saddle to begin the long climb into the hills.

'Where's he going?' Gayle asked Karen as she watched him leave.

'Away into the hills to begin with and then up north somewhere. Who knows if we'll ever see him again,' Karen replied.

'So, he's not going to say goodbye then?'

'No, he's leaving. He's already said goodbye in his own way.'

'How do you know?' Gayle questioned.

'I finally got him to talk these last few months. All he wants is for this year to be over and get as far away from this place as possible.'

'Did he really hate us that much?' Gayle questioned.

'It was not a matter of hating anyone. More a case of not connecting with anyone,' Karen replied.

'He's a strange one, that one.'

'A very lonely one, actually, life has not been kind to him,' Karen told her.

'I don't doubt it,' Gayle said.

For reasons Karen could not explain, she felt his isolation at the moment. She had failed to reach him and felt she never would. Having enjoyed every moment of secondary school, she felt Ben had lost and left behind just so much. As much as she was looking forward to moving on with the next stage of her life, she knew she would miss this place and could not imagine what it was like for Ben to just walk away without a backward glance.

As everyone celebrated around the bonfire that night, Karen looked to the hills when she saw the light of a campfire on a rocky outcrop high above the town. She imagined it was his way of saying goodbye and that he was okay. She knew his campfires were normally hidden away from the work. She thought of Ben sitting beside the fire looking down upon everyone. She knew he would stay up there tonight and look down on the celebrations of the end of their secondary school education and consider whatever was going on as lost. Part of her wanted to be up there with him if only to have someone to share the event with him but she did not want to miss this night with the people she had spent most of her life with.

In the morning, he would be gone and she wondered if she would ever see him again.

# CHAPTER FIVE

## *The missing years*

Ben disappeared after that. The house was locked up and the horses he didn't take with him were passed to other properties to care for. He had dropped by Karen's place when he knew that she would not be there to tell Ian that he was heading north with a couple of packhorses and would be gone for some time, possibly years. Ian told her that he had two good horses and appeared to have plenty of provisions. Nobody knew exactly where north he was going other than he was going via the mountains in the hope of picking up work along the way.

Karen went by his house to see what had become of it only to see it overgrown and neglected. Neighbours had cut back the grass from time to time to reduce the fire risk from long grass but apart from that it had been left. Some of the gates and fences were showing signs of damage and in need of considerable repair. The screen door hung at an odd angle, having been slammed to destruction by the wind that whistled through the place. It was always a sad place, so neglected. It had always been a sad place with the dark stained timber almost lost among the overhanging trees. She hoped that one day Ben would return and do it up a bit.

Looking over the property one day, she toyed with the idea of buying and restoring the house herself. She saw the potential of the place if the trees were cut back to lighten up the house and the gardens renovated. The stained timber beams of the house had a certain rustic appeal, which could be heightened by a stained picket fence to replace the broken post and rail fence that circled the entire property. With the fences replaced and painted and stained and the outbuildings repaired, the property had potential to come to life again. It was her vision for the place for a few brief moments before walking away leaving it for the moment to fall further into a state of neglect. Karen made herself a promise that if she ever saw Ben again, she would talk about doing the place up, giving him a hand if need be. She did not know how he would like the idea but she knew she could use the idea to connect with him.

One day, Ben's father wandered into town to find the house locked up and abandoned. Few in town knew he'd left and even fewer where to. Harry turned up at her house asking after him. Karen was on a rare visit home from university when he turned up. She had not seen him for years and barely recognised him except from an old photograph Ben had shown her back at high school. She told Harry of Ben's departure, which saddened Harry.

'Are you certain? I was sure he still had a year to go,' Harry questioned.

'I'm very sure. We went through school together.'

'Oh, okay. If you see him again, tell him I called, will you?' Harry asked.

'I'll do that, Mr Templeton, but I'm not sure when or even if he'll be back. The last time I spoke to him, he intended to be away for a year or more. I'm sorry you missed Ben but I will tell him you called if I see him again.'

'Thank you. So am I, so am I,' Harry replied.

'If you leave me your number, I'll see to it that he gets it when he's back and he can call you.'

'I don't have a phone where I live. You tell him I called, hey, and tell him I care, despite what he may think of me.'

'It's not a problem. I'll make sure he gets the message,' Karen told him.

'You don't know where he went then?'

'No. The only thing he said was that he was heading north with a couple of packhorses but didn't say where.'

There was a sadness about Harry that had been matched only by

Ben's. It was hard to imagine such sadness and isolation in a family as was in theirs.

*

It was almost three years before Karen saw Ben again. She opened the door to the house in the hills she was sharing with some friends from uni in the hills to the east of the town. Gayle had opened the door after hearing someone knocking above the incessant rain. 'Do you want something?' she asked as he stood, dripping water from his long coat at the back door.

'I've just come to let you know the river is up and you had better sit tight until things ease. I'll come and get you when the river drops.'

'Thank you for your advice but we are leaving in the morning so you go and play cowboys or whatever it is you do in this weather.'

'What's going on?' Karen asked and then saw Ben at the door.

'The river is rising and is in a bad mood. I was telling Gayle that you should stay put for a few days.'

'And I told him we are leaving in the morning,' Gayle snapped.

'Like I said, the river is up and is in a dangerous I am urging you to sit tight,' Ben told her again.

'Is Loudon Bridge under yet?' Andrew Henley questioned.

'No, but the water is close to the top and under a lot of pressure; it may not even be there in the morning. I don't recommend you attempt it,' Ben replied.

'Noted but we're big enough to take care of ourselves. If there is nothing more?' Andrew asked Ben who turned to leave.

'Ben, I'll be here.' Karen pushed past Andrew to tell him.

'Good, you do that. I'll be back as soon as I can,' Ben replied before walking off into the rain.

'What is wrong with you people? Can't you see that he is trying to help?' Karen told them.

'But we don't need his help; I know this country every bit as well as he does,' Andrew replied.

'I doubt that very much. I'm staying,' Karen told him.

'You do that,' Andrew snapped at her.

*

Shortly after first light, there was another knock on the door as they packed their gear ready to leave. Andrew opened the door to Jack and Maureen Carmodia.

'Going somewhere, son?' Jack asked. 'The river is up; you're wasting your time,' he added.

'That's for me to decide. That idiot Templeton told us the same thing last night but that's for me to decide,' Andrew replied.

'And you chose to ignore good advice. Then you go alone, I won't stop a fool,' Jack told him. Andrew did not reply as Jack pushed into the house. 'I hope you had no intention of ignoring Ben's advice? He didn't come here looking for bed and breakfast,' he questioned Gayle when he met her in the doorway. 'When Ben says stay, you stay,' he added.

'But you know how he overreacts to things like that,' Gayle said in her defence.

'Do I? Right now, he is out there and if he calls in telling me that he thinks I should stay put then I will stay put. You think about that,' Jack replied.

'Anyone for breakfast?' Maureen asked as she pushed past them into the kitchen with fresh ham and eggs, breaking the tension of the situation.

Karen was quick to join her to give her a hand.

'Don't mind Jack. He has a lot of time for Ben and not a lot of time for those who don't. You weren't planning to drive out with them, were you?' Maureen questioned.

'No, I learnt to trust Ben completely some time ago.'

'I thought you might have. A night alone with him tends to change peoples' view of him, doesn't it?'

'Yes; how did you know?'

'Till now I only just suspected but your survival had Ben written all over it.'

'He made me promise not to tell anyone and even made up the story I used. I didn't want to deceive anyone but it was important to him that I tell no one.'

'I know that too. Ben wants to help and in return only asks for respect. You have given him that – it means more than you know.'

'The fact that he came here today tells me he cares. He wasn't expecting to be invited in for tea but he did expect to be listened to.'

'It takes some people longer than others.'

Ben returned the following morning just after first light where

Maureen made him a hot breakfast. He was still wearing the same clothes he was wearing the last time he was there. He smelt of dampness, an earthy smell and that of a smoky fire from a damp night in the open. Maureen and Karen took no notice but others turned up their noses at him, offended by the smell.

'How is it out there?' Jack asked as Ben hung his coat on the back of the laundry door.

'As bad as I thought. Loudon Bridge is not under but the approaches are and if the rain doesn't ease soon, I think it will let go or at least shift. Crossing it is not an option. There is the cattle bridge but it will need roping. I got hold of the SES last night; they will be on the other side to meet us if we want to get these people out.'

'Good we'll do that but not till you've had a good breakfast. Karen, you can go with him and give him a hand. Take Maureen's horse, she'll follow later,' Jack told her.

'Sure, if that's what's needed,' Karen replied.

'Good, how are the cattle?' Jack asked.

'Good, they are all up on high ground. I'll head up to Tweedales after I'm finished here to keep an eye on his sheep as he has a few fences down and has the other lot on the other side of the river and can't get to them. They are right for a moment but he'll rest easier knowing someone is looking out for them.'

'Good, good, you just give us a call if you need a hand.'

'No, we should be right.'

*

Sometime later, they went down to the river where Ben had rigged ropes up to allow safe crossing of the narrow bridge. The approaches were covered by nearly a meter of water, which meant a damp crossing for everyone. Ben worked waist-deep in the chilling water, apparently oblivious to the cold. Karen strung a tarp in the trees and got the fire going while Ben worked the ropes.

When he finished, Ben stood in the front of the fire, his clothes steaming. He changed his socks and boots but remained in his damp jeans. When he was dry, he made some fresh damper some of which he buttered before handing to Karen.

'This brings back memories,' Karen said.

'Yes, it does. From a very long time ago.'

'It seems like yesterday. Where have you been the last couple years?'

'About,' Ben replied without looking at her.

'Where, Ben? You can talk to me,' she pleaded.

'Queensland and a bit in between.'

'It sounds amazing. You must tell me about it some time.'

'You know where I live,' Ben replied.

'Yes, I do and now that you are back, I will call in when I head home.'

'Thanks, but you don't have to do that.'

'No, I don't but I want to. It's good to see you again,' Karen told him.

'You too,' Ben replied.

The others arrived shortly afterwards and Andrew smelled the damper.

'So, you can cook too, bush boy. Any left?' he asked.

'Not for you there isn't,' Jack said from behind him without knowing how much was left. Later, Jack made sure that Karen had an extra slice of the thick bread, smothered in homemade jam. 'He's not a bad cook, is he?' Jack said.

'He's a very good cook,' Karen replied.

'Past experience then.' Jack winked.

'Yes,' Karen replied with a secret smile.

*

When the SES was ready, Ben led Andrew across the bridge first. Jack and Ben then took it in turns taking each one across on horseback until only Karen was left. She hesitated until Ben rode up and offered her his hand. She climbed up behind him and put her arms around his waist. Instead of being repulsed by the smell and the dirt of his clothing, she embraced him, knowing the dirt and the damp were part of who he was. There was something about him and sharing these brief moments with him that she cherished for some reason. When they reached the other side, she reluctantly slid off the horse and looked up at him.

'Thank you. It was good to see you again,' she said with a smile.

Ben looked down at her with those same sad empty eyes of his.

'You're welcome. Take care now. I'll catch you again one day,' he told her, meeting her gaze for a fleeting second before waving to the SES chief and heading back over the cattle bridge. He rode off into the rain and the mountains without a backwards glance.

# CHAPTER SIX

## *Michael*

A rough-looking guy walked into town after hitch-hiking along the coast road. All he had was the clothes he was standing up in, a sleeping bag, a plastic ground sheet and a pack on his back. His jeans were faded and worn as the steel toe-capped work boots on his feet and the old shirt and hooded jacket he wore. He looked like trouble. The locals spotted him straight away as he walked the last few kilometres into town. He soon began knocking on doors looking for work. His presence in town was not welcomed as everyone was suspicious of strangers, especially those who appeared to have little means of support. He said he was hungry and looking for enough work to get a meal and a place to sleep if he could. A few people were willing to give him a go with odd jobs here and there while they kept a close eye on him. The local police also kept a close eye on him as he camped by the river on the edge of town before moving to the town's small caravan and campground. He took what jobs he could get, which included clearing drains around properties to clearing blackberries that were taking hold on the edge of some properties.

Someone suggested Ben might need a hand and told him to go and talk to him. Ben had seen him around town and knew the police were watching him having spoken to the police about him. Sergeant Barry Wright was an old-school country cop who knew his district very well and did not take well to strangers making sure he knew where they were or at least where to start looking for them. At the first sign of trouble, he moved them on. He knew that Ben was doing it tough and did not like Michael at all initially and kept a close eye on him. Michael got used to Barry stopping him and was always straight with him which Barry began to warm to and over time they developed a degree of respect for each other. For his part, Michael avoided the hotel and the football club even though the sport had been his life years earlier.

'I haven't got much myself; all I can offer you is the same meals I have and a place to sleep,' Ben told him.

'That's fine. I'm not looking for anything else.'

'Another thing, don't go near the house. My dog Jesse will stop you cold.'

'Not a problem,' Michael told him.

He got Michael to work for a couple of days, shifting timber and rebuilding one of the neglected stockyards. Ben paid him what he could which was not a lot but Michael did not seem to mind as Ben fed him as well.

Slowly, the two of them began to talk.

'What has brought you here? You're not a usual itinerant – you are too well educated to begin, so what's your story?' Ben asked as they ate the lunch that Ben had made for both of them.

'I was a smart-assed teen who wouldn't listen to his parents and got in with the wrong crowd. I started hanging out in all the wrong places and was doing drugs and the whole bit. It all started at school where I thought I was pretty cool and I finished on the streets where I was basically living most of the time. My girlfriend, who was a junkie, got pregnant and was really sick and ended up hospital. We'd been living rough and had no way of dealing with any of the issues; we didn't even have a proper place to live let alone raise a family. Her family found her and rescued her from the hospital and slammed a restraining order against me. She lost the baby a few weeks later.

'My old man caught up with me at a police station at around the same time. He tried in his own way to get me to get my act together. I know it broke my mother's heart. In the end, he told me not to expect any help and that I deserved everything I got. He didn't faze me because we had not got long for years. I continued to live rough sleeping in factories and derelict houses. I was living on handouts and collecting the dole from time to time.

'Once I ran into an old football mate from my school days. I was the original bad boy and I seriously thought he'd think I was pretty cool. He didn't. He told me to look at my reflection in the window of the café we were standing in front of and then look at his uni mates he was having coffee with. I'd become a homeless junkie and didn't even know it. He didn't want to know me and told me how it was; I felt I had two choices, either stay and continue to live the way I was, which was in a downward spiral, or leave. I started walking, picking up what work I could for meals and a place to sleep.'

'So where are you heading?'

'I'm not sure really. I always wanted to see this part of the country so I headed east I guess. I guess I will keep heading east and follow the coast north.'

'Are you heading for Sydney?'

'No, there is no point heading there, I will only drift back into the same place I was in Melbourne. I was hoping to find work on a farm or something like that where I will be outdoors and can stay away from drugs and alcohol.'

'Fair enough. I can tell you now, you will get short shrift if I find you with either. Alcohol took my old man; if you start it here, you are back on the road.'

'Understood. Thanks for giving me this, man,' he said, holding up his sandwich and tea.

'It's all I have.'

'I get that but it looks like you're building something here.'

'I have to make something of it for myself.'

'You're doing that alright, good on you; it would be easy to walk away.'

'I did initially and walked most of the way to Queensland and back before I started working on it.'

'You've lived rough too then?'

'I guess I have, yes. I never lived on the streets like you but I've slept under bridges and the like from time to time.'

'I thought there was something different about you. I, for one, would like to help you make your dream.'

'Yeah, well, I don't have anything much to pay you with so you have to move on tomorrow.'

'I understand that, man. Thanks for the work though.'

Before he left town, others began to offer him work too as they saw he was reliable and stayed away from trouble and their daughters. It took a while for people to warm to him and they to him as he kept very much to himself as he worked when he could and slept out when he had to. Everything he owned he carried with him in a well-worn travel pack. The more he worked, the more work he got and was able to afford to rent an old caravan at the back of the caravan for a while.

Staying around town as long as the work lasted, Ben found his tour guide business and breading programs somehow growing in parallel so he was able to offer Michael more and more work. Being away on the tours or delivering horses, Ben employed Michael to keep things moving on the property such as feeding horses and cleaning stables and pathways. It was not just a case of leaving Michael to it but they discussed tasks and introduced him to the daily tasks on the property teaching him how to work the horses.

Michael was a natural with the horses and took any activity in his stride. He seemed to enjoy the tasks that Ben thought he would baulk at, happy to muck out the stables and walk the horses in any weather. Ben knew it was a risk to trust an ex-junkie with his emerging business but there was something about Michael that made Ben think he needed a bit of responsibility. Michael was just happy to have work, a place to sleep and food to eat. He took Ben's trust seriously and did everything that was asked and never ventured near the house. In time, the two struck up a friendship. Ben was always apprehensive about leaving Michael alone in the place but the police knew about him and often dropped in to see how he was going. With time, the visits from the police came in the form of friendship rather than watching him as he gained their respect. Sometimes, they dropped in on Micheal when he was home to catch up as he slowly gained acceptance.

When Ben bought groceries he would often buy a bit extra and give them to Michael, which he always appreciated when he received them along with his pay. The two of them would often then talk before Ben returned home.

# CHAPTER SEVEN

*Working together*

A year later, Ben was running a touring company taking people in the high country. He conducted guided horse-riding tours of the south-eastern high country and was much in demand. A couple of botanists were undertaking an extensive study of the flora of the high country and hired Ben to guide and support them on a month-long expedition. Ben was happy to help but needed to hire extra staff to assist. With Michael taking care of things at home, he needed someone to cook and take care of the camp while he was out with the botanists during the day. He also required that person to return home to re-supply the camp, which would require staying out alone overnight. There were a number of people in the district who would have been qualified and happy for the work when he got a call from Karen.

'I heard you're looking for someone to help out with the botanist's tour of the high country.'

'You're well-informed,' Ben questioned.

'I don't miss much, you know that.'

'No, you don't. So, what's your question?'

'Would you hire me?'

'I would but there are better-qualified people that you out there I can call upon.'

'I know that but I really want to do this.'

'Why? You are not studying the field and you of all people know how harsh it can be up there.'

'I'm always looking for money for uni and it would be an opportunity to do something completely different, which means I get a real break and earn a little money as well.'

'It doesn't pay a lot. My margins aren't that great,' he warned. 'This is not a hobby, it is my business. I will need you to do what I ask. If this works, I get more work – if it doesn't, it will make other work hard to come by.'

'I fully appreciate that, Ben, and I will do everything that is asked of me. I'm not some little princess who can't handle a little dirt or rain.'

'I know that, I just wanted to be sure that you knew that. I'm still not convinced why?'

'I would like to get to know you a little more, to see how you operate. It's been a few years since we caught up and I would really like to spend some time with you.'

'That's better; it seems an odd request. Okay, I'll tell you what. I am going up to the camp to set up and store some supplies next Thursday. You turn up at six a.m. and we'll take a look.'

Karen arrived in jeans and a jumper over elastic-sided boots, ready for work, but she still looked good somehow Ben thought as he looked at her also briefly. She immediately began to help with the horses as it proved to be a long day with the camp being almost inaccessible by vehicle and she understood why he preferred to use horses. Isolated on the edge of the high plains proper, it was a crude wrought iron structure with a fireplace and an earth floor.

It had no doors but was accessed via a simple windbreak built out from the main walls of iron built onto a rough-sawn timber frame. The only window was a hole cut in the wall with a couple of shutters to keep out the wind. A crude table made of rough saw timber was built in the floor. Sleeping accommodation consisted of a couple of platforms built into the sides of the structure making for a rough cold night without the right gear.

'This will be home for the few weeks we are here. Food will be stored in the food safe, which will hang in the tree. Showers consist of a bucket hung in a tree behind a canvas screen so I suggest that you have a shower while we are out in the field. You'll be first up in the morning to make breakfast and you'll be last to bed after everything is packed away after tea and breakfast is prepared. The middle of the day will be yours but if the weather catches us out, you'll be alone for the night too. It is going to be a bit rough so what do you think?'

'I'm in,' Karen replied without hesitation.

'Really?' Ben questioned.

'I told you that you would not put me off,' Karen replied despite the huge knots in her stomach.

'Okay, I'm hoping I'm not making a mistake for both of us but the job is yours if you are still interested.'

'Thank you. I'm looking forward to it,' Karen lied.

*

The work proved to be as exacting as Karen imagined. Out of her swag before first light, she got breakfast underway with Ben before he went off to prepare the horses for the day ahead. The mornings were a hectic time as they attempted to get everyone fed and out to make the best of the morning light. After they left, Karen sat down with a coffee and took a breath before cleaning up everything after breakfast. She warmed some water and then took a bucket shower before going for a walk, exploring the area around the camp and beyond. At lunchtime, she would get a radio call from Ben to tell her how he expected the day to go and she would prepare the evening meal accordingly. It was a long few weeks but she enjoyed it. She did not see a lot of Ben but when she did she saw a person at home in his own environment much as he was when she first spent the night with him.

Ben was very pleased with the way Karen worked. Always happy and polite, she had everything ready when it needed to be and went out of her way to make sure everyone was as comfortable and as well-fed as she could. She also took time to make sure her clothes were clean and her hair done which showed Ben that she knew how to take care of herself and present a professional attitude to his clients besides that she was rather easy on the eye as well.

Heading back to pick up supplies was a personal challenge as she had to stop on the return trip to camp alone overnight but she took on board everything that Ben had told her and accepted the challenge. She woke in the morning still wondering what Ben liked about camping out alone but did admit to herself that it was as bad as she had first thought. Ben was delighted to see her return on time with everything he had asked of her.

When the botanists left, they took their time to walk the horses down and do a bit of sightseeing for themselves on the way down the mountains. Deciding to rest the horses, they stopped at the pool in a mountain stream. They watered the horses from canvas buckets Ben carried for them.

They then went swimming in their clothes before stepping up onto the bank to dry off.

'This is great, thank you for bringing me here,' Karen told him.

'The pleasure is mine. Listen, I'm going to take off for a while so that you can get changed and go skinny dipping if you like. There is a place I need to check out in that valley and I will be gone about an hour so you enjoy yourself and then I'll be back to cook us tea.'

'Thank you, but why would I want to go skinny dipping? It never occurred to me to want to.'

'It is one of the privileges of isolation. There is no one up here but me. You'll see me before I see you, have no concern on that point.'

'I don't have any concerns at all.'

'Good. You enjoy yourself then,' Ben told her before climbing on the back of his horse and leaving it to her.

True to his word, she heard and then saw his horse return an hour later.

'How was it?' he asked.

'It was good; it was not like anything I have done before. Thank you.' She realised that she had just confessed to swimming naked in the open and felt a little embarrassed.

'You have done some really good work this last fortnight. I really appreciate that.'

'Thank you; I had a good time too. I wouldn't mind doing it again sometime.'

'This time next year, you will be earning a lot more than I could ever pay you so I think that this was really a one-time only.'

'Is that why you took me on? Because you knew it would be the last?'

'To be honest, I have not come up with a definitive answer as to why. It was a business risk but employing you was not a business decision so much as following a hunch that maybe we would both get something positive out of it.'

'Well, I was hoping to get a real friendship with you out of it.'

'I think you have that. I have enjoyed your company on this trip.'

'I may not work for you again but I do hope I can do another trip like this one day or at least ride the hills with you again.'

'You know where I live,' he told her as he prepared tea.

They sat around the campfire, watching the sunset as they ate tea and then settled down for the night under the stars. Alone together under the stars, they talked a good part of the night as they watched the fire burn down from the warmth of their swags. Karen lay in her swag and watched the stars, feeling happy to have been able to contribute to what Ben was doing and happy to be able to share the stars with him.

'This has just been the best day; thank you. I will remember it for the rest of my life.'

'I'm glad you are enjoying it. Tomorrow we will head home and get you paid and get this stuff cleaned and packed away for next time.'

'I'll give you a hand if you like?'

'Thank you but I have it covered and besides, I can only pay you up until lunchtime tomorrow.'

'Don't worry about the money; I do it as a friend.'

'Well, you are working for practically nothing as it is. I will not even ask as a friend. The offer is, however, greatly appreciated.'

'I really want to see you succeed and if I can help in any way, you only have to ask,' Karen offered.

'I appreciate that; perhaps we can do it again one day when you're on leave or something like that.'

'I would like that, thank you,' Karen replied.

# CHAPTER EIGHT

*Catching up*

Their next meeting was an unexpected encounter in the city when Karen was having lunch in a park close to the uni. It was one of the few times Ben went near the city because it held no attraction for him. Ben saw her sitting in the park wearing jeans, a long-sleeve white shirt and comfortable shoes, her hair tied back in a ponytail. She was one of the better-dressed uni students he had ever seen.

'Hi,' he said when he recognised her sitting with friends just off the edge of the path.

'Hello, Ben. It's good to see you. What brings you to town?' Karen asked, standing up to greet him. Ben wore cord trousers and a plain blue shirt over the top of polished elastic-sided boots and carried a brown leather satchel. He looked ready to do business.

'I have a couple of appointments to get to today. The first one in about twenty minutes is with some of the tourism people about promoting the business and the district. How are you going; you can't have long to go with your studies?'

'Yeah, good; I'll be finished at the end of the year and then I'll have to get a real job,' Karen replied.

'I can't see that being a problem – you have really good people skills and some of my clients still speak highly of you.'

'Thank you. Oh, Ben, this is my friend, Tracy,' she said, introducing her friend from her first days at uni.

'Hello. Nice to meet you, Tracy. You will have to both excuse me I am on a tight schedule but it was good to catch up.'

'Yes, it was. You're not going to be around later, are you? We could catch up for tea or something?'

'I would like that but I have to make a start back at the end of my last appointment; I told Michael I'd be back early tomorrow so he can get away in the afternoon. He's heading to New South Wales tomorrow to deliver some horses for me.'

'Another time perhaps?'

'Yeah, if I am ever in town again, I'll give you a call.'

'Do that. I would love to catch up.'

'Sure. All the best with your studies. I'll see you later,' Ben said before walking off, looking a little self-conscious.

'So, who is Ben?' Tracy asked after he left.

'A guy I know from home; we went to school together.'

'He appears to be a little more than that.'

'I worked for him last summer.'

'So, he's just a friend?'

'Yeah, that's all.'

'Are you sure?'

'Yeah, why do you ask?'

'Because you and I are friends and if you ever look at me the way you just looked at him, you and I are going to have to talk.'

'I have no idea what you mean,' Karen replied, her face suddenly flushed. She seemed lost for a moment; it made Tracy wonder who this Ben was.

# CHAPTER NINE

*New start*

Gaining immediate employment at the end of her studies, she had little time for a break before starting with the company she and Gayle had done their industrial experience with. Both were employed on their graduate program, which fast-tracked them into an auditing and consultancy role. For a time, she shared a flat with Gayle for a time before sharing a place with Tracy and another girl from the same company when Gayle took a place in St Kilda. Gayle and Karen kept in touch, often working on the same or similar contracts and often went out socialising together but even then, it was obvious that they were moving in different directions. Karen preferred Tracy's company as she was not as wild and enjoyed having friends around as much as the city night spots.

Everything went well enough during that first year as she applied what she learned in uni. The rewards were there in the form of a very good salary package given she was a new graduate but a lot was asked of her for that reward. She worked long hours to meet demanding deadlines and for a time, she thrived on the pressure. There were endless meetings often going late into the night. She learned to eat meals when she could get them and had many a meeting of lunch or dinner in a café or restaurant. She learned to drink wine, where the better places in town were and how to use her expense account to cover her business expenses. Living in the city, she had no room or need for a car, using public transport or one of the company cars.

Sharing a flat with Tracy and Julie, she was able to save a good part of her wage, which she invested in a growing stock portfolio. She was careful with her money, taking her lunch rather than buying it unless it was a business lunch, which was all too often.

Her main form of recreation was drinking red wine, which she shared with Tracy from time to time. It was all innocent to enough at first but it became every Friday night and Saturday night and then last thing each night. Friday night drinks went from being an opportunity to unwind occasionally to being an essential part of her weekly routine as the pressure of work built up. It changed her as much as she denied it.

On her rare visits home, she slept, unable to rise before midday as much as she wanted otherwise. At first, her mother took little notice of the glass of wine she had with lunch and again with tea. Over the next year, she watched Karen change with the pressure and success of work and the amount of wine she drank.

Tracy was the first to question her drinking and Karen did not appreciate it.

'I work hard; I think I am entitled to have a drink occasionally.'

'No one is denying that but you are drunk most weekdays all weekend.'

'I am not. I never wake up with a hangover and I can always remember where I've been and what I've done,' Karen replied.

'Yes, but you are still drunk.'

'So what if I am? That is none of your business.'

'Perhaps not but I'm your friend and friends look out for each other.'

'Well, thank you for caring,' Karen said before storming out of the flat, taking her clothes with her to visit her parents that weekend.

*

After a long drive in a hire car, she arrived home, exhausted well after tea having eaten little since lunchtime. Wound up but exhausted at the same time, she dropped her bags in her old room while her mother put the kettle on. Her mother was a little surprised when she returned to the kitchen with a bottle of red but then thought it may be something to add to lunch or tea the following morning. Karen opened the bottle without a second thought and poured herself a long drink, promptly downing it in a couple of swallows.

'Enjoy that, did you?' her mother questioned.

'Yes, I needed that it's been a long week,' Karen replied as she poured herself a second glass before sitting down at the kitchen table.

Fiona made a pot of tea, which she poured for them by the time Karen had finished her second glass, the effects of which were beginning to tell as Karen slumped at the table.

'When did you last eat?' Fiona asked.

'Lunch time, I think. I picked up a coffee on the way,' Karen replied with an excaudate wave of her hand, unaware of her own gestures.

'Let me fix you something,' Fiona suggested.

'No, I'm okay. Really, I'm fine,' Karen replied, her voice slurred and her eyes noticeably bloodshot.

'You need to eat something, especially if you are going to drink that stuff,' Fiona told her.

'I'm going to bed; it's been a long day,' Karen said, standing up and grabbing the bottle, deciding to leave her glass as she headed for the door. 'Good night,' she added from the doorway.

Karen woke late the next morning, feeling very unwell and immediately retreated back to sleep but was forced by hunger pains to get up. Staggering into the kitchen with the same bottle of red wine, she put the kettle on and then went to pour herself another glass.

'No, you don't,' Fiona said grabbing the bottle off her.

'Hey, that's mine,' Karen snapped.

'That's what concerns me. You drink and don't eat. You haven't eaten since lunchtime yesterday and yet you're about to have a drink.'

'And?' Karen questioned.

'And you are well on your way to becoming an alcoholic if you're not one already.'

'That's rubbish. One bottle of wine over a weekend doesn't make anyone an alcoholic.'

'It does if it's your only nutritional intake for the weekend.'

'I'm going to eat.'

'Then eat,' Fiona told her.

'What is your problem? You have been on my case since I got home,' Karen asked, her tone short.

'I haven't been able to. You have been too drunk.'

'I have not been drunk.'

'No? Well, you certainly do a good impression of it these days. Look at you; you're a mess. You need to take a look at your life because, at the moment, it is clearly not working. I suggest you get a grip and get back in control before that bottle takes over your life and becomes your life – and it's a lot closer than you think,' Fiona told her.

Karen stormed out of the kitchen in defiance, telling her mother she was going for a ride. Changing into jeans, jumper and riding boots, she saddled her horse and took her for a ride, almost inevitably heading for Ben's.

Ben was working with one of the young colts when Karen arrived. He walked over to her with the colt as she rode up to the fence.

'Hello, stranger. What brings you here?' he asked.

'I was out riding and just happened to be passing,' she lied.

'Of course, you were. What's up?'

'I needed some air.'

'I was about to put the kettle on. Interested?' Ben offered.

'Sure.'

'Unsaddle your horse in the yard next to this one; get this one used to a trained horse. I'll put the kettle on,' Ben told her.

Karen took her time to settle her horse before heading to the house to find Ben setting up a table on the back verandah, inviting her to take a seat. He had made a couple of sandwiches and plate of homemade fruit cake and a pot of fresh tea.

'So, what's happening with you? You look a bit stressed,' Ben questioned.

'I am. I just had a bit of a fight with Mum.'

'What about?'

'She says I drink too much.'

'Do you?'

'I don't think so. What is it with everyone? So, I have a drink. What's wrong with that?'

'Don't come here expecting me to hold your hand and say it's okay if you become a drunk, no matter how well you hide it or how graceful you are at it. Now, have you asked yourself why? You look really tired.'

'I am tired,' Karen replied, feeling suddenly exhausted.

'When did you last eat?' Ben asked, offering her a sandwich.

'Lunchtime yesterday.'

'And a drink?'

'Last night.'

'Then something's wrong, isn't it?' he asked, holding her gaze.

'Yes,' she admitted after seeing the concern in his eyes.

'Then find out whatever it is and change things. You are so much better than this.'

Karen didn't reply for a moment then looked at him. 'Thanks, Ben. You're right. No offence, I didn't expect you to care – I wanted you to but I didn't expect it.'

'Well, just don't tell anyone. I'm not supposed to be a very caring person.' Ben smiled.

'It's a good thing that we know each other better than that. Promise me you will always be honest with me. I value your friendship so please tell me how it is,' Karen told him, which seemed to embarrass him.

'Oh, I won't let you get away with anything. I care for you too much for that,' Ben replied without making eye contact. His words shocked her a bit and took a while to process them.

After that, the conversation lightened up considerably and they talked about what was happening locally and what Ben was doing with the place. Ben's father had finally caught up with him long enough to hand the property over to him debt-free. The place had been fairly run down when he had returned from his long walk north. Since then he had begun to work on the place, repairing gates and fences. Many of the outbuildings had been repaired but most were still a work in progress. With his guiding business and horses, he was generating a decent income but most of it was still being ploughed back into it in the way of improvements and restoration. Ben walked her through the property and was pleased at how well it was looking since he had taken over the property.

Karen returned home with a different attitude. She was noticeably more relaxed when she sat with her mother after she got back.

'So, how is Ben?' Fiona asked.

'Who said anything about Ben?'

'That was where you went, wasn't it?' Fiona questioned.

'Yes.'

'And what did he have to say?'

'Much the same as you. He was straight with me and you are both right; things aren't right and I need to make some changes. I'm sorry for how I reacted. I know you that you care,' Karen said, taking her mother's hand.

Fiona patted her hand. 'I'm glad he was able to help.'

'I'm glad you have both been there for me, I really appreciate that.'

'You're welcome.'

*

That night they were joined by Karen's brother Ted (Edward) who was a couple of years older and by then had completed his studies in agriculture and was gaining experience on other properties before one day taking over the family cattle stud. The two of them had always been close for some reason and Karen always valued his opinion so she listened when he spoke. He was very different to her older sister, Joanne, who seldom could not get far enough from the land and had begun working as a business analyst in Sydney after completing her studies and seldom returned home for more than a few days at a time.

'So how are things with that boyfriend of yours? When is he coming over to join us for tea or a barbie?' Ted asked her.

'Mark is working; he is heading up a couple of major accounts at the moment and is putting in the time to tie all that together.'

'Mark? Who's Mark?' Ted questioned.

'Mark is my boyfriend, the one that lives in St Kilda.'

'I thought you were seeing someone from around here.'

'No. I have a friend Ben Templeton who lives near here.'

'Ben, yeah, that's him. I thought you were seeing him, not this Mark character.'

'No, I'm going out with Mark.'

'So where does Mark fit into this picture? You never bring Mark home and when you are home, you head straight for Ben's. Can you explain that because I'm a little confused or is it you who is confused?'

'I'm not cheating on Mark if that's what you're implying?' Karen questioned angrily.

'I'm not saying you are but perhaps you need to make up your mind before you lose both of them,' Ted told her.

'And perhaps you need to mind your own business,' Karen snapped.

'Perhaps I should but you need to be careful, sis. I'm not sure Mark would understand about Ben. I know I don't,' Ted replied before leaving her at the table. Karen didn't reply but stared at her plate.

'He means well,' Fiona said, patting her hand.

'I know; I also know he's right. How did I manage to make my life so complicated?'

'I don't know. We are here for you, Karen. Not just Ben.'

'I know that too. Ben deserves better than this.'

'So do you.'

'Do I? I am making such a mess of this.'

'It's nothing that you cannot fix.'

# CHAPTER TEN

*Turning point*

When Karen returned to work, she began making time for herself and did not go for the usual Friday night drinks, leaving work as soon as she could. She kept up the unrelenting demands: working long hours, often taking work home and working six days a week. By staying away from the clubs and bars, she kept herself from drinking but felt it could only be a matter of time. She returned to working fifty weeks a year or more, her only real break was for Christmas and again in September after the financial reports had been sorted. There was a new position created in the company's Sydney office, which she was told she may be offered which only heightened her stress levels.

'How are things with you?' her boss Tina asked when she found Karen at her desk after six p.m. one night.

'Not too good. Is it possible to get someone to share the load? There is too much work here for one person,' Karen asked in reply.

'I was wondering how you were going. I'll see what I can do.'

'Is it possible to do a little more than that please?' Karen added.

'Okay, talk to me. What happening with you?' Tina said, pulling up a chair opposite her.

'It's this job – it's become my life instead of my job. I need a break to be able to leave work at work and get a life. I work late here and often as not, take it home with me. I just don't have time to myself. The only break I get is Friday nights when it is compulsory drinks; the problem is that it's not a real break at all.'

'I had noticed your absence lately,' Tina said.

'There are some issues around that, which have nothing to do with the people that I go out with.'

'You can't always stop at one.'

'No. How did you know?'

'Because I've been there. Mandy can start full-time with you tomorrow and I will send Jarred to you on Wednesday. Don't take any crap off him – he either works for you or he's out the door. Be blunt with him; it is the only language he understands.'

'I'm not sure that's a good idea.'

'Don't you think you can handle him?'

'Oh, I can handle him but he is not going to like it.'

'It will be made crystal clear to him that your team is his last. If he doesn't conform, let me know and he will find himself cleaning out our old files with Keith. Given that I won't have to fire him, he'll leave of his own accord.'

'Thank you.'

'We'll talk again. For the record, you are doing really quality work. As for that thing with Gayle, she may be a hard hitter and get things done but the follow-up work you do is what makes it every bit as vital. Don't take not being offered the position in Sydney as a poor reflection on your work; quite the opposite, in fact.'

'Thank you but I would not have gone to Sydney.'

'Can I ask why not? Is it too far from home?'

'No, too far from the country. I need some space.'

'Then take Friday off and head home or wherever you need to go; we owe you plenty of days. I'll cover you.'

'Thank you. I will see you on Monday then.'

'Yes, we'll meet with your team and lay out what's expected.'

*

Gayle's move to Sydney was good for her as she seemed to thrive on the bustle. Karen had gone to Sydney for a few days working holiday but liked Sydney even less than Melbourne. The move did not bring them closer together but drove a subtle wedge between them that was not obvious at first.

That year, Tracy married Phil. The wedding was a nice distraction as Karen helped her with the wedding, becoming her only bridesmaid on the day. Karen also helped Tracy decorate the small terrace in Carlton where Tracy and Phil would spend the first few years of their married life before buying a place of their own in the suburbs.

Tracy's wedding also meant that there was one less person in the house. With Julie increasingly staying with her boyfriend, Karen spent more and more time alone apart from her time with Mark. When Julie was home, her boyfriend often stayed and Karen had to endure the sounds of their lovemaking while she tried to sleep. It was more isolating than being in the flat alone.

With her relationship with Mark not going well, Karen went home more often if only for twenty-four hours to take a break. After the long drive home late in the night, she would share a hot chocolate with her mother. In the morning she would be gone, leaving on her horse or in the ute, seldom returning till late. One day, she returned within the hour.

'This is a surprise; what brings you back so early?'

'Ben is away for the next four to five weeks working with horses in New South Wales. Can you believe it?'

'Yes, I can actually. Those horses are his livelihood and so what's your problem?' Fiona questioned.

'I need to talk to him,' Karen replied, looking lost.

'What about?'

'Everything and nothing. You know what it's like.'

'Do I? Isn't that Mark's role? He is your boyfriend – or isn't it that kind of relationship?'

'No, Mark is not the best listener. Ben understands me.'

'So, what is Mark's role then? Bed partner?'

'No, I haven't slept with him,' Karen snapped in her defence.

'So, he's not your confidante or your lover, so what is he?'

'My boyfriend.'

'But you enjoy his company, right?'

'Not anymore. Things aren't going that well at the moment.'

'So, what is Ben then?'

'Ben is a friend.'

'Okay, I can understand that he's a friend; what I would like to know is what is it that he gets out of listening to you?'

'I listen to him; we work the horses together and talk for hours.'

'That much I know. People have seen you together. Have you ever considered that perhaps he may want to be more than friends?'

'No, he would have said something; he's always been honest with me.'

'I think Ben would be very guarded about revealing his feelings for you. Do not take what you have with Ben for granted; in the meantime, I think it may be time to talk about where you are going with Mark or you will be having sex with him in some attempt to save your relationship with him that may not be worth saving?'

'That is not going to happen. I think that is all Mark wants; sex, not a relationship. He says things are getting too serious and I'm too clingy, yet we hardly see each other.'

'Oh, Karen, you deserve better than that,' Fiona said.

'I hope so. Not a lot is going that well at the moment.'

*

Karen tried to talk about their relationship but the only solution he could think of for saving it was to have sex, not talk. After arguing the issue, Karen decided to end the relationship then and there. Mark was at best indifferent and walked out with barely a kiss on the cheek for her efforts. Karen was devastated and feeling fragile but even more so when she saw Mark walking hand-in-hand with a girl from another office a few weeks later and then heard that they were living together. Every assumption she had about their relationship had been wrong, believing once that Mark had real feelings for her. Rumours were heard around the office that she was frigid, which hurt and were quickly shut down by Tina but it was all a bit much for her.

Believing things could only improve from that point, she was walking between meetings with Mandy and some clients when she ran into Ben. Completely thrown by the encounter and feeling very vulnerable, she hesitated in saying anything to greet him, sending all the wrong messages as she seemed embarrassed by him.

'Um, hi, Ben,' she said, barely making eye contact.

He hesitated too.

'Hi,' he said before moving on when it appeared she was not going to introduce him to anyone.

She rang him several times that night and the following night before she finally caught up with him.

'Ben, I'm sorry about what happened when we met in the city. I just wasn't expecting to see you, that was all.'

'That much was fairly obvious.'

'Ben, please don't,' Karen pleaded.

'Make this harder than it needs to be?'

'Ben, I'm apologising here,' Karen told him.

'Are we friends?'

'Yes, we are.'

'It didn't look that way to me,' Ben replied.

'Ben, I'm sorry. I made a mistake.'

'Did you? Am I going to be met as a stranger next time we meet in the city? Are you embarrassed to know me?'

'No, I'm not,' Karen replied. 'It's complicated,' she added.

'Actually, I think it's rather straightforward. I'm either your friend or I'm not.'

'You are, Ben. You are.'

'Am I? I'm not so sure anymore. Goodbye, Karen,' Ben said and hung up. Karen sat staring at the phone for hours afterwards, numb with grief.

*

A few weeks later, Karen went home for a weekend away. She got up early and saddled her horse then rode up into the hills where she could look down on Ben's place. For the first time, her heart ached at the loss of a friend. She sat there for hours looking out at his house and thinking before reluctantly climbing back on her horse for the long ride back home. Arriving back just before lunchtime, her mother was a little anxious.

'Where have you been?'

'I went for a ride.'

'That much I know. Where did you go? You were not with Ben because I saw him in town?'

'No, I went up into the hills,' Karen replied.

'Are you okay?' Fiona questioned.

'Just tired.'

'Aren't you going to see Ben?' Fiona asked.

'No. Ben and I had a falling out a few weeks back. We haven't spoken since.'

'Karen, I'm really sorry to hear that. Surely it's something that can be fixed?' Fiona told her.

'I just don't think I have the energy at the moment.'

'But don't you think he is worth it?'

'He's not my boyfriend.'

'But he is a friend and from what I've seen, a good one.'

'He is but a lot of things aren't working at the moment. I need time to myself but I will call him before I leave,' Karen promised.

Later, she went walking along the river and then up to a high knoll where she got a different view of the town and once again found herself looking down on Ben's place and wondering. At that moment, she wished she had a drink and longed for a nice glass of wine to sit and simply enjoy the view. The longing turned into an all-consuming craving and she wanted to walk back into town and buy a bottle of something but she knew that if she started, she would not stop. So strong was her desire for a drink that it seemed to consume every fibre of her being, curled up beneath a tree and waited for the craving to pass. When the cravings subsided, she looked around and realised she missed the bush and the open space more than she could have imagined and began to cry. Riding in the hills or walking along the river was when she was truly relaxed.

Karen left a message on Ben's answering machine before heading back to Melbourne.

Back at work, Tina dropped into her office to talk about how she was going.

'Your team is working well,' she offered.

'Yes, they are. You have given me some good people,' Karen replied.

'There is a but in there somewhere, isn't there?'

'Yes, there is. I have been doing a lot of work trying to sort things out. It's not the job as much as I thought it was. I enjoy my job, I really do, especially now that we have the resources right.'

'So, what is it, you think? I know you have been going home a lot lately. Is there a guy involved?'

'Not as such, no. The guy thing will work itself out one way or the other. The truth is, I haven't been going home to my parents as much as it may appear. What I have been doing is heading into the country or down on the coast, staying in cabins and caravan parks.'

'It's a little bit off the country girl thing, is it?' Tina asked.

'I think it is a lot of the country girl thing. I am basically looking at my options. I can't unwind in the city without drinking, which brings its own problems. I need space. Getting away most weekends has eased the pressure but I need to do something a bit more permanent in the longer term.'

'You're leaving us?'

'Basically, yes. I have to for my own emotional health.'

'I can't say I am not disappointed but I respect your decision. I take it you haven't got anything tied down yet?'

'No but I am seriously looking.'

'Well, we'll keep this between us until you formally resign. I hope that you will give us enough notice to do a proper handover.'

'I have already made that known to the people I have been talking to.'

'Good, I appreciate that.'

'Tina, I won't give you any less in the meantime,' Karen assured her.

'It never occurred to me that you would. You are one of my better players; you will not be easily replaced.'

'Thank you but you are being far too generous.'

'Don't you believe it? That is why I need your input about your replacement,' Tina told her.

'I'll do all that I can.'

'That's all that I ask. And good luck with the job hunt.'

'Thank you,' Karen replied.

*

A few days later, she got a call for an interview for a two-year contract position down in the western district. Based in Hamilton, the position paid well and would give her time out on her own to find her place in the world. It was going to take her a long way from home.

Karen had rung Ben a few times during the weekend before getting him to talk to her.

'I don't know, Karen; I'm just not sure there is any point. We appear to be going in different directions. Your life is in the city and mine's here. We are just too different.'

'No, we're not. Our difference is what makes us good friends.'

'But you will meet somebody and you'll get married one day and I'll be alone.'

'But I'm not seeing anyone; Mark and I broke up ages ago and right now, I'm not looking for anyone. You are crossing bridges before you get to them. Even if I got married, you and I can still be friends,' Karen assured him.

'That's just it, we can't and I doubt your husband could either. It's just not working. You have a good life,' Ben told her before hanging up.

For Karen, Ben's rejection had been a huge blow and she wanted to give up and look more seriously at the position in Bendigo.

When the call came offering her the position, she took a couple of days to consider it as another offer had also come through, which she had made them aware of. Taking a couple of days off, she went to her talk with her mother. She told Fiona about Ben.

'What are you going to do?'

'I'm going to accept the position in Hamilton. It's a long way from here but perhaps that is the point.'

'Well, if it's what you want?'

'It's what I need right now.'

Two days later, she left home and headed west, passing the mountains that were now covered in the first of the winter snows. On a ridgeline a couple of kilometres away, Ben rode alone the snow line in search of cattle. Even from that range, he recognised Ben. It was not the quickest route to the highway so she knew she was on that road to look at the mountains. He stopped and waved to her, not expecting to be visible at that range, but then she stopped, got out of the car and stood on the side of the road. Karen looked at the dark figure silhouetted against the snow line and raised one hand high above her head a waved slow and long, tears in her eyes. The man on the horse sat high in the saddle and waved back.

\*

It was a full two years before Ben saw her again. During that time, he continued to work for Neil from time to time but never visited the house, making only a rare visit to see Fiona as the snow began to fall again a year later to ask after her. Fiona told him it would be at least another year before she was likely to be back. Ben thanked her. She saw him ride out alone into the winter winds which tossed light snowflakes about and wondered what he was thinking, thoughts that he would never share. At that moment, she felt his isolation and knew that perhaps Karen held the key to that lonely man's heart. She knew too that that night he would sit alone in a mountain hut up where the wind blew hard and snow laid heavy on the ground, lost in those solitary thoughts of his.

Fiona called Karen to tell him about his visit.

'He misses you, you know?'

'I miss him too but things are going well for me at the moment and our lives are heading in different directions. I think some things are just better left slide.'

'Can't you write to him at least?'

'I can do that,' Karen replied.

Karen sat in front of her computer for several nights wondering what to write but could not think of anything. In the end, her letter was more like a postcard than a letter, telling him she had found a small unit to rent, the job was going well and she had managed to find a nice coffee shop to work. Ben's reply was just as brief, saying that he was happy that things were going well. She could not blame him for not replying with any more enthusiasm as it appeared they were moving further apart with every passing day.

The job itself had gone well in that she was achieving of all the objectives the economic development unit. Her immediate director was very pleased the business strategies and her professional interaction with the local business community. Her late evening presentations were always well-attended and follow-ups usually produced results. Having met a series of objectives, she had received a number of performance-based bonuses.

As good as the job was, she did not really connect socially with anyone. One of the women owned a holiday house in Port Fairy, which she offered to Karen for the weekend from time to time. Karen gratefully accepted the offer but did not feel comfortable enough with anyone from work to invite them to join her. The problem was that while she got on well with people, she couldn't say that any of them were friends. She went for drinks after work and stuck to mineral water, engaging in conversation but never talked about anything of consequence. Occasionally, she accepted invitations to barbeques and dinner but still never connected with anyone on a personal level.

When not working, she sat in a coffee shop in town or took drives in the country, sometimes doing a round trip to Mt Gambier to sit in another coffee shop or pick up a book from a seven-day-a-week bookshop. When she spoke to her mother, there was little enthusiasm in her voice when she spoke about anything but her job. Karen had been there for a year before she decided to take up the offer of the house for a weekend. She left work one Friday night for the house on the eastern beach. It was not a long trip so she was in time to go into town for tea at the hotel where she sat alone and listened to the juke box before making her way back to the house. That night, she sat alone in the dark and listened to the surf and sipped a slow glass of wine and tried not to think of another. Sitting alone in the dark, it was not how she imagined things would work out. Instead of having a new start, she was more alone than ever and was not who her idea of success was. Karen was sitting alone again over a cup of tea in the main street the following morning when the woman she rented the house from suddenly sat down in front of her.

'What are you doing?' she asked, staring at Karen.

'I'm having a cup of tea,' Karen replied.

'Yes, on your own.'

'And your point being?' Karen questioned with immediate regret.

'You didn't hire my place to sit alone and look at the sea?' Eleanor questioned.

'I did actually.'

'Why?'

'I've got no one, I guess.'

'I didn't think so. You look totally miserable,' Eleanor told her.

'Thank you for pointing that out.'

'I only said because it is time to take stock. I've thought you were happy sitting here on your own then I would never have said anything. Is there someone missing in your life?'

'Sort of.'

'What do you mean sort of?'

'There is this guy from back home. We used to be great friends and we used to spend a lot of time talking and writing to each other.'

'What happened?'

'We met by chance in the city once and I was with some people from work, heading back to the office from a meeting. I got embarrassed when we met and I almost completely ignored him and he felt embarrassed and we did not part on good terms.'

'Have you tried talking to him?'

'Yes, I have but we have been drifting apart and moving to this job certainly hasn't helped.'

'What if you were to move back closer to him?'

'That would help.'

'Then you should consider it because at the moment while you are good at your job, I get the suspicion that you are only just passing through. There is nothing here for you, Karen, not in the long term.'

'I know,' Karen replied.

Two days later, there was a knock on the front door. She opened it to see Ben standing in front of her.

'Hi. I was just passing I thought you might like to walk in town for a coffee,' he said, delivering his well-rehearsed line. Karen was so stunned to see him there she did not reply at first. 'Another time, perhaps?' he then offered.

'No, Ben, I'm sorry – it's just that you're the last person I expected to meet me at my front door. I'd love to go into town to have a coffee unless, of course, you would like to come inside for one?'

'No, in town is fine,' Ben replied.

'I'll get my coat,' Karen said before quickly turning away and returning just a few minutes later with her coat on.

They walked in silence for a few minutes before Karen looked at him.

'Can I ask, were you really just passing or is there another reason you are here? It's just that this appears to be a long way out of your way.'

'I heard on the grapevine that you were sitting out here on your own, so I thought I'd drop over and see how you are.'

'You hardly have been passing – you must have driven half the night. What is it, ten hours from your place to here?'

'Something like that.'

'You drove all night?'

'Pretty much.'

'But why, after I made such a fool of myself the last time we met?'

'Sure, and if that is the worst mistake you ever make in your life you are way ahead of the rest of us.'

'Are you saying you forgive me?'

'I'm here, aren't I?'

'Yes, and it's good to see you again.'

'Thanks. It's good to see you again too but I thought you were a bit smarter than this.'

'How do you mean?'

'I'm the loner, not you. I enjoy being alone. What are you doing here on your own besides being miserable?'

'But I'm not miserable.'

'No?'

Karen looked at him. 'You read me too well at times.'

'I'm a friend, Karen, and I don't like to hear that you're not happy.'

'And you drove all this way to tell me that?'

'I drove all this way to say that you have friends and that this friend will happily drive anywhere if only to sit for a while over a coffee and talk so that you're not alone.'

'So, what do you do when you feel lonely? Who do you call?'

'You already know the answer to that.'

'Yes, I do and that's what makes you such a good friend. You are always putting others before yourself. It is good to see you. Thank you for coming.'

'Not a problem. The next time you are feeling down, you know my number. Just call and you know if I can I come and we can just sit and talk.'

'Thank you. You amaze me – I'm so grateful to have you as a friend,' Karen told him.

They made their way to a café where they sat and talked and enjoyed the moment knowing that one day, she would find someone and these moments would be rare if at all. What was important was that Karen needed someone for now and that he got to share the moment with her.

After coffee, they went for a walk along the docks and sat on a park bench overlooking the water and continued to talk.

'Are you doing anything for lunch?'

'Nothing planned.'

'Then let me make lunch back at the house for the two of us. The balcony has a great view of the bay and is sheltered from the cold.'

'That sounds good but I have to get back tomorrow.'

'Where are you staying tonight? There is a spare room if you want it?' Karen offered.

'I have booked a cabin for the night in town so that I can get back tomorrow afternoon.'

'But tomorrow is Friday. Surely you can give yourself a weekend off once in a while?' Karen asked, unsure of why she was so disappointed that he was leaving so soon.

'Michael is going fishing with Fred and Max. I promised him the time off to spend with the guys – it's important to him.'

'I understand. Well, we'll enjoy the time we have then,' Karen told him, trying to maintain a smile.

Karen made a late meal for them over which Ben told her how the business was developing. Michael continued to prove himself with the horses taking over a lot of the basic tasks so that Ben could concentrate on training and selling the horses.

'I thought he would have moved on long ago but he seems determined to stay,' Ben told her.

'It's probably because he has a good boss who is willing to give him a go,' Karen offered.

'Yes, well, maybe but I'm not paying him a lot.'

'But you are paying him what you can and as you've said, as your income increases, so does his wage. Remember, he didn't arrive with much and I think he is working for a lot more than money.'

'I hope so. I would hate to lose him.'

'Perhaps you should talk to him so that you both know where you are going.'

'I will do that because if he does leave, I'm going to have to hire someone. Anyway, enough about me. What about you – what are you doing besides sitting alone drinking coffee? How is the job going?' Ben asked her.

'The job is good but I am looking at my options.'

'You're not looking at returning to the city, are you?'

'No, I've done my time there. Would you mind if I found something closer to home?'

'Why would I mind? It's your career.'

'It's just that I haven't been the greatest friend of late and we might run into each other a bit more often.'

'It's a bit hard running into you around here – it cost me a fortune in fuel,' Ben replied and Karen immediately went red with embarrassment.

'I'm really sorry about that. You know you didn't have to come.'

'I know but friendships should be able to survive a few rough times. You go where you need to go, I'll cope. Just remember me when you meet someone. I would still like an invitation to your wedding and a chance to say goodbye,' Ben said with a smile.

'Why would you say goodbye?'

'I think your future husband could cope with your friendship with Tracy but I'd only be competition if only in his eyes,' Ben told her and she looked at him.

\*

The following day Karen called her mother.

'Have you spoken to Ben lately?'

'Yes, we see him from time to time and we always stop to say hello.'

'Did you tell him I was down here alone and feeling sorry for myself?'

'No, but you've just confirmed what I suspected.'

'How could you? How weak and isolated does that make me look?'

'I take it his visit didn't go well then?' Fiona questioned.

'I'm not saying that and don't change the subject. Why on Earth of all people would you tell Ben Templeton?'

'I thought that was obvious.'

'It may be to you but in case you have forgotten, the two of us had a huge falling out some time ago.'

'Yes, I know that?'

'So how was sending him to Port Fairy going fix that?'

'Did it fix it? Are you talking again?'

'Well, in fact, we are but that's not the point. How was your bully him into driving all that way knowing how much I had embarrassed him?'

'First, I didn't bully Ben into anything. I told him you were not travelling too well and could do with a friend right now. He didn't hesitate he said he would leave that night and be there in the morning.'

'He said that?'

'And did it too by the sounds of it.'

'Yes, he did,' Karen replied and was silent.

'Are you there, Karen?'

'Yes, I'm here and I'm still mad at you. Why would you do such a thing?'

'Because you two have been friends for too long to let this thing between you go unresolved. Now, it looks like mission accomplished, wouldn't you say?'

'Mum, just don't. It's more complicated than that.'

'Only if you want it to be, Karen,' Fiona told her before hanging up.

\*

A couple of days later, she called her old boss Tina to see if there were any jobs going. Tina was delighted to hear from her and was happy to catch up. There was a bit of project work on and Tina was happy for her to return on a casual basis to work on some of the short-term contracts until Karen could sort out what she wanted to do. Karen decided to take up the offer and resigned, returning to Melbourne a fortnight later where she quickly settled in. She enjoyed the work, especially when she found she could get away on time most nights. By deliberately avoiding the usual networking, Karen was able to avoid drinking again but it was not easy, living in a unit on her own.

The company had a couple of longer turn contracts at that time and some of the organisations were looking to take those positions back in-house. One of them was Economic Development and Tourism. Tina decided to talk to Karen about them.

'It is a good position and while it does not come with a contract salary, it is a job that really suits your qualifications and experience and it is also closer to home,' she told Karen.

'Why are you telling me this?'

'For a number of reasons; they want us to fill the position full-time and I want to put someone in there who will reflect well on this company so that we will be the first company they reach out to when they are next looking to fill a position.'

'Any other reasons?' Karen questioned.

'I think you need to have a look at the position and the lifestyle it offers. You have some unresolved issues back home and you to be close to home to do that. Bairnsdale is close enough to home to do that yet far enough away if things don't turn out exactly how you hope.'

'That's just it. I'm not sure how I want things to turn out.'

'Then it is all the more reason why you should go and settle into the job and allow yourself time to settle in and then once you are established to work on those things, having a secure base to work from.'

'I will need time to look at the position and think it over.'

'Take your time but I do need an answer by the end of the week. You do understand that I do not think you have a future in the city. Now, I can no more recommend some of the city girls for this job any more than I could have sent you to Sydney instead of Gayle. You can see that now, can't you?'

'Yes, I can. Thank you,' Karen replied.

*

Karen looked over the job description and took the opportunity to visit the shire offices and talk to the CEO and Director of Corporate Services. The meeting went really well as they told her they liked her style and would be happy for her to start on a contract basis with a six months' review with the intention of her joining the shire on a full-time basis or leaving if all parties were not happy without any form of recrimination from either side. Karen did not accept straight away but decided to call in on her mother and talk about it given that she was not far down the road.

'I'm going to accept the position in Bairnsdale.'

'And Ben, when are you going to tell him?'

'I'm not for the moment. Right now, I have to concentrate on getting this job up. When I'm settled then I will sort things out with Ben.'

'Moving back this way will be a start.'

'Perhaps, but Ben is not the reason why I'm moving back. The position is the best for me at the moment. The job is the thing that is important; it gets me out of Melbourne again and gives me a stepping stone to other things if I want it.'

'I don't doubt you but Ben is also part of it, isn't he?'

'I'm really not sure; Ben is not the main priority at the moment – work is.'

'Fair enough,' Fiona replied.

*

That Friday, she walked into Tina's office with a letter in her hand.

'Is this what I think it is?'

'Yes, I'm accepting the position in Bairnsdale; it's time to move on and we know the city is not the place for me,' Karen told her.

'Then close the door. I think this one deserves a drink if that's not going to cause you problems.'

'No, I want this drink. I don't need it,' Karen replied.

'They rang me and I sang your praises so it is up to you now.'

'I'll try not to let you down.'

'You won't; you know your stuff. Now may the future be all that you hope for,' Tina said handing her a glass.

'Thank you,' Karen replied.

*

It didn't take long for Gayle to hear that Karen had given notice and was soon on the phone.

'What's this about you leaving? Did you get a better offer?' she questioned.

'Not in monetary terms but certainly in lifestyle.'

'You're going home?' Gayle questioned.

'Not so much home but back to the country. I had two offers to consider – one at Bendigo as well as Bairnsdale.'

'Then why not Bendigo? Or did you want to be close to your parents?'

'No, Bendigo was a purely financial position whereas Bairnsdale is Tourism, Economic Development as well as being part of the financial management team. Being close to my parents is a bonus and I know the area and have a good idea of the tourism infrastructure already.'

'I thought we made ourselves a promise to leave and never return?' Gayle asked.

'Perhaps but it is a promise I couldn't keep and besides, I'm going back on my terms – nobody else's,' Karen replied.

'That's true enough; well, I hope it works out for you. I really do.'

'Thank you.'

'I'll come and visit,' Gayle told her.

'You do that; I'll have a bed for you as soon as I am set up.'

# CHAPTER ELEVEN

*Return to town*

Moving into her new position, Karen kept a low profile at first, attending local meetings and introducing herself afterwards as she got to know the various groups in the area and gain an understanding of the environment in which she saw them operating in. From the outsets, she began to look at making alliances between groups to create tourism packages. With food and wine being the obvious, she also looked to link the tour operators with the food and wine groups so that no one group operated in isolation and the tourist public got the wider picture of what the area had to offer.

At one of the meetings, she ran into Ben who said hello just before the meeting started but it was not like old times; there was a distance between them this time. Ben remained, as always, on the fringes but now when he spoke, people listened. Karen listened too as he spelled out the issues as he saw them and he proved to have a real handle on the issues of balancing tourism and the environment, understanding the need for yearlong employment over seasonal tourism-based employment. It was not surprising given that his own business was a mix of both but he understood the bigger picture better than most. At times he was the voice of reason in a room full of emotion and strong wills. He proved to be an excellent chair of the local business group despite being outside of his comfort zone.

They met again at the Omeo meeting which was always going to be difficult because of the nature of the area and what was seen as the old guard and those welcoming change. Ben sat with Jack and together, they were a force that held their ground against the onslaught of a newcomer who seemed determined to push some radical changes. The need to retain Omeo's traditional base was the focus of their argument. While not wanting to stifle the development of Dinner Plain, they were determined that Omeo would not be reduced to being a satellite of it. At the end of the meeting, they had won the argument being seen as the voice of reason by most sides of the argument. All of this was a side of Ben she had longed believed was there but was possibly forced due to the impact of economic change upon his own business.

Other meetings followed from that which resulted in tourism and economic development strategies. It took months to get the first of it into draft form and longer still for some of the strategies to be adopted but it did result in a number of more focused tourism campaigns that reached a new target audience. Financially, the program was managed and financed in part by the use of specific grants that the various grants were assisted to apply for. Karen found that Ben understood the process very well and ensured the forms were not only complete but very well put together with detailed submissions and financial reports where required. It was what she had long suspected he was capable of but had not seen to that point.

'These are really good. All the boxes are ticked – it should have a good chance of gaining funding,' she told him.

'Well, that's because you have shown us how. All we've had to do is follow your lead.'

'Thank you. On a personal note; Ben, are we okay? Would you mind if I dropped in to catch up one day?'

'Of course, you know where I live,' Ben replied.

'Yes, I do. I'd love to catch up next time I am in the area,' Karen told her. 'It would be good. I wouldn't mind hearing what you've been up with the rest of the property, and I've heard some good things about what you're doing of late.'

'Yeah, I would be happy to show you around if you're interested,' Ben told her without committing himself.

'I am, Ben; I would really like to reconnect with you,' Karen told him.

'I thought we were already doing that,' Ben replied.

'You know what I mean. We were closer than this once.'

'Yes, but one of us moved away and I don't mean to Melbourne.'

'So, it's all my fault is it?' Karen asked, trying not to sound hurt.

'Karen, I don't think you have known what you've wanted for some time and it appeared that I was an embarrassment to you. Now, I didn't mind being introduced as some old friend from back home but not to be acknowledged or introduced at all that was different.'

'I know, Ben, and I am sorry. Things a different now I promise. I'm a different person in the country.'

'Then welcome home,' Ben said without enthusiasm, his guard still up.

\*

Karen visited Ben a couple of times and they sat on the rails of a fence and talked. Ben welcomed her, letting his guard a little more each time. Once he stopped to see her after work, which was a nice surprise, but he declined to enter the cottage and talked at the front door before leaving.

One Saturday, Karen finished work and went for a drive and almost inevitably ended up at Ben's after initially heading for her mother's. She found Michael clearing the front paddock, trimming around the posts.

'Hi, Michael. Is Ben about?'

'He's due back soon with some horses from the high paddock. If you head down to the river bridge, he should be along shortly and he will be holding them in old yards down there,' he replied.

'Thank you,' Karen replied and parked her car near the house before walking through the yards, escorted by one of the kelpies who met any visitors. Ben's dog, Jesse, was on guard on the verandah, watching her without moving.

The walk down to the river was pleasant. The country on the opposite bank rose steeply, which was part of Ben's place and why people didn't want the property over the years. The old timber bridge was built in the 1890s from rough-sawn logs milled locally. Since then, it had survived fire and flood and had once served as a link with a number of small remote mines in the high country, which had long since closed.

At the edge of the clearing near the bridge stood an old stockyard that had been built in the 1920s to replace the one burnt down the previous summer. On the river flat, beside the river, was the old firepit, over which many a story had been told when cattlemen and miners met over a tea and damper.

Ben had left his cooking gear in an old heavy timber chest beneath a small tin shelter on the edge of the clearing. Karen found the billy, some tea and sugar. She filled the billy from the river and hung it over the hot coals. She soon had warmed up from a small fire lit in the pit. While she was waiting for the billy to boil, Karen sat and stared into the flames.

Her thoughts were broken by the distant crack of a horse heading to the river bridge. The billy was close to boiling so she dropped in some tea leaves and opened a tin of homemade biscuits she had brought with her before standing up to catch a glimpse of Ben descending through the trees.

After what seemed like an age, Ben appeared through the trees, a small group of horses in front of him. The horses moved unhurried under his guidance, allowing them to make their own way down the steep slope. Crossing the earth-covered timbers, the horses made a unique sound as they moved into sight. Karen was captivated by what she saw as Ben as he followed them into the clearing. For the first time in her life, she saw Ben as a man, unashamedly masculine. There was something earthy and rugged about him that captivated her eyes. For the first time, she saw him not so much as a friend but as a man who could make love to her. He had changed and she did not know why – it frightened her.

'Hello, Karen. What brings you here?' he asked from the back of his horse after closing the gate behind the horses.

'I was just passing. Would you like a cuppa?' she asked, holding up the billy.

'Sure, but do you want to explain the "just passing" again because the road ends at my front door.'

'Okay, I came to see you and now I have,' she said, not making eye contact or looking at him because she felt his masculinity in a way she never did with Mark.

'What is that supposed to mean?'

'I missed you, okay? I'm back. You can't stay mad at me forever,' Karen pleaded.

'I'm not mad at you, Karen, what made you think that?'

'I've been back in the area for a while and we met a couple of times but you haven't called or anything.'

'I thought I would give you time to settle in first. The last thing you want is for me to be calling at all hours just to say hello. Besides, phones work both ways.'

'That's true. I should have rung if was so important.'

'Yes, you should have. Do you want that cuppa now?'

'Can I ask what's wrong? You look as nervous as a kitten,' Ben questioned, looking at her but Karen could not or would not make eye contact.

'You've become a man,' is what she wanted to say but would sound crazy because he was a man just as long as she was a woman but for some reason, she had not seen it until now.

'What is it?' Ben asked again.

'I just wanted to make sure that we were friends again,' Karen replied.

'But we are friends, Karen. Why can't you look at me? What's wrong?' he asked, looking at her even more intently.

'It's not you, okay. It's just something I have to work through. I promise it's nothing for you to worry about. When I've worked through some things, we'll talk, okay?' Karen replied, standing up.

'Take as long as you like. I'll be here when you're ready to talk – I'm a good listener.'

'I know, Ben, and it means more than you know,' Karen replied, then kissed him on the cheek before hurrying away leaving Ben to ponder the change that had seemed to have overcome.

# CHAPTER TWELVE

*Together*

Karen rang Ben a couple of days later after taking a couple of days to think. She invited herself to his place to talk to him over afternoon tea. She arrived to find lunch set out on a table on the back verandah overlooking the small houseyard. Ben came out to meet her. They sat together while he served her tea and wonderful sandwiches.

'What was it you wanted to talk about? Does it have something to do with the other day down by the river?' he asked when they had eaten.

'You're right, it does have something to do with the other day. You have always been a friend that I have taken for granted at times when we had such a falling out and for that, I am very sorry. When I met you down by the river the other day, I wanted you to know that I would never take you for granted again. When I saw you, I got confused about you – about us,' Karen began.

'What do you mean, confused? I don't understand,' Ben questioned.

Karen stood up and walked to the edge of the verandah. Ben walked over to her.

'What is it?' he asked.

'There was something I wanted to do down by the river,' Karen told him, taking a step towards him. She leaned towards him and kissed him full on the mouth, holding him gently for a moment. Ben held her too then.

She suddenly felt Ben pull away sharply.

'What the hell was that for? If you're going to say goodbye, say it but never kiss me like that, not if it's goodbye. I don't want to know you like that not if this is goodbye,' he snapped.

'Is that what you think this is? Do you think I'm saying goodbye?'

'Well, aren't you?' Ben questioned with hurt in his eyes.

'Ben, no, I'm not saying goodbye. I would never kiss you like that if I was saying goodbye.'

'Then what was that about?' he asked, looking confused.

'I want to go out with you. I want to be with you,' Karen replied, stepping closer to him but he stepped away, looking at her with wild eyes. 'Ben, please say something,' Karen pleaded, fearing the worst.

'Why are you doing this?' he questioned as Karen saw him struggling to get his thoughts together.

'Because I want to; you and I have been friends for a long time. Down by the river the other day, I realised that we could be so much more. Ben, we can only find that out if we try.'

'Karen, I don't want to lose you and if this doesn't work between us that is what will happen. I will lose you.'

'You are already assuming it won't work. Have you ever considered what would have if it did?' Karen asked him.

Ben paced the verandah, stealing quick glances at her, his mind in complete turmoil. 'Karen, you of all people know that I'm no good with people. I am so completely different from you. You know what people think of me.'

'You say that but these last few weeks you have been the voice of reason in meetings where people listen and respect what you have to say.'

'But you are asking me to be in a relationship with you,' he pleaded.

'Yes, I am but we are already in a relationship – we are already good friends; I'm only asking you to take it to another level. Ben, we could have a real future together, the two of us; now, isn't that worth taking a risk on?'

'I'm just not sure; I just can't think straight just at this moment.'

'Are you saying you don't want to go out with me?'

'No, I'm not saying that at all, I just need time to think about it. I'm sorry it's not the answer you are looking for but you have had time to think about it, I need the same. I'm just a little thrown. I expected to say goodbye to you one day when you met someone but not this.'

'Okay, Ben, I understand, I assumed too much. I will be at Mum's for the rest of the day and you have my other numbers; please call.'

'I will, I promise. Karen, please don't be angry with me.'

'Ben, I'm not angry with you. You need time, I can see that. We'll talk soon,' Karen replied before walking away, feeling very emotionally exposed.

*

Karen was in a very subdued mood when she arrived at her mother's a few minutes later.

'What's wrong? You look a million miles away,' Fiona asked when Karen walked in the door looking a little distressed.

'I'm not a million miles away, I'm just over the hill actually.'

'Ben?' Fiona questioned.

'Yes, I kissed Ben and asked him to go out with me.'

'And he didn't react well, I take it?'

'He had no idea. He thought I was saying goodbye. Now he needs time to think,' Karen replied, unsure of how she could have read the situation so wrong.

'I can't say I'm surprised. I didn't think he would have seen it coming. Of course, he needs time to think, you've been planning this for some time but Ben has been holding on to little more than hope.'

'What do you mean? I only decided I wanted to go out with him a couple of days ago.'

'Moving here was not about Ben?'

'No.'

'Karen, please, you wouldn't have taken the job had it not been for Ben?'

'It wasn't like that at all.'

'Wasn't it? In all the times you have been coming home to see us, you have spent most of your time with Ben. Since Mark has been gone, it has been more so. You haven't mentioned Ben's name but you have always been around there. Now, I know the job was part of it but Ben has been a part of your plans a lot longer than you're admitting at the moment,' Fiona told her.

It was Karen's turn to be silent and think, having not considered Ben to be such a factor in her job selection.

'Karen, it's okay that you need him but just remember he's had a lot of negative input into his life and it is going to take some time for him to get used to having someone love him,' Fiona added.

'I really want to know what that's like.'

'And that's okay but just be careful. Make sure you save the physical for when you are married,' Fiona told her, which caused Karen to blush.

'I have no intention of sleeping with him.'

'Perhaps not at the moment. You really need to be careful because you may only get one chance at this.'

'I know, that is why I want to give him space. At the end of the day, he might decide he doesn't want to go out with me anyway.'

'Come on, you don't think that for a minute.'

'No, but I also know that nothing is certain in life. When I left here, I was certain then that I would never be back.'

'But that's because you never really left. Through work and uni, you have always returned most of the time to see Ben but sometimes it was just your horse. Hamilton was not the city but it was not home either. The country never really left the girl.'

'That's true; Ben is part of it, I'll admit that, but as much as I tried, I never got to a point where it was home.'

*

Ben did not call that day and Karen's heart sank until some flowers arrived at her office Monday morning. She was delighted if not a little embarrassed when one of the customer service girls carried them into her office with a knowing smile. He had sent a note with it asking her on their first date to Carlo's at Lake Entrance that Friday. The note made her whole week and others in the office noticed it too, gently teasing her.

At exactly seven p.m., Karen walked into the restaurant looking for Ben. Being their first date, she went all out to impress. She chose a dress and coat that she knew she looked good in but could wear flat shoes with so that they could go walking near the beach afterwards. She put on bright red lipstick for the first time, which was highlighted by her fair complexion. She found him waiting for her at the table. He stood up to meet her.

Dressed in deep blue trousers, a dinner jacket over the top of a freshly ironed white shirt, he looked as good as she had ever seen him and she liked what she saw.

'Hi, it's good to see you,' he said, holding out his hand to her, which she accepted. Ben surprised her by kissing the back of it. 'I wasn't sure if you'd come,' he added.

'Why wouldn't I? I asked, you remember?' she replied as Ben invited her to sit. The one thing Karen had noticed was the total lack of physical contact between them in all the years they had known each other. Ben's kiss of her hand was a significant gesture by Ben, which had her wondering. She reached for his hand across the table after they had ordered and he accepted her hand, holding hers gently.

'Are you okay?' she asked as Ben seemed unsure whether to make eye contact or not.

'Yeah, I'm okay. I'm just wrestling with the fact that you are here and that we are on a date. I never believed that it would ever happen.'

'Did you want this to happen before I asked you?'

'Of course, I did.'

'Then why didn't you say something?'

'Because it never occurred to me that you would want to,' Ben replied without looking at her.

'Why not? We are friends and you are one of the most caring and loyal people I have ever met.'

'You seemed happy enough with us being friends. I didn't want to spoil that.'

'Where do you fit into that same equation? What about what you wanted?' Karen questioned.

'That doesn't matter.' Ben shrugged.

'That's just it; what you want does matter – it matters to me. There are two people in this relationship now, not one. I am not the only one in this relationship. You need to tell me what you want and don't be afraid to disagree with me,' Karen told him. She noticed the trembling in Ben's hands and his efforts to hide it. 'Ben, it's going to be okay,' she said, giving his hand a reassuring pat.

Their meals arrived and the conversation lightened, Karen telling Ben about the small cottage she bought above the river. Being on safe ground, Ben became more animated as he quoted much of the history of the fishing cottages along the river. When Karen told him the address, he knew the cottage and was able to tell her a great deal about it including its approximate construction date and the man who built it. In the years that Karen had known Ben, he had always such an amazing grasp of the local history of the area and could often connect that history to a wider social and political history. It was his stories that attracted people to his high-country rides where he connected people with their surrounds and the people who had gone before them. His knowledge also made him a popular speaker with local historical societies, a role that surprised her a little but having heard she never tired of him.

Later, they went for a walk along the beach. She reached for his hand and turned to him as he leaned against the sea wall. 'I don't bite, you know,' Karen said, wrapping her arms around him, leaning into him and holding him close.

'I'm sorry,' Ben replied.

'What are you apologising for? I won't break my promise,' Karen told him.

Ben gingerly wrapped his arms around her. 'I don't want to disappoint you.'

'You are here with me and I'm not the least bit disappointed. I like physical contact with the people I love. You will get used to me in time,' Karen said, holding his arms about her. She felt the power in his arms and knew she could lose herself in those arms; she felt the tension and uncertainty in his touch. 'This is nice,' she said, looking into his eyes that were so full of fear and uncertainty.

'It is,' Ben replied, looking into her eyes for the first time.

'You are a beautiful person, Ben Templeton,' Karen told him and then kissed him. Ben returned her kiss this time and it was all that Karen had hoped. His gentle lips were full of warmth.

'Now, that was better than our first kiss.' Karen smiled.

'Yes, it was,' Ben replied, holding her close. 'Can I tell you something?' Ben asked after a quiet moment.

'Sure.'

'Many years ago, I was walking alone on this very beach. I remember seeing a young couple. The girl reminded me so much of you that I wondered what it would be like to walk along the beach with you like that.'

'Really? When was that?'

'Towards the end of year twelve.'

'After you saved me?'

'Yes.'

'And you've kept that dream to yourself ever since?'

'No, I forgot about it soon afterwards and did not remember it until just now,' Ben replied.

'Why didn't you say anything at the time?'

'There was no point. I was the last person you wanted to be rescued by and you were leaving anyway just as I was.'

'So, you let your dream just die?'

'Yes.'

'Well, this is real; is it as good as your dream?' Karen asked.

'Better,' Ben replied and Karen could feel her heart skip a bit. In the time it had taken to have tea and walk along the beach, her world had changed. Ben had entered her life.

'I'm glad,' Karen replied, holding him close. 'There is so much you have hidden away. What other dreams have you hidden?' she asked.

'None that I can remember.'

'Or will admit to? You have had to bury so much in order just to survive. I hope that I can unlock some of those dreams so that I can see a sparkle in your eyes again,' Karen told him, which caused Ben to blush. 'Ben, can I ask you something?'

'Sure.'

'What did you think when I arrived tonight?'

'Just how good you looked. In all the years I've known you, I have never seen you wear red lipstick like that before. Can I ask why?'

'Because I knew or perhaps just hoped that you would notice and that I would get kissed by you tonight. What did think when I first kissed you? I know how you reacted but what was your first thought?'

'You took my breath away. For a split second, I thought it was the most incredible thing to ever happen to me but then I thought you were saying goodbye and then thought that you were about to break my heart.'

'That is the thing I would never do. I have taken you and our friendship for granted up to this point; I don't want to ever do that again. I want you to know that I care for you a great deal and that I am here for you and I won't leave the moment things get tough.'

'Thank you. It is not going to be easy with me – there have been dark times and places in my life and I know that I am not free of them. I don't want to frighten you, just warn you that I'm used to handling things alone.'

'But that is what I'm here for now, so that you don't have to do it alone anymore,' Karen told him.

# CHAPTER THIRTEEN

*The past catches up*

They had not been going long when Ben's past caught up with him. Karen was giving Ben a hand to clear out one of the back rooms of the main stable one weekend when Karen found an ornate walking stick.

'What's this? You know, it reminds me of the one Reverend Alexander used to have,' Karen said with a smile of discovery until she saw the look on Ben's face. Ben's face was ashen his eyes fixed on the cane. 'Ben!' Karen called in alarm.

'It is the one he used to have,' Ben replied without taking his eyes off the cane.

'How did you get this?' Karen asked, not believing for a moment that he had stolen it but for other more sinister reasons. As much as she did not want to know the answer, she knew she had to get him to talk about it.

'It doesn't matter. This has been a mistake, you should go. I don't want you to come back here again,' Ben told her as he reached for the cane.

'I'm not going anywhere until you tell me what this is all about,' Karen told him, deliberately pulling the cane away from him.

'You have no idea what this is about and it's better if you don't. Now please give me the cane and leave.'

'Ben, I have to know especially if this is the thing that is going to split us,' Karen replied.

'If you care you won't do this.'

'I'm doing this because I care. You know, of all the people in the world, you can trust me. Trust me now, trust me with this. Ben, we can talk about this and get through this together or you can close the door on me and be forever in bondage to whatever this represents. Let me in; please,' Karen pleaded as she sat with him.

'Don't leave; I am sorry. You are the one person I know that I can trust,' Ben told her with his head bowed.

'I'm not going anywhere. What happened, Ben?'

'Reverend Alexander used to beat me with it. He took over my care after my father made some arrangements with him before he left. My physical needs were met. There was food in the cupboards so I was not hungry It meant that I could cook my own meals but I didn't mind that. It would have been okay if it had been left at that but the problem was that he took particular interest in my spiritual well-being as he called it. His idea of my spiritual well-being was to lecture me endlessly about how worthless, lazy and sinful I was.

'To be honest, I didn't take much notice at first but then he began finishing it with a slap with a leather strap. I thought I must have done something to deserve it so I took it at first but the sermons and beatings got worse and worse. I tried fighting back once but he beat me to a standstill, I could barely move when he left,' Ben told her, his voice as distant as his eyes. Karen could only listen in disbelief.

'I stayed away from home as much as I could. I went home to change, grab a few things and hide out but then he began to arrive at all hours so I began sleeping in the hills. The Reverend knew and I knew that one day our paths would cross and it was going to get ugly. We did and it was. He raved and swung at me sure enough but this time it was pure madness. He kept laying into me with anything he could and I knew that if I didn't fight back he would kill me. It became a bar-room fight with no rules. At some point, he hit me with that cane and broke my collarbone. I was insane with pain and somehow, I got the cane off him and chased him out of the house, telling him never to return. He never did. I haven't seen him since,' Ben said with a voice so distant that Karen wondered if she would ever reach him again.

'How old were you?'

'I was fourteen. I have had trouble trusting people since then.' He shrugged then his whole body trembled and an animal escaped him as the pain came to the surface. He fought back the grief that threatened to overwhelm him. Karen squeezed his hand, not knowing what else to do as he fought to contain the pain of those memories.

'I'm here, Ben; I'm still here,' she said as she watched Ben push all that emotion back down before continuing. It all but broke Karen's heart.

'I hid that cane in here and then went into the hills and stayed with old Joe Hamill until my shoulder healed. I came back to an empty house and went back to school. Nobody did a damn thing about it and in time I forgot about it until just now.'

'I'm so sorry, Ben. I had no idea.'

'You weren't meant to. I was ashamed that people would think that badly of me, that they thought I deserved that, so I kept to myself. The Cambodia's figured it out and your father suspected something so he gave me what work he could, thinking it would help, which it did.'

'He never said anything.'

'He wasn't meant to. I asked him that what went between us stayed between us.'

'And you've carried those memories alone since?'

'Pretty much.'

'Did anyone else beat you?' Karen asked, hoping he would say no.

'My father did; that's why he left. I wanted to talk about my mother but he could not stand hearing her name so he beat me senseless. When I woke up, he was gone and I ran away. When I got back, he was gone and then the Reverend turned up.'

'How on Earth did you survive?'

'I don't know, to be honest.'

'Is there anything I can do?'

'You can help me find the Reverend. It is time I gave this back or, as you say, it will hold me in its grasp for the rest of my life.'

'My mother has contact in the church she can help. Are you sure you are strong enough to do this?'

'No, but I have to do this.'

'I will do anything and everything and everything I can do to help.'

'Thank you.'

'Come on, we need to get out of here and settle. I don't want to leave like this,' Karen told him.

'Sure, I'll put the kettle on while you wash up,' Ben replied, indicating the semidetached laundry.

Karen sat with him for a couple of hours while he talked and she listened. She had long known that he was alone and isolated but had no understanding of the pain and emptiness in his life. All the time, his voice was etched with such pain it took everything she had to stop herself from breaking down.

\*

Karen fled to her mother where she fell into her arms and sobbed.

'Mum, he has been so terribly hurt. He has been physically and emotionally abused. He's been so hurt by people who were supposed to care for him.' She cried as proceeded to tell Fiona what Ben had told her.

'Karen, Ben was very good at keeping family secrets. I don't know what he went through but he has done it tough, tougher than most. The thing for you is, are you going to be strong enough to work through it with him?' Fiona asked in reply.

'I think so. He is such a strong person. Now he wants to return the cane to Reverend Alexander so that he can put it behind him. Can you help us with that?'

'I'll make a few calls and see what I can arrange. I hope that Ben can put this behind him when he does meet the Reverend because a major confrontation will not do either of them any good.'

'I know that. Ben and I will do a lot of talking before we get there to ensure we can all get out of this thing with as much dignity as possible.

\*

A few weeks later, they arrived outside the manse in Bairnsdale to meet with Reverend Alexander. Karen could see the intensity in Ben's eyes to end the years of pain and regret. She held his hand as they walked to the front door.

Ben introduced himself and Karen when they were met at the front door.

'Reverend and Mrs Alexander are expecting you,' a well-dressed woman said before directing them through the offices, which the manse now served, to where the Alexanders were waiting.

'Mr and Mrs Alexander, thank you for seeing us,' Karen said to open the conversation.

Reverend Alexander invited them to sit with them. 'Now, what can we do for you?' he asked.

'You may not remember me but I have something of yours,' Ben told him before pulling the cane from the bag he was carrying and placing it on the table in front of everyone. Reverend Alexander went white. 'It's yours, not mine and it's time to give it back,' Ben added, pushing it across the table towards him.

Reverend Alexander didn't move while his wife looked at the cane and then at her husband.

'The stories were true. You beat him with that and he took it from you?' Mrs Alexander questioned.

'Yes, and what's more terrible, I had managed to forget about it until just now. I don't know what to say,' Reverend Alexander told him.

'Reverend, I am not here for retribution. Karen found this when she was giving me a hand to clean up a storeroom at my place. What I am hoping is that by returning this to you we can both put a very dark period of our lives behind us. My apology to you is having kept what does not belong to me and to apologise for whatever I did to cause you such rage.'

Reverend Alexander sat motionless for a few moments as everyone waited for his reply. He looked at the cane and then looked at Ben for the first time since he arrived.

'This cane was a gift from an esteemed colleague, which was supposed to be a symbol of ministry, of caring for people, a symbol of pride in what I have done as a minister of the cloth. What it is now is a symbol of the brutality it brought to your life; that I brought into your life. I have, over the years, tried to forget it and the past it represents since you took it from me. Now you have brought it back to me and I am deeply, deeply ashamed. I am also deeply humbled by your actions and I am in awe of your courage. I have nothing to offer you apart from my deepest apologies and to tell you that you have nothing to apologise for. It was my own rage that caused your beating, not anything that you did. Given all that, I will, if you wish, accompany you to the police to fully report what took place and to accept fully whatever comes from that,' Reverend Alexander told him.

'There is no need for that. I came here not for retribution but to confront the past so that I may be able to put this thing behind us. You have acknowledged the past and so I am able to accept your apology.

My only request now is that you give me your word that you not use it on anyone else ever again.'

'You have my word. Now, there is something I must do,' Reverend Alexander said, standing up and sliding the cane from the table. He walked over to a blue stone pillar and leaned it against the stonework at an angle where he smashed it with his foot. He then picked up the pieces and returned to the table, a number of brass ornaments hanging from the remains. 'This now needs to be burned. If you take one piece and I the other, we should burn this thing together so that you know that it is gone forever. Will you do that?' he asked.

'Yes, I will,' Ben replied and stood up. The women stood too but the reverend waved them down.

'This must be between us, if you'll excuse us for a few moments,' Reverend Alexander told them before the two men walked away.

When they had left, Mrs Alexander turned to Karen.

'What an amazing person Ben is. Are you a friend or a little more?' she asked.

'We have just started going out together.'

'This is a huge test for your relationship then. I am sorry that you have to carry this. You must be a remarkable person too to be able to share this with him.'

'Ben is the remarkable one. He has always looked out for others when the whole world turned its back on him. His courage to go on is, as I said, amazing. I believe he will be stronger again for having gone through this.'

'I have no doubt about that. When they return, I hope that you will join us for afternoon tea. I know that sounds trivial, given what is happening here, but there are also things I would like to say to Ben and then to both of you. I hope that you will stay and take the time as this is not something to just walk away from. This is the beginning of the healing process, not the end.'

'I know that too and I am going to see it through with him,' Karen told her.

'Then you need support too, away from Ben. I want you both to leave here with some tools to allow you to move on because you may feel very empty when this is over.'

'I don't doubt that.'

'If you'll excuse me, I shall make the tea.'

'Please, let me help. We can talk then too,' Karen offered.

'Certainly.'

When the men returned, the women could see that both men had been crying.

'Karen, this is a man of great character and courage. You must be very proud of him.'

'Yes, Reverend, I am. I am dating one of the most amazing people I have ever met,' Karen replied with tears in her eyes.

'Please, join us,' Mrs Alexander said, indicating the table set for afternoon tea. They filled their cups and took a moment to reflect before Mrs Alexander turned to Ben.

'Ben, I have my own apology to make to you. There were all kinds of stories about what happened to that cane and my husband's outburst. I did not listen to any of it nor follow the call of my own heart to confront Bill with what I knew and suspected in my own heart. I put my loyalty to Bill ahead of others and ahead of my own call to ministry; in doing so, I did you, Bill and myself a great injustice. I can only apologise to you and ask your forgiveness,' she told him.

'Apology accepted. Thank you for saying so. I should have said something to others and asked for help. Had I done that, this would never have dragged on this long,' Ben replied.

'Ben, you were a child under the care of others; it was those adults around you, myself included, who let you down. You must not carry this. Today, you have placed your burden at our feet but it was never your burden to carry; that burden is where it belongs. I hope that from today, you'll be free of that and that freedom will allow you to love and be loved by this remarkable person that you brought with you today.'

'She is remarkable,' Ben said, looking at Karen squarely, taking her hand and squeezing it gently in the rarest of public displays of affection, which she cherished. 'You have all been full of my praises for doing this today but it is for selfish reasons and I was not always as forgiving. There was a time that I hated you, Reverend, for what you did. I hated you, Mrs Alexander, for doing nothing and I hated you, Karen, because you were and are so beautiful,' Ben told them with tears streaming down his face but waved off any attempt to comfort him. 'At some point, I knew I had to stop hating and trust a little. Then came this person knocking on my door, insisting that she become my friend. She showed me another way to match what I had read in a small bible the reverend had given me when I was young and before all this went so far off track. I'm no saint so please forgive me for the things I thought about each of you.'

Everyone was silent for a moment.

'What is remarkable is that you had some whisper of faith and that you and you alone acted upon that faith. Karen could have knocked on that door forever but it meant nothing until you opened it. You chose to forgive; no one could make that decision for you, that is what makes us think highly of you. Had you opened that door to Karen and not come to that point of forgiveness, you would be here now and you would be dragging Karen into that hate and two lives would be adrift in the pain of the past. Instead, you can both move on from here because of the forgiveness you have in your heart. You can build something new for both of you from here. It is no accident that you are here any more than it is an accident that Karen is here with you. If you ever need anyone at all to talk to then I am here twenty-four hours a day seven days a week – that is my commitment to both of you.'

'Thank you, Mrs Alexander, it means a great deal,' Ben replied.

'Is there anything that I can do at this point?' Reverend Alexander asked.

'Yes, there is one thing. I have not been able to find my sister Helen. I want to know that she is okay if at all possible, to meet her. My father refuses to tell me anything and neither will any of the agencies I've spoken to.'

'In that case, I will not rest until I find her. I can't guarantee anything after that but I will try to speak with her, find out how she is first-hand and ask her to meet with you. The final decision will not be mine to make but I will do what I can,' he promised.

'Thank you. On that positive note, I think we might leave; we have a way to travel.'

'Certainly,' the reverend said and they stood and shook hands, not in confrontation but with real respect. Mrs Alexander offered her embrace and both Ben and Karen accepted.

'I will be in touch as soon as I know anything at all,' the reverend told him.

'Thank you both for today. I feel I have turned a corner in my life and the road ahead is clearer for it,' Ben told them.

'I believe we all have. Thank you, Ben. God bless,' Mrs Alexander told them.

Karen turned around when they got to the car to take another look at the Alexanders' and could see that the reverend was crying. She felt sorry for both men and could only admire Ben's courage all the more.

Ben sat slumped in the car on the way home, his eyes as distant as ever. At one point, he drifted off to sleep, exhausted by the events of the day. It was not a peaceful sleep though as he was jittery and his voice whimpered occasionally. Tears rolled down her face and she so much wanted to comfort him but did not know how.

# CHAPTER FOURTEEN

## Helen

It was looking good until Ben received news that his father had died. For Ben, it was hard because he was the last living link to his family. There had been no word of Helen but he did wonder if she knew anything of him. There was nothing he could do about it for the moment.

'I can't make tea on Friday, my father died and the funeral is Friday so I won't be able to get back on time,' Ben told Karen when he called her that evening.

'Not a problem. I'm coming with you.'

'You don't have to do that.'

'Yes, I do. He's the last family you have at the moment. Let me know what time you're picking me up.'

'The funeral is in Mallacoota so it will be an early start.'

'It doesn't matter. You tell me a time and I'll be ready.'

'Okay, I'll call you back.'

His father's solicitor rang to arrange a meeting prior to the funeral. He met the solicitor at his office in town when Ben was presented with a box of photographs and a number of letters for him to read. Some of the letters were to his father from Helen going back a couple of years. It was, as Ben had suspected, that his father knew where Helen was but would not share any details of her. They went over the details of the funeral, which had been arranged sometime before his death and was already paid for. It was all a bit clinical with arrangements in place for the disposal of his assets, which were few in number.

The funeral was to be a graveside service at the small Mallacoota cemetery under the gumtrees. There were few people expected and there was no church service. They were just to meet the hearse on the gravel path that ran down the centre of the cemetery. Ben waited at the graveside for the undertakers to arrive when another vehicle arrived. A young woman with long dark hair got out of the car escorted by an older woman. The two of them walked arm in arm towards the grave. The young woman looked up at Ben as they walked towards him.

'Are you Ben Templeton?' she asked.

'Yes I am,' Ben replied, not sure who she was.

'My adopted name is Eleanor Helen Dingy. I was born Helen Templeton.' She hesitated. 'I'm your sister. This is my adoptive mother, Gina,' she said, sadness suddenly filling her eyes.

Ben stood motionless just looking at her for a moment. 'I spent years looking for you.'

'I know; Reverend Alexander found me and told me about you a couple of days ago just as I was told of Dad's death,' Helen told him.

'This was not how I wanted to meet you, not after all these years,' Ben told her, his face grief-stricken.

'I know but perhaps it was what Father wanted. He was a sad lonely old man the few times I met him.'

'He was that,' Ben replied as the hearse pulled into the cemetery gates.

It was a little too much for Helen, clinging to her adoptive mother as the hearse pulled up in front of them. The attendants carried the coffin to the grave and placed the coffin on the white straps of the elevator.

A minister said just a few short words; there was no eulogy, just a statement and a prayer as the coffin was prepared to be lowered.

Tears rolled down Helen's cheeks as she placed a small bunch of flowers on her father's coffin. 'Goodbye, Dad,' she said before turning to Ben, expecting him to make a similar gesture but he just stared dry-eyed at the coffin, his face blank as if watching a length of wood going into the ground instead of a coffin. Karen looked more upset than Ben was as she held on to his arm all the more saddened by Ben's lack of emotion.

Watching the coffin descend to the bottom of the grave was

devastating for Karen. How could it be at the end of a man's life, the only witnesses to his passing were his estranged children, two outsiders, a solicitor and a couple of funeral attendants? His passing was not witnessed by a single friend or workmate after a lifetime of work.

Helen knelt at the graveside and cried for so much more than the passing of her father, her mother laying a comforting hand on her shoulder. Ben could not be more distant looking without really seeing his thoughts very much his own.

*

After the funeral, Helen walked with Karen to the car as Ben just stood silently beside the grave, telling Karen he would join her shortly.

'Can you tell me something? I'm his sister and we haven't seen each other in twenty years but he hasn't even offered me a hug. He didn't even shed a tear at his father's grave. Why is he so cold?'

'There are reasons for that. Ben has had very little positive physical contact with anyone since your mother died. He finds physical contact very difficult.'

'Was he abused or something?'

'It is best if you talk to him.'

'He was, wasn't he?'

'Yes, he was.'

'By whom?'

'You need to speak to Ben about that.'

'But I'm asking you.'

'Yes, and I'm telling you to speak to Ben.'

'What I can't figure out is my father never spoke of him. I believed he was dead for many years.'

'You knew your father?'

'Sort of. I visited him on several occasions; I even visited the place we grew up in.'

'You visited Ben's?'

'Presumably but I never saw him, obviously.'

'He owns the place you grew up in.'

'He can't. I've been there several times.'

'You need to talk to Ben then,' Karen replied as Ben arrived.

'The undertaker has arranged some lunch for us where we can talk and then we can visit Harry's place afterwards,' Ben said.

'Why don't you call him Dad? He is your father, after all.'

'Harry stopped being my father a long time ago.'

'So, you didn't speak. At least you got to live with him for all those years, which is more than I had.'

'Harry walked out on me. I've seen him half a dozen times since.'

'You were fostered out then too,' Helen said hopefully, thinking they had another experience in common.

'No, I wasn't.'

'Then who did you live with?' Helen asked but Ben turned away and began shuffling through some papers.

Helen went to challenge him but Karen took her arm and guided her away from him.

'Why won't he answer me? Is he always this rude?'

'Helen, he lived alone. He's lived alone since your mother died but doesn't like to admit it still.'

'He was abandoned? My father abandoned Ben?'

'You need to talk to Ben.'

'Yes or no?' Helen insisted.

'Yes, he did,' Karen admitted.

'So that's why Ben is so distant. How did he survive?' Helen asked but Karen turned away to hide her own tears. 'Karen?'

'I can't tell you. Please, don't ask me,' Karen replied.

'But you know, though, don't you?'

'Yes, I do. Please, do not judge Ben. He is a truly wonderful person, I promise you that; it's just that not many people ever get close enough to see it.'

'But you have?'

'Yes.'

'How?'

'By chipping away at his shell for many years. Helen, I have known Ben since the middle of high school and I've just really got to know him in very recent times. He has built up a lot of walls to protect himself. Please, don't judge him. You are his sister and the walls will come down for you but not yet. He needs time.'

*

They went to Harry's rough windblown house near the beach. Helen took Ben's arm and they walked down to the beach.

'Harry told me that is where we grew up. Is that true?' Helen questioned.

'No, I have only ever been here once looking for you. It turns out that you were here the day before – not that Harry told me that.'

'Where did we live?'

'Come to my place and I'll show you around.'

'Can I? Karen wouldn't mind if I came and maybe stayed a night or two?'

'No. Why would she?'

'She doesn't live with you?'

'No,' Ben replied, clearly surprised that she would suggest such a thing. Helen apologised for her assumption.

*

Karen stayed in town with Gina.

'This is difficult for both of them,' Gina said as she passed Karen her coffee.

'Yes, I can imagine just how difficult. Ben has been looking for her for years but his father would not tell him anything and the authorities were reluctant to facilitate the meeting.'

'Yes, we know. Reverend Alexander met with us a couple of days ago. There seems to be some history between Ben and the reverend?'

'There has but not all of it good, I'm afraid.'

'I suspected as much. What do you think Ben wants from meeting Helen, do you think? They are both too old to start living as families and Helen has her own commitments now.'

'Ben does not want to interrupt or change anyone's life – he only wanted to know she was alright and now to know the truth about their family,' Karen replied.

'Up until a few weeks ago, Helen was almost certain that Ben was dead. Now not only is he alive, there is so much for them to catch up on – especially, as you say, she has yet to see where she grew up.'

'He knows that. He wants to fill in the gaps and move on,' Karen replied.

'I hope it works for both of them because the little I've seen suggests that they have had very different experiences growing up. The years and experiences won't be easily reconciled.'

'I don't doubt that but it is a journey they must take if they are to move on.'

'You are right of course; I just hope that it is not too painful.'

\*

'What happened to you while you were growing up, Ben?'

'How do you mean?'

'This is one of the biggest days of my life, having buried my father and meeting you. I am hanging on by fingernails but you seem so distant and in control. It is like you have gone into overload and shut down.'

'Perhaps I have. I have always known you were alive so for me, that journey is now at an end and a new less certain one has begun.'

'Perhaps I can understand but we buried our father today. I know he wasn't much of a father to us but it tore my heart out to know he is gone but you stood there emotionless. Why? What did he do to you?'

'He did nothing, which was the problem. I was basically left to bring myself up after our mother died. He was never home; I saw little of him over the years. I know he was lonely after she died but so was I. Getting through each day took everything, I had so I pushed everyone aside. What I feel about Dad's death is nothing other than to say that the struggle to earn his love, respect, whatever, is over. Am I sad that he's gone? I just don't know.'

'Ben, I'm so sorry.'

'You weren't to know.'

'Karen seems nice. How did she get past all the walls you built up over the years?'

'I'm not sure about that either. All I know is that she was the one person who gave a damn over the years. We've been friends since high school. She helped me get on the road back to civilisation again.'

'She must be a special person.'

'She is. Now, tell me about you; how was growing up for you?'

'Gina is the only mother I have known; I don't even have a picture of our mother. Gina has been my strength, my friend and my mum since I was two. I have been fortunate in that I was adopted into a loving family, growing up with two sisters and a younger brother. Bobby was adopted but Stella above me and Evie who is younger are Gina's. I have loved every day I have spent with them.'

'Is there someone special in your life, apart from your family, of course?'

'There is and when the time is right, you will meet them.'

'Them? There is more than one?'

'In time, Ben, in time. I have to reconcile the past before I can open that door to you but I promise at the right time it will be opened to you,' Helen told him but Ben had no way of knowing what that meant and how it would change his life; all he could do was trust a woman he hardly knew.

A few days later, Helen arrived with Karen who met her in town, sharing a brief coffee with her before proceeding on to Ben's. He had breakfast waiting for them laid out on the rear veranda complete with space heaters when they arrived.

Ben met them at the front of the house and escorted them down the side lane and into the house garden via the little wooden gate. He was dressed as Karen so often met him in clean work clothes and that Akubra hat sitting low on his head. Helen did not appear to notice, her attention trying to take in the detail of the house. They walked the stone path to the back of the house where breakfast awaited them. Helen thought it an odd way to introduce anyone, let alone family to his place but did not say anything at the time as he sat them at the table before immediately serving breakfast as if they were guests at a formal function.

'This is lovely, thank you,' Helen replied when he served her fresh bacon and eggs on a plate itself warmed by an iron serving tray.

'Do you remember anything of this place yet?' Ben asked.

'This view of the garden is vaguely familiar but I remember a darker place almost buried in the trees,' Helen replied.

'Many of the trees have been removed as the result of storm damage and to let a little lighter in the place. These views you may remember because we used to play here and in the sandpit to the left of the gate. I've changed nothing since I took over the place. Not that much has changed apart from the restoration work, of course.'

'I do vaguely remember this but it was such a long time ago. Breakfast is superb, by the way, although I normally don't eat much for breakfast but thank you nonetheless. It is a nice change.'

'Ben is quite the cook. You should see what he can do over a campfire.'

'You show me at some stage,' Helen suggested.

'Any time; in the meantime, I'll show you around the place after breakfast,' Ben told her as he sat with them.

Helen stepped gingerly into the kitchen and looked around, trying to make sense of the images as memories of the past and as a sense of who Ben was now. Karen followed, taking in the same images, equating everything she saw with an image she had of Ben. The kitchen was dominated by a line of windows, which opened out onto the back verandah and the wood stove at the opposite end of the room. A bench seat ran the length of the wall beneath the window and an old hardwood table dominated the space of the kitchen. A small side table and kitchen cabinet in the kitchen were the only other pieces of furniture in an otherwise sterile kitchen. There was no colour in the room and a lifelessness Helen could not explain.

'How long did you say you have lived alone in this place?'

'Since I was twelve. Why do you ask?'

'Because there is a sadness about this place that you can feel,' Helen replied.

'I've tried to keep the place nice,' Ben said in his own defence.

'I'm not saying you haven't, it's just that there is no colour in the place. It's as if the colour in your life has gone,' Helen replied. Karen stepped up to his side and gave his hand a reassuring squeeze, knowing Helen didn't mean to hurt him.

They continued the tour via a doorway that split the kitchen, opening onto a lounge room on one side and a second small room that served as an office on the other, leaving another room, which could only be accessed via an almost hidden door. The rest of the house was laid out differently to most with a second half added to the right of the rear kitten door. A number of rooms had been added with a separate roofline on the side of the house which included two additional bedrooms, bathroom and laundry. The verandah continued along the extension, which was partially covered in places.

Ben left them to wander while he cleared away the breakfast dishes.

'Do you remember any of it?' Karen asked as they wandered through the various rooms, most of which were empty.

'A little of it; I'm not sure if I remember it or just want to remember it,' Helen replied.

'That's understandable. I don't think a lot has changed; Ben has made every effort to keep things as they were.'

'Perhaps that's the problem, everything looks so old. It's like this place is a monument to someone or something but no one remembers what. I know that sounds cruel but that's what it looks like,' Helen told her. 'Can I ask a personal question?'

'Of course.'

'What exactly is your relationship with Ben? You seem to be close in some ways and at first, I thought you might have lived together or something but you haven't been inside the house before, have you?'

'No, I've never been in the house; he has always met me on the verandah. He is a very private person; I respect that.'

'But if you are his girlfriend, aren't you offended by not being allowed in the house?'

'It's not a case of not being allowed, it's a case of just not being invited and not pressing the point.'

'Do you think he's worth it though?' Helen questioned.

'Definitely,' Karen replied without hesitation.

'Why if he is so closed?'

'Because behind all his barriers is a really loyal caring person.'

'And you love him, don't you?'

'Yes, I do,' Karen replied.

Helen looked at her a moment before continuing their walk through the house.

*

Later, they rode along the river together, taking a gentle pace. Ben was more relaxed once on horseback, showing the first physical gestures of affection towards Karen as they rode along, reaching for her hand and at one time touching her knee as their horses came close together. Karen was delighted by the touch as it showed a renewed confidence in her and their relationship as if letter her into his house had opened him up on a number of levels.

Over a campfire and the inevitable pot of tea, Ben told Helen of her mother. Karen sat at a discrete distance, making some spicy scones for them to have with the tea, utilising an old family recipe.

Karen served scones and tea on the edge of the river. It was only then that Helen took in the real beauty of that place.

'It is so beautiful here; you must love this place,' Helen said.

'We do,' Ben and Karen said in unison, both laughing at themselves.

'I'd love to ride up into the hills one day when I have a bit more time. Do you know the hills very well, Ben?' Helen questioned.

'I know the hills well enough. I'll take you for a ride up there one day and even arrange an overnighter at one of the huts if you like,' Ben offered.

'That would be great. You won't get lost though, will you?' Helen asked in reply.

'There are few better than Ben in the mountains. You have no worries on that score.'

'You do have confidence in my brother; I'm impressed.'

'Ben is impressive; there is no one better to be in the mountains with. I've known Ben for a long time and there is no one I would not recommend him to. Ben is a member of Mountain Rescue, which is local to this area. Membership to that team is by invitation only and Ben has been part of it as long as I have known him,' Karen told her.

'Really?'

'Yes,' Karen assured her.

'Karen, please, she doesn't want to know that stuff,' Ben snapped.

'But I do. I want to hear about the good stuff too. Who is Mountain Rescue?' Helen asked and Karen was only too willing to oblige talking about his lengthy involvement in the community. Ben got uncomfortable and went for a walk with his dog Jesse further along the river.

'There appears to be different sides to Ben. One that is so cold and distant and another that fully engages with his community. How do you deal with that?'

'Because that is who he is. The community has never embraced him because he kept them at bay and has hidden his secrets so well. He went through some very tough times and did not like people knowing. I've only found out about some of the stuff he went through and I used to see him every day at school. In spite of what he was going through, he always helped people in any way he could. He would find people, even locals, lost in the hills and would get them home. When animals were out on the road, Ben would help the owners return them. When there were floods, he would call on people and help move stock to higher ground. He was so self-reliant and good with horses, he was accepted without question by Mountain Rescue. Ben is a survivor and as such guards his heart. It was his way of staying connected to a community that did embrace him.'

'Okay, I get that but what do you get out of it? You admire him and may even love him but you are very different people and I can't imagine he has a lot to give you or with respect in the bedroom or is that one of your secrets?'

'No, it's nothing like that; Ben and I have never shared a bed. I worked for him on one of his guarded tours to the high country when I was in uni and I got to see him in his element, we were able to sit under the stars half the night and I got to like him a lot over those conversations. I had a successful job with a management accounting firm in Melbourne for a couple of years after uni. That success came with a price and I began to have problems with alcohol. I wasn't getting drunk or anything but I was beginning to drink out of need, not for pleasure. Ben and I talk, we always have, and he was straight with me and helped me get through that. We've been through some tough times together including a long search for you. There is no one I would rather be with.'

'I can see that; it sounds like you are good for each other,' Helen told her.

'I think so,' Karen replied.

When the time came for Helen to leave, it was not difficult for both of them. They looked at each other for a moment and then embraced. 'Thank you for coming. I hope you found it helpful.'

'It was, to see into your world. I'm sorry that I don't remember much of it.'

'It was a long time ago and we have lived very different lives,' Ben replied.

'I know; I just never imagined how different. I would like to spend more time here with you and get to know you and see your world if that's okay.'

'Any time, you only have to call and there will be a room ready for you.'

'Thanks, Ben. I appreciate it.'

# CHAPTER FIFTEEN

*Change*

Caught up in a series of business meetings out of town, they had not seen each other and then with Ben being away for weeks in New South Wales, they had not seen each other for over a month. They had called each other regularly but it was hardly the same. Karen had dropped into the bakery to pick up some afternoon tea to share with her mother before later calling in on Ben when he was up at the post office. To that point, they had always been discreet about their relationship, going to great lengths to keep their relationship private. Now they were face to face on the street.

'Boy, I've missed you. I didn't realise how much until just now,' Karen said, unsure of what to do next.

'I've missed you too,' Ben said, stepping up to her and discreetly taking her hand.

'Oh, what the heck,' Karen said and leaned forward and kissed him on the lips. Instead of pulling away, Ben briefly returned her kiss.

'Wow, that was almost worth being apart for,' Karen told him.

'It was; wasn't it? It is so good to see you,' Ben replied.

'Now the whole town will know. Do you mind?' Karen questioned knowing that people were looking at them.

'Not any more I don't. Besides, we're not sixteen anymore.'

'No, we're not,' Karen replied, looking at him intently for a moment. 'Listen, Mum is expecting me. Do you want to come over for afternoon tea and maybe stay for tea? I'm sure Mum won't mind,' Karen offered.

'I've still got a few things to do. I've been waiting on these parts for a couple of days so I can't make it until tea if that's okay. I don't want to put you off but I've had a hopper offline for a few days.'

'Ben, it's okay, you have a business to run. I'll see you at Mum's for tea then,' Karen said before giving a second quick kiss, which caused Ben to blush before he too returned to his vehicle.

*

It didn't take long for Karen to reach her mother who greeted her warmly.

'I met Ben in town. I hope you don't mind but I invited him for tea?'

'Of course not, you know he is always welcome and he doesn't need an invitation from you either; he is welcome at any time. I take it you two didn't just shake hands when you met this time?'

'No, we kissed. How did you know?'

'Because the phone hasn't stopped ringing; your secret is well and truly out there now.'

'I hope you don't mind. We didn't do anything that would embarrass you. It was a kiss, nothing more.'

'I didn't think it would be. You two are adults now and you have handled yourselves with such dignity. I wondered when you were going to come out with it because I had not heard so much as a rumour until a few minutes ago. This will change your relationship, you know that, don't you?'

'Yes, I do but I also think that Ben is ready because he kissed me back.'

'Then I am happy for both of you. You have missed him, haven't you?'

'Yes, I really have this time. I think we are closer after meeting Helen. Working through that has brought us closer, which I enjoy.'

'Good for you, you have put a lot of work into the pair of you. It's good to see that he is responding to you. I must admit that I was beginning to wonder.'

'Me too; it was as though we had reached a point at one stage that I didn't think we were ever going to get beyond. Having dealt with some of his past has made room for us.'

'That's good. Have you considered where this may be going between you two? You are hardly children anymore.'

'Yes, Mum; I'm not walking into this blind. We have a long way to go before we can consider anything permanent.'

'It may not be as far as you think.'

'Well, we will cross that bridge when we come to it.'

'I'm sure you will but just keep your head up – it may be closer than you think,' Fiona told her.

'What makes you say that?'

'As the barriers come down, you are getting closer and once enough of them come down then you need to consider where you are going from there.'

*

When Ben arrived, Karen ran out to meet him. It was good to see Karen excited about their relationship. From the kitchen window, Fiona watched Karen greet Ben with a kiss that he seemed happy enough to reciprocate. The two of them stood close and talked for a moment before going into the house. Once inside, Ben cooled in his responses to Karen, appearing very conscious of being observed by Fiona and appeared afraid of offending. As much as Karen tried to reassure him, Ben remained extremely reserved and even more so when Ian arrived. Fiona tried to reassure him that they were happy that the two of them were together, fully accepting their relationship. Any physical contact between them vanished after Ian arrived, Ben barely making eye contact with her until he left, very conscious that he worked for Ian.

For his part, Ian was pleased to find Ben at the house and even more so when he realised Ben was staying for tea. The two men talked over tea, the two of them comfortable about talking about work but there was little recognition given to the fact that Ben was there as Karen's partner and not just as a worker. Karen knew why but could not help but feel left out.

When he got up to leave, she went to his side and took his hand, determined to walk him hand-in-hand to the car. Ben was extremely self-conscious as he reluctantly took her hand.

'You don't be a stranger now that you've been once. Drop over any time. You know you are always welcome,' Ian told him.

'Thank you, I appreciate it,' Ben replied as Ian looked at him.

'It's good to see you two together at last,' Ian then added.

'Thank you,' Ben replied, barely making eye contact but it was the approval he needed and Ben physically appeared to relax if only a little.

It got better between them after that with Ben being freer to be with her and being more open with her. He accepted her hand and later her embrace and kiss before leaving.

Ben invited Karen out on the lakes for a day's fishing on a hired motor launch. Fishing was not something she enjoyed nor did she believe that Ben was interested in but decided to go along anyway.

'He's taking you fishing?' Fiona questioned.

'Yes.'

'How romantic.' Fiona smiled.

'Romantic is not what I'd call it but he is determined to make a day of it so what can I say?'

'Be brave, he means well,' Fiona assured her.

'Yes, I know, I just hope I don't disappoint him with an appearance of enthusiasm.'

*

Karen dressed to fend off the cool breeze across the water, with a windproof jacket over a polar-neck sweater as she arrived at the jetty where Ben met her in a beautiful timber motor launch dressed in a vintage jacket and tartan cap. He greeted her with a warm smile and assisted her onto the motor launch. Karen had to smile as he appeared to be making a real effort to make the day enjoyable and memorable and to that point, at least he was succeeding.

It was a pleasant day for just cruising around the lakes, stopping occasionally in one of the small coves or exploring one of the smaller islands where they dropped in a couple of lines. To her surprise, they hooked a couple of good fish. Ben then took her to a fishing hut where he promised to cook her fresh fish. To her surprise, it was not just fresh fish on a basic grill but lunch sitting on the jetting complete with fresh salads and bread he had waiting in the fridge along with a good couple of bottles of wine.

'I must admit that this is very pleasant. I had no idea you were a fisherman.'

'I'm not, I had backup, and there are a couple of fresh fish fillets in the fridge,' Ben admitted in reply.

'Well, your plan worked. You continue to surprise me; this is not something that I could not imagine you doing, which makes this very special.'

'Thank you. I was hoping you were going to enjoy the day.'

'I enjoy spending time with you anywhere. I don't know what made you come up with the idea but I'm impressed – there is this whole other side of you that is such a romantic,' she said which caused him to blush. 'Hey, don't be embarrassed. It wasn't said to embarrass you but to thank you. I always wanted a guy to take the time to do special things for me. This is really great.'

They sat on the jetty to eat the fish and salad and then sat dangling their feet in the water, watching the water and waving to the occasional boat that passed by.

'You have put a lot of effort into today. Thank you, I really appreciate it,' Karen told him.

'The pleasure is mine; you have spent enough time sitting on my verandah or wandering around the yards. It's also a thank you for being with me; it's been tough the last couple of months. I thought it was time to try something a little different so I made a couple of calls and here we are.'

'This was done by doing a lot more than just making a few phone calls. You must have been planning it for weeks. Ben, I told you when we got together that I was here for you and I meant it. You don't have to reward me for staying with you during the tough stuff; I want to be there for you. I love you and that is a reward in itself.'

'You do?' Ben questioned, a little surprised by the statement.

'You know I do and if didn't before this, I'm telling you now that I love you, Ben Templeton,' Karen said and then kissed him.

As the evening began to cool and shadows lengthened across the lake, it was the end to a perfect day.

'I guess we should get going shortly to get the boat back,' Karen said, not wanting the day to end but needing to get back to reality.

'There is no rush – I have arranged for the boat to be collected from here and the ute is parked up behind the hut.'

'You have thought of everything,' she said, wondering if Ben would try some form of sexual advance towards her but found that when he kissed her that night, his hands did not wander as she may have thought but held her as gentle as a child.

# CHAPTER SIXTEEN

## *Family*

Ben went to Boronia to meet the rest of Helen's adoptive family. The family home was modest but well-kept and deceptively large allowing everyone space when they needed. One of the first people Ben was introduced to was Helen's adoptive father, Charlie. He was a bit reserved but there was something about him that Ben knew he was a person he could trust. He showed Ben about the place and filled him in on what he knew following the accident.

He had time with Karen who showed him about, including things like her local school and the like. Back at the house, they sat and talked until the rest of the family arrived. Eve embraced him like a long-lost friend, which caught Ben off guard and tried not to react. Stella was a bit more conservative looking at him summing him up before offering a polite kiss on the cheek in greeting. They were all talking excitedly when a little boy peered around the corner of the kitchen door.

'Hello, who is this?' Ben asked, looking at the little boy.

Helen put her arms out to him and the boy reluctantly left his shelter by the door and pattered up to her followed by a tall fair-haired man.

'Ben, these are the special people I was telling you about. This is my son, Joel,' Helen told him as she held the little boy, which shocked Ben as much as he didn't want it to.

'Hello there, little Joel,' Ben said to the shy little boy who replied with a smile.

'When you are ready, we need to show him the real high country. It's part of his heritage,' Ben told her as Joel made tentative steps towards Ben. Ben opened his arms to him and Joel accepted a short embrace from him before racing back to his mother.

'There is someone else in my life,' Helen said as she cuddled her little boy. 'Ben, this is my husband, Martin,' Helen said, inviting Martin to join her. 'Ben, I'm married. I was a teenage bride,' Helen told him, looking for Ben's reaction who tried not to look shocked but could not help it. He stood to meet Martin with a firm handshake.

'Martin, nice to meet you,' Ben told him.

'Likewise. I'm looking forward to getting to know you. Helen has told me a lot about her big brother. I hope we can be friends.'

'So do I. Life has certainly moved on a great deal since I last saw Helen – in fact, she was younger than Joel. It doesn't seem quite real just yet,' Ben replied with surprising honesty.

'It's okay, man. You are part of our family now,' Martin told him as he sat beside Helen, placing a reassuring arm on her shoulder.

'Thank you; I appreciate what you're saying. Thank you for your welcome and for allowing me to interrupt your lives as I have,' he told them as they rallied around him ensuring everyone knew he was welcome.

Later, Ben and Helen were able to talk alone as Martin took Joel to the park for a late play.

'We've missed so much of each other's lives, haven't we?' Helen said in an attempt to get Ben to talk.

'Yes, we have. My one hope was to meet you before you were married and maybe witness that. I understand that's happened and you have a family of your own now and I have no wish to take any of that from you.'

'But you are disappointed?'

'Yes, because unlike you, I knew that you were alive somewhere. I have looked for you for years. I had hoped to meet you before we both finished secondary school but there were those who were determined that that would not happen. I'm not disappointed in you or that you're married and have a son, I think those things are all great it's just that if others had just spoken up earlier, I may have been able to share them with you.'

'I know what you mean. If I had even thought you were around, I would have changed things but neither of us can change any of that now. All I can do is be there for you when it happens for you.'

'I guess but you'll be waiting awhile.'

'I don't know about that.'

'How do you mean?'

'Ben, life has a way of working things out. Your life is turning around at the moment; Karen is a big part of that. I believe the best is ahead of you, Ben, not behind you.'

'I hope so because I really have missed you.'

'I know you have and I appreciate all the years you spent looking for me, I really do. I know you are my brother and that you love me. You will be so good for Joel and Martin. They will love going to your place and riding the hills if they are welcome?'

'You know you only have to call and everything will be there for all of you. You only have to ask and I'll do everything I can.'

'Thank you. We'll have good times ahead, Ben; look to the future, not the past.'

'Thanks,' Ben told her and they embraced.

They went out and found Martin and Joel and they all played together in the park. Joel was usually shy around strangers but Helen noticed how quickly he warmed to Ben who appeared to delight in his nephew.

'You have made quite the impression on Joel because he doesn't take well to strangers. I do hope that we can all get to know each other as family. Martin and I are talking about having another child soon so I hope you have room in your heart for more of us.'

'Yes, I do. Helen, I can't promise to come to the city too often because my property is a seven-day-a-week business so visits like this just have to be rare but I do hope that you will all come and stay sometime.'

'We will, Ben. Joel loves horses and I think he would like nothing better than to be led around on horse by his uncle and see how they are fed and watered.'

'I'd love to do that.'

'And don't worry about Martin, he is very supportive. He knows what we've lost.'

'Thanks, Helen, for everything,' Ben told her and Helen patted his knee in recognition.

Ben called in on Karen on his way home, sharing tea with her in town. As he told her about meeting Helen and her family.

'I've missed so much of her life and never got to see Joel as a baby. Those times never come again.'

'I know, Ben, but there is time to get to know them now that you've met them and Joel sounds like a really nice little boy.'

'He is. I hope that they will come and spend some time with us. I really would like to teach him to ride and take his parents into the mountains and show them around.'

'You will, Ben. I will keep in touch with Helen and arrange for them to come and visit soon,' Karen promised.

Karen felt deeply for his loss, knowing it could never come again. It made her think about her relationship and her life with Ben. She was concerned for Ben but agreed with Helen that his best was ahead of him and she was linked to that future.

Later, they changed the subject, holding hands across the table. They went into town for coffee and cake after cleaning up the tea dishes. Walking along the street in the evening hand-in-hand with Ben was one of those things that Karen loved.

# CHAPTER SEVENTEEN

## *Lifetime changes*

Karen had her own plans for meeting Jack and Maureen Carmodia as they were the nearest thing to family he had. She had thought of inviting them to Ben's for tea one night but knew they were not a couple who travelled a lot and had not got around to asking them. Karen had joined Ben for a trip to Omeo when he decided to drop in on Jack on the way home, catching Karen completely off guard.

Her heart racing, Karen faced going into the house to meet her.

'Come in, Karen, sit down and put your feet up; I'll make us a cuppa in a minute.'

'Thank you,' Karen replied, stepping gingerly into the kitchen.

'Don't look so nervous. I won't bite,' Maureen assured her.

'I'm sorry, thank you; I'm with Ben.'

'I know.'

'Ben and I are going together.'

'I know that too. How are things going?'

'Well, I think; I just wasn't sure if you knew.'

'Or approved?'

'Yes; you are the nearest thing to family Ben has got.'

'You don't need my approval. I thought you and Ben should have been together years ago but you had other things in your life. I know you moved back to be with Ben and I know you are committed to him. I also know that he thinks the world of you. You don't need my approval.'

'Thank you but I still appreciate your acceptance of us as a couple. Has he talked to you about us?' Karen questioned.

'He didn't have to; he has been different since you teamed up. He is in love with you, you know?'

'Do you think so?'

'Yes, I do. Haven't you seen that?'

'I'm not sure. He's hard to read at times and he is not too forthcoming about how he feels about anything.'

'Perhaps but trust me, he loves you. Are you two going to get married, do you think?'

'I'm not really sure; we've only been going out a short time,' Karen replied immediately in her defence.

'Where do you think you'd live if it does get serious between you two?'

'At Ben's – it's his life's work. It will be easier for me to move and commute than Ben so I wouldn't want to live anywhere else. He needs to be where he works and I want to be there with him,' Karen replied immediately before realising what she had said.

'You really have thought about this, haven't you? Have you told Ben?'

'Yes, I've thought about a great deal. Ben needs time to come to that conclusion for himself.'

'I think it's time you talked to Ben. He has shown me the preliminary plans for the house he is planning to build for you.'

'I had no idea but I don't need a new house; Ben's place is fine.'

'Then you need to tell him that. Do you love him?'

'I had no idea about the house,' Karen replied.

'You didn't answer my question.'

Karen turned away, suddenly unsure of herself for a moment before meeting Maureen's gaze. 'Yes, I do love him; very much,' she replied with tears in her eyes.

'I thought you might. Neither of you are teenagers anymore. Do you think you are ready to marry him then?'

'Yes, yes I am. I came here hoping for you'd accept Ben and I going out together and now I've basically told you I'm ready to marry him. I have no idea how I came this far so quickly,' Karen told her.

'I don't think it has been all that quick if you think back. Moving back this way wasn't with the idea of being Ben's friend, was it?'

'No. I've tried to convince myself that Ben wasn't the reason that I came back because I had a number of good offers on the table at the time. I could have taken any one of them.'

'But this one was close to Ben?'

'Yes. I had messed things up between us and I wanted to make it right. I wanted to move back this way and I hoped I could work things out.'

'You took a bit of risk then?'

'Well, yes and no. I always thought that Ben and I had the sort of friendship that could survive if I was honest with him and I think he responded to that.'

'Ben seemed to have responded very well to that.'

'I have been very fortunate. Ben has been incredibly understanding. I'm not sure how he has put up with my indecisiveness.'

'You are being too hard on yourself. I've heard you have been through some tough times with Ben – you are good for him. You would not be the person you are if you had not moved away and done what you've done. It has taken some courage to admit to Ben that you needed to fix things.'

'It was selfishness more than courage that motivated me. I want to share a life with him.'

'It still took courage though. It's never easy to say sorry and harder again to step out on a journey when you are not sure where that journey may end.'

'Well not until now at least.' Karen told her with an attempted smile.

'You'll tell me what happens won't you?'

'Of course. Thank you for everything,' Karen told her and Maureen took her hand.

'You are welcome, dear; now, tell me what will you do when you move into Ben's place?' Maureen asked and with that, the distance between them evaporated as they talked about the house.

Karen told Maureen, her plans were similar to what Ben intended for the place and she knew he would really like the changes she planned for the place.

'Ben will love it because it does not involve making the place unrecognisable but enhances what is already there. If you don't marry, he should employ you to do it up for him.'

'I would do the place for nothing.'

'I'm sure you would, just as I'm sure you will. I would love to see the results.'

'I'll make sure you get an invitation to an open house.'

'You really do love your man, don't you?'

'Yes, I do,' Karen replied, smiling this time and Maureen then knew that Ben would not be living on his own for much longer.

\*

Jack and Ben arrived a short time later in full voice as they talked about a group of wild brumbies that were causing a bit of concern on the north end of Jack's lease. They were talking over a couple of strategies for capturing them or moving them on. Jack greeted Karen warmly as ever. For some reason, Jack had always accepted and welcomed Karen whenever they met.

'It's good to see you again, Karen. How is the job going?'

'Good, thank you.'

'I hear you've finally got some of the more extreme elements together. You are doing a great job. Perhaps now just maybe we will see some balance in the argument for the development of the region.'

'Thank you, Jack, we've made a start but there is a long way to go yet,' Karen replied.

'I have no doubt. You didn't come here to talk work; it's good to see you two together at last.'

'Thank you, Jack. I was hoping you would approve.'

'You don't need my approval, Karen; you are one of the good ones,' Jack told her.

'Thank you.'

'You're welcome, my dear. Now, where's that cuppa?'

'Cuppa's on the way. You men sit down. Have you come up with some ideas for dealing with those brumbies?'

'Yes, we think so; we'll get the boys together next week and go after them. We'll drive towards The Bend and coral them there. We'll keep the best of them and sell the rest off. I've already arranged for Dodson's trucks,' Jack replied.

'Sounds like you have it all organised?'

'We have a plan. I just hope the brumbies appreciate it.'

\*

Karen didn't talk a lot on the way home as she processed the conversation she had with Maureen.

'Are you okay?' Ben questioned after sitting in silence for a time.

'Yes, I just have a lot on my mind at the moment.'

'Can I help?' he offered.

'You already are. I've got some things to think about, that's all.'

'Okay, you know where I am if you need to talk.'

Karen did not reply at first but reached for his hand, which she took from the steering wheel for a second, to receive one of his love you squeezes that told him she was alright.

When they pulled up at Karen's place she stopped and turned to him.

'Would you go out with me Friday night? We'll do the whole-dress-for-success look and make a night of it?'

'Of course. Do you want me to pick you up?'

'No, I will meet you there. Say, seven-thirty?' Karen suggested.

'I'll be there.'

'Good, I'll see you there then,' Karen replied before giving him a brief kiss goodnight.

∗

The restaurant was where they had their first date where they watched the surf while they enjoyed their meal. It had become something of a favourite place for them for their formal nights of getting away to really enjoy a meal together. Karen had gone all out with her outfit for the evening, dressing to impress in a full-length evening gown and shawl. Ben had dressed in new suit and tie, which Karen just loved. They sat down and ordered their meals from the attentive waitress.

'Okay, what's on your mind?' Ben questioned when they sat down.

'What makes you say that?'

'Come on, Karen, you have pulled out all the stops tonight. This is our favourite place and you look as fantastic as ever. So, what's up?'

'I've been thinking a lot about us lately.'

'And what have you come up with? It's good between us isn't it?'

'It is, we worked through some tough things together and we've come out the better for it. What do you think about the idea of us getting married one day?'

'Yes, I've thought about it and I've got some plans drawn up for a new house if you would like to see them? I was thinking that maybe in time you might consider it after I've built it.'

'I'm sure it would be great but I don't need to see the plans or watch you build a new house unless you want to build a new one of course. I like your place just as it is.'

'You do because I don't really need one; I just thought you may want a new house to move into if we get married. What are you trying to tell me?' Ben said suddenly very uncertain of where the conversation was going.

'You're in love with me, aren't you?' Karen asked.

'You know I am.'

'Good because I'm in love with you too,' Karen told him.

'So, if you don't want a new house, what do you want?' he asked.

'Ben, I want to marry you.'

'What? Now, you mean?'

'Yes. Why not? We love each other and I don't need a new house any more than you do,' Karen said as she got out of her chair and went to him.

'You want to marry me now?' he asked, a little stunned by her standing up to give him space to take in what she was saying.

'Yes, I do. Ben, I said when we got together, I told you that I thought we had a future together. For as long as I have known you, I have been looking for someone who could love you and now I know that is me. When I saw you arrive down by the river, I saw you not just as Ben but as a man I want I want to be with. I knew then that one day we could be lovers and not just friends. On our first date down on that beach when we held each other and kissed properly for the first time, a big part of me knew then that this day would come. We can build a life and a family together if we want.'

'You want a family with me?'

'I love you. Of course I do. One day, when we are ready, we can raise a family together in our house on the edge of town. After all you've been through, I think you be a great dad to our kids,' Karen told him.

'You really want this, don't you?' he asked, stunned by what she was telling him.

'Yes, I've been thinking about this a lot lately. Do you realise we haven't spent a night alone since that night alone back in the mountains after the botanist tour?'

'You remember that?'

'Oh, I remember it; it was one of the best nights I can remember lying in my bedroll next to you, looking up at the stars, talking into the cold early hours. It was amazing.'

'It was, wasn't it?'

'I want to do that again but next time, I want to sleep with you, not a couple of meters from you. I trusted you then; I love you now. I want to wake up with you on a mountainside again without recrimination or regret. We can only do that if we are married. Ben, the very best is ahead of us,' Karen told him.

'Do you really think so?'

'I just said so, didn't I? Now, my question to you is do you want to marry me? You don't have to give me an answer now; take as much time as you need,' she asked, leaving him no doubt about her attentions.

'I don't need time to think about it,' Ben replied and then pulled her in slowly and kissed her with the first real passion he'd ever shown her, causing her to catch her breath even though it was still with all the gentleness she knew him for.

'Wow.' Karen gasped. 'I take it that was a major yes.'

'Didn't I do it right?' he asked with a smile.

'Oh, yes, you did. You did it very right.'

'Good because my answer to you is yes.'

'We have just got engaged? We're getting married?' Karen said as she took it all in. She held him and realised others were watching. They returned to their seats where they held hands as they were approached by a waitress with their meals.

'I don't mean to intrude but that looked like some good news?' she asked.

'We think so; we have just this minute got engaged.'

'That is good news. Congratulations.'

'Thank you very much,' Karen replied with a smile.

'You are most welcome,' she replied.

'When do you want to get married?' Ben asked as they began to eat their meals.

'As soon as we can. If we are going to get married then let's get married. I don't want a long engagement. I'm owed some leave so let's make it three months from now. Can you wait for that long?'

'I would wait forever for you,' Ben told her holding her close. 'I love you, Karen Rossiter.'

'I will be Karen Templeton soon.'

'You don't have to change your name for me,' Ben told her.

'I want to change my name. I want people to know that there is a new Mrs Templeton in town.'

'I'm sure the old Mrs Templeton would have loved you,' Ben said with tears in his eyes.

'And I would have loved her; now, I'm going to love her son,' Karen replied as she held his hand across the table. 'I'm going to love you for the rest of my life. I am going to have your babies and we are going to raise them together and watch them grow up. One day, they will have children of their own and then you and I will be grandparents together,' she told him softly and tears rolled down his face.

'You are all my dreams come true,' he told her, which made Karen's heart skip a beat as it was, she wanted for him.

Word quickly spread across the restaurant of their engagement a waitress arrived with a small bottle of champagne as the public address system turned on.

'Ladies and gentlemen, we have a couple with us tonight who have just got engaged. Could you please raise your glasses with the management and staff of Carlo's to wish the couple all the happiness in the world for their new life together?'

Everyone in the restaurant applauded and wished them well. Ben was very embarrassed but Karen loved it.

'Thank you very much. We appreciate it,' Karen replied with a blushing smile before they returned to their seats.

'We should call your parents.'

'I would prefer to go and see them; they need to hear this face-to-face. I'll call them and tell them to wait up for us,' Karen told him.

'How will they react to the news?' Ben questioned.

'I'm sure Mum will be okay with us but Dad never says much,' Karen replied.

'It will be interesting what Jack makes of us,' Ben said.

'I'm sure that Jack and Maureen will be delighted.'

'What makes you say that?'

'Maureen asked me about us. She told me about the house and we got talking about you and me. I hope you don't mind?' Karen explained.

'Not at all; I wondered where all this came from.'

'It wasn't just my conversation with Maureen, I had been thinking about us a lot lately. With everything that was going on with Helen,

I've been thinking that it's our time. It's our time to be married and our time together; then our time to have a family.'

'I think you're right. Where would you like to get married? We could have the reception here if you like?' Ben suggested.

'Actually, I was thinking more like getting married at Mum's. For as long as I can remember, I've always wanted to get married in the rose garden at Mum's in the spring. It will mean a small guest list because there isn't a lot of space but it also means we don't have to have a whole lot of people that we don't know either.'

'That sounds fine to me; I can't say I like the idea of the big public formal thing.'

'I didn't think you would be. This is going to be our wedding; nothing will happen that you don't want to happen.'

'Thank you,' Ben told her.

'We are a team now. Let's go tell some people.' Karen beamed as she stood up to leave.

*

Fiona was waiting for them, having set out the table for a large supper with all the trimmings. From the moment they got out of the car, she knew that they had news. Their usual relaxed manner was replaced by tangible tension between them. Both of them looked amazing, Ben looking very smart in his suit and tie and Karen in one of those stunning metallic gowns. They held hands as they headed for the house.

'Ian, our guests have arrived,' Fiona called. Ian was quick to gain a glance of them through the window.

'Looks serious.'

'Think so,' Fiona responded as she went to put the kettle on.

A few moments later, Karen led Ben into the kitchen.

'Come in, the kettle's on,' Fiona told them. 'Aren't you two dressed to the nines; what's the occasion?' she asked.

'It has turned into one. Mum, Dad, Ben and I went out to tea tonight and after some discussion, we have decided to get married. I know that we haven't been going out long but we are hoping for your blessing,' Karen told them.

No one said anything for a moment until Ian smiled and opened the fridge and pulled out a bottle of champagne. 'I think we can do a little better than a cup of tea, don't you?' he said, holding up the bottle in triumph.

'Congratulations. Of course, you have our blessing,' Fiona said as she embraced Karen, almost bringing her to tears.

'Absolutely. Congratulations, Ben,' Ian said, offering Ben a firm hand, which Ben met with a firm handshake.

Ian opened the bottle and began filling glasses while Fiona reached out to Ben for a hug, who surprisingly accepted her embrace.

'Thank you; your acceptance of us is important,' Ben told her.

'You are not just accepted, Ben Templeton; you are loved and we are thrilled to have you as part of our family,' Fiona told him.

'What's with the champagne? Were you expecting something?' Karen questioned.

'We've been expecting this for some time. The only one's surprised by your news is you two.' Fiona smiled. 'Now, have you called Jack and Maureen?'

'Not yet,' Ben replied.

'Come on, I'll show you where the phone is,' Fiona told him as she led him to the phone in the passageway.

Jack and Maureen were soon on their way. They were delighted by the news, arriving with an esky ready to celebrate. Maureen greeted Karen with a hug.

'Congratulations, my dear,' she told Karen before embracing her.

'Thank you for everything.'

'Oh, I didn't do any more than listen.'

'Yes, you did and the few words you said gave me the courage to talk to Ben as you suggested and now, we are getting married.'

'Then you are most welcome, dear. You two will have a good life together. He's loved you for a long time.'

'I can see that now; I just can't work out how I didn't see until now.'

'Ben is hard to read at the best of times and more so when it comes to matters of the heart,' Maureen told her.

'He has a good heart.'

'He does and you are the centre of it,' Maureen told her before embracing her again before Jack gave her a hug.

'This is a very fine thing you are doing; I am happy for both of you,' Jack told her.

'Thank you, Jack. I'm going to marry a very fine man,' Karen replied.

'Yes, you are indeed. One of the best,' Jack replied as Karen saw a much softer side to Jack than she had ever see before.

Karen rang Brendan and Ben rang Helen who was delighted by the news.

'Oh, Ben, I am so happy for you. Didn't I say to you the best years are ahead of you? Karen is such a great person. I'm sure you will be very happy together.'

'Thanks, Helen.'

'Are you having a get together at some point? I would love to come and meet everyone.'

'I wasn't planning to but under the circumstances, we'll talk and I'll let you know,' Ben told her.

*

The following morning Ben told Michael who was delighted with the news.

'That is really great news, mate. I am really happy for you.'

'Thank you.'

'If I can give you a hand with anything, you know you only have to ask,' Michael offered.

'Thanks, Michael. I may hold you to that.'

'Please do that. I'd love to help in any way you need. Are you going to stay on the block and are you going to build another place?'

'Karen's insisting that we stay. We are do some work on the place but as she said, it's where I live and work so it's where she wants to be,' Ben replied.

'I told you she is one of the good ones.'

*

When Karen caught up with them for lunch, Michael greeted her with the recently found broad smile of his and the two of them embraced.

'Congratulations, Karen, you are marrying a very good man.'

'Thank you, I think so too.'

'Ben tells me you are going to be living on the block.'

'Yes, we are. I think we can make it a happy home again.'

'I'm sure of it with the two of you in it. Now, if you need a hand with any of the renovations or if there is something I can do for the wedding, just call.'

'Thanks, Michael. I really appreciate it,' Karen told him.

# CHAPTER EIGHTEEN

## *Gayle*

Gayle made a surprise a couple of days later after Karen had tried to contact her but only got her message bank and answering machine. She turned up at the front desk just before five p.m. to invite Karen out for drinks and go out for tea. They went to a café nearby that served great coffee, Karen explaining that she seldom drank these days.

'It's good to catch up again. It seems like ages since you returned this place. How's the job going?' Gayle asked without taking a breath.

'Good, it's all that I hope and a little more. It has some unique challenges because things are done a little different out here.'

'I can imagine.' Gayle smiled. 'Hey, you wouldn't believe who I saw on the way into town: Ben Templeton. I thought he'd disappeared into the hills or something. I haven't heard much of him since Mum and Dad retired. I was thinking of giving him a call and catching up for old time's sake. What do you reckon? You were friends or something, weren't you?'

'We were,' Karen began to reply but was cut short by Gayle.

'We should invite him out for tea if we call him now. You don't have a mobile number, do you?'

'Gayle, he is already coming for tea, if you are joining us. I assume you are staying tonight.'

'I want to, yes, if you have the space?'

'You know I have and you know you are always welcome.'

'What do mean he's coming to tea? What, at your place?'

'Yes. I need to head home soon to put tea on for both of us. Ben has a meeting later tonight and we are having tea together before he does.'

'You said you were friends; it sounds like you still are?' Gayle questioned.

Karen did not answer straight away but looked for words.

'What is it? You're beginning to scare me.' Gayle smiled, hiding her concern.

'Gayle, I've been trying to contact you but all I got was message bank.'

'Yes, I know and I couldn't get back to you because I was out of the office and my mobile has been playing up. What's going on?'

'I was trying to contact you because I have some news,' Karen said, taking a breath. 'Gayle, Ben and I are engaged.'

'You're what!' Gayle screamed, gaining the attention of everyone in the café.

'Ben and I got engaged on the weekend, which was why I was trying to get hold of you,' Karen told Gayle who was still looking at her wide eyed.

'Why? Why Ben Templeton of all people and why the sudden desperation? Any number of people would jump at the opportunity to go out with you to marry you, to do whatever with you whenever you want it.'

'Okay, stop right there. There is no desperation. I'm in love with Ben and the great thing is that he loves me. We have been friends since high school.'

'I don't doubt you but what do you two have in common? You're everything he's not. Listen, if he is really that good in bed then hey, sleep with him but you don't have to marry him. Trust me, it is less complicated.'

'Gayle, it is not like that at all. I've never slept with him. It's never been like that between us but it is something that I am looking forward to. It's the differences that make us great. Our strengths complement each other,' Karen replied.

'That all sounds so wonderful but I just don't get it. Karen, you are giving up your whole life for him.'

'No, I very nearly gave it up for Mark and he only stayed with me because he wanted to sleep with me.'

'And like Ben doesn't? I just don't get it.'

'Gayle, it doesn't matter. You don't have to understand how we work. All you need to understand is that I'm going to marry Ben and we are going to make a home together,' Karen told her.

'I apologise. You are right. This is just a bit of a shock, that's all. I had no idea you were seeing Ben. Why didn't you say anything? I thought we were friends?'

'We are and I should have told you but I needed Ben in ways I did not understand for a while and I didn't think that you would understand. I realised that he needed me too, which was hard to resist.'

'He must be special if he was able to capture your heart. I'm happy for you, I really am.'

'Thank you,' Karen replied.

'I wonder if he knows just how lucky he is. He has got one of the good ones,' Gayle told her.

'That's okay because I got one of the good ones too.'

'That's one of the things I admired about you. You always went after what you wanted with such courage and conviction but didn't stand on a lot of toes doing it. It couldn't have been easy coming back here.'

'It wasn't but I had to give this job a go and to make a place where Ben and I could have a chance to get to know each other and find a place where we could be,' Karen replied with tears in her eyes.

'So, moving back here was about Ben?'

'Yes, but it took me awhile to come to terms with that and admit to myself.'

'You must have realised he was part of it though?'

'We weren't talking at the time because of a fight that we had but I had to come and know that I gave us a chance.'

'You really do love him, don't you?'

'Yes, I do.'

'Does he know what you did to get you two together?' Gayle questioned.

'He does now but he didn't see it coming at the time. He was so shocked when I asked him to go out with him; he really didn't think it was ever possible.'

'Did you ever think so? Back in high school, I mean?'

'Not really because I thought we would both have to change a lot for anything to happen between us.'

'And now you are going to marry him. Are you going to live in his place or build something new?'

'We are going to do some renovations to his place and then it will become our home. With a bit of work, it will look lived in and loved just like the people who live in it.'

*

To Gayle's surprise, Ben had rung the doorbell and waited for Karen to open it to him before entering the house. He kissed Karen briefly at the door and then eyed Gayle wearily when he entered the kitchen, offering a polite hello before adding a bottle of apple cider to the table.

'Karen tells me you two are getting married. Congratulations,' Gayle called.

'Thank you,' Ben replied making a hesitant return to her sight.

'Ben, you have got one of the good ones here but I'm also told by a very reliable source that are one of the good ones too. What can I say but wish you both the very best? If anyone can make it, you two can,' Gayle told them.

'Thank you, Gayle. I hope that you will be joining us for our wedding?' Ben suggested, knowing that Karen would want her there.

'I would not miss it for anything. I know we haven't seen a lot of each other in recent years but I would like that to change. I could come home for you two.'

'I'd like that; you would be welcome any time,' Karen replied, looking to Ben for his response to which he was quick to agree.

'Of all the people we went to school with, I could never have imagined you two together but then you both were your own people and somehow you got it to work. Now that I've got my head around it, I really do want to wish you all the very best.'

'Thank you. I think you know us better than you think,' Karen told her.

Over dinner, Gayle watched as Ben relaxed a little and began to interact with Karen more freely, then began to see them as a couple who were planning their lives together. She saw a softer side to Ben and could see that Karen really did love him.

They talked about old times and their plans for the future. Gayle was quietly impressed by Ben's business plans as he seemed to have it figured out. They talked about their dream to have children and Gayle tried to imagine Ben with children but just could not see it, yet Karen was quite clearly looking forward to the idea.

When Ben got up to leave, he offered Gayle a friendly handshake but Gayle pressed for an embrace.

'I am happy for you, Ben.'

'Thanks,' Ben replied after reluctantly accepting her embrace. 'I'll see you later, I guess,' Ben told her as Karen took his arm and walked him to the door.

They spoke for a few moments before she kissed him goodnight. That was when Gayle saw them as a couple very much in love.

# CHAPTER NINETEEN

## *Families and engagements*

There was a time when Karen and her sister Joanne had been close but that had been a long time ago. When Joanne went to university, she effectively left her family behind her, seldom returning home as she pursued a career in academia. She preferred the company of her academic friends to her family being uneasy with people outside a select group of friends.

When Joanne arrived for Karen's engagement party, there was no emotional reunion, only a polite kiss on the cheek.

'Congratulations, sis,' she said not knowing how much Karen hated being called sis.

'Thank you,' Karen replied without conviction.

Later, Karen heard Joanne talking to her parents.

'What is she thinking, giving up everything to marry some local hillbilly? What sort of life can she hoped to have here? Is she that insecure that she can't let go of your apron strings?' Joanne questioned.

'Now, you stop right there, miss. You know little about Karen or her life; don't come in her questioning her life or telling her, us or anyone else for that matter what's wrong with her life. We don't see you from one year to the next so what do you know? If you want to know about her life, you ask before you judge and then you be damn careful because unlike you, she has remained a member of this family since going off to university,' Ian told her.

'That's a bit harsh,' Joanne replied.

'Is it? I think your father is spot on with his comments. You don't know what's going on. The only time you see Karen, you criticise her; you back off until you know what you're talking about,' Fiona told her.

'You either support Karen or you leave. It's that simple,' Ian told her.

Joanne fell silent. Karen was even more wary of her after that. She could not understand why Joanne seemed so embittered after all these years and knowing so little of Karen's career. Joanne still did nothing to enhance her own beauty but surely Joanne had to have put that behind her by now as it was not an issue with Karen. With Ben due to arrive soon, she knew Ben would be wary of her anyway but she knew he would be quick to pick up on the lack of support from Joanne. He would be defensive and Karen wondered how that would translate if Joanne crossed him. She did not have to wait long.

*

Ben returned dressed very smartly in trousers, an open shirt and fashionable yet comfortable shoes. Karen thought he looked great and made it known to her at the time as she took his hand as she circulated with him.

As expected, Ben was wary of Joanne, sensing her disapproval. He kept close to Karen, not that he was afraid of her but to avoid the confrontation that he knew would come if she found him alone. Joanne chose her moment when Karen was on the phone and Ben was getting some air on the verandah.

'So, you are going to marry Karen, are you?'

'That would be the idea, yes; do you have a problem with that?'

'I do, in fact. Have you got any idea what she is giving up to be with you?'

'And what would that be?' Ben questioned, knowing what her list would be. Joanne gave him a great list, which gave the impression that Karen was giving up her life for him to live in an impoverished backwater with an ignorant hillbilly.

'If you cared for Karen, you would end this,' Joanne told him, finishing her critique of their relationship.

'A couple of facts for you, Joanne. I love Karen and I have no intention of ending anything. Why can't you support Karen's choice and celebrate instead of trying to destroy it?' he began but Joanne tried to cut him off.

'I think I know Karen a little better than you. I am her sister.'

'I haven't finished yet. At the end of the day, I don't care what you think of me but if you use me to some score with Karen, I will wipe the floor with you.'

'You know, you are so arrogant. How dare you speak to me like that?'

'I'm arrogant? You are the one who is asking me to end my engagement to Karen. You do not speak for Karen.'

'Are you sure?'

'I am,' Karen said, stepping up beside him. 'You do not know me and you certainly do not speak for me. This is my engagement party you are no longer welcome. Please stay out of the way,' Karen told her coldly before leading Ben back into the house.

'You know I don't like you to smoke near the house,' Fiona told her.

'Finish your cigarette and then leave. You are not welcome here,' Ian told her, dropping her bag at her feet.

'That's a bit harsh, don't you think? Besides, it's late.'

'Then go to a motel.'

'So, the princess wins again? Typical,' Joanne snapped.

'It is not a contest. I warned you, now it's time for you to leave and you don't get an invitation to the wedding. Don't come. You have a lot of bridges to mend to make up for challenging Ben. Think long and hard before to speak to either of them again. Now leave,' Ian told her before walking away.

'Whatever it is between you, sort it. You are the only one who stands to lose out of this. Karen is engaged to her soul mate. Very few people get that opportunity to do that. Your criticism won't split them up, it will only turn them further against you.'

'Mum, don't lecture me; I get the picture.'

'Do you? Because you are making decisions about your future, not theirs,' Fiona told her before walking away.

❉

Karen's brother Edward, or Ted, was delighted by the news of their engagement when he arrived at the house and gave Karen a bear hug before giving Ben a firm handshake.

'Welcome to the family, brother.' Edward laughed as he shook his hand. 'I always said you two should be together. I couldn't be happier for both of you,' he told them, taking them under his big arms. Karen was naturally delighted by Ted's response.

Ted really was a huge man like some of his uncles; full of humour and energy. Later that night, Karen was delighted to see Ted and Ben talking and laughing together, knowing that a real friendship had begun between the two of them.

'Thanks for taking the time to talk with Ben the way you did tonight. I really appreciate it,' Karen told Ted later in the evening.

'I've always said you two belong together. He is the real deal, is your Ben and I could not think of anyone I want to see you married to than Ben. I hope I see a lot of both of you from now on.'

'Consider it a standing invitation to drop in for cuppa or even stay a couple of days if you wish.'

'Thanks, sis, but Ben has already said as much.'

'I thought he might have.'

'You think a lot the same, you two. Are you going to give me some nieces or nephews one day?'

'Definitely but not for a year or two.'

'You are going to be a great mum and despite Ben's background, he's going to be alright dad too so don't you worry on that score.'

'I'm not. He is a good man – you both are.'

'Thank you, sis. I love you,' Ted said and gave Karen a big hug, which she loved, having always got along with him.

\*

Michael arrived with Melanie and they were greeted with great warmth by everyone when they arrived at the house. After a year of quiet persistence, Melanie had finally agreed to go out with Michael and was delighted to receive an invitation to the engagement party. The two couples talked for a few minutes before Ben asked Michael to one side.

'Michael, I have a huge favour to ask to do with our wedding?'

'Ask away. You know I will do whatever I can to help.'

'Good. Would you mind being my best man?'

'Ben, that is not a favour; that is a privilege, I am honoured to be asked.'

'You'll do it then?'

'Absolutely. I'll help out any way I can and even organise a bit of a buck's night and I promise not to do anything to embarrass you.'

'Thanks, Michael. It's a big ask but you helped me a lot these last years and I can't think of a better man to have at my side.'

'Thanks, Ben, it means more than you know. Is Karen happy with your choice of best man or haven't you told her yet?'

'She is more than fine with it. She knows we have travelled some similar roads.'

'Yeah, she is good like that. Karen is a keeper, Ben; you are a lucky man.'

'That I am.'

# CHAPTER TWENTY

*Making house*

'You'd better come over and see where you are going to live. We can have a look a look at the place and see what things you want to change. It's only been me there for a long time and as Helen pointed out, it's very dull.'

'Ben, don't take offence at what Helen said, she was only saying as she saw it. Ben, I'll have a look at the place but I don't want to turn your world upside down – I just want to live with you.'

'But you already have turned my world upside down the moment you agreed to marry me,' Ben told her, which caused Karen to blush.

'We'll have a look it but like I said, I don't want you rebuild it, just let a bit of light in and put a bit of colour into the garden.'

'We'll see. Bring your best colour chart and we'll start painting,' Ben suggested.

'Wait, I'm not talking about painting anything inside or out. We may repaint some of the rooms in the same colour to make over tired paint, that's all,' Karen replied.

'I don't mean to put to you on the offensive, it's just that I don't know how to make things right for you.'

'But that's just it, there nothing wrong for you to fix. I told you when we got engaged that if we were married today, I'd move in with you tonight; that still stands. When I told you I didn't need a new house, I didn't mean for you to spend the same amount of money doing the one you have up. Ben, it will be our house; not mine, yours and mine. I already have my own place and I don't want to live there when we are married. I love you and want to live with you. You don't have to make this bigger than it is.'

'I'm sorry, it's just that, I don't know, that maybe...'

'That I'll wake up and realise that I'm living at your place and think I've made a mistake?'

'Yeah, something like that?'

'Ben, I've known you for a very long time. I know your place and if I had any doubts, I would not be here with you and I would have said something about the house.'

*

They began work on installing timber louvers on the extension of the verandah to the bathroom and laundry area. After consulting with some of the local builders, they decided upon and ordered wooden louvers to add a bit of privacy to the verandah and the rooms. The louvers were considered in keeping with the style of the rest of the house, which had been built in stages and linked by the verandahs. Steps and handrails were added to the centre and the end of the building to provide access to the rooms and the clothes lines at the end of the building. The timber was stained and coated with a fire-retardant mixture, greatly reducing the risk of loss to all but a major fire. The laundry was originally a two-roomed building with the kitchen being in the half closet to the main house. Originally built of mud brick, it was later converted to a bathroom and the exterior covered in weatherboards to match it in with the main house, which had been extended twice.

Ben was completing the installation of panels in the lower half before installing rails and pivots for the louvers on the top. With screws and washers lined up on a bench on the verandah, he reached up behind him, unaware that Karen was there, his hand brushing her clothes over her breast as he reached for a synthetic washer. He was aware of something soft and looked up to see the back of his hand brushing against her breast.

'Ooh, that's very nice but perhaps we'll save it for our wedding night.' Karen smiled, choosing to laugh it off but it was Ben who was shocked and very apologetic.

'Karen, I'm sorry, I swear I wasn't trying anything. I didn't know you there. You have to believe me,' he said, jumping to his feet and looking at her.

'I do believe you, Ben. It was one of those wonderful accidents that comes from working close together.'

'But I should have looked and I should never have touched you like that. I promise I will never touch you like that again,' Ben pleaded, his voice full of desperation and fear.

'Ben, stop. It was an accident. You will touch me like that again because I want you to,' she said and stepped up to him and took his hands in her own. 'You have to know something about me, about us. I know that you have had a lot of rejection in your life and have had whole lot of terrible things said about you, most of which you believe but I don't. What that means is that I have not rejected you and that I will not reject you because I love you. These hands are part of you and I love all of you. I don't want you to be afraid to touch me to hold me any more than I want you to be afraid to kiss me,' Karen told him and took him in her arms only to feel him trembling.

'I'm sorry,' he whispered.

'Don't be, I'm not. I love all of you, Ben Templeton, and want you to love all of me too,' Karen told him.

They continued to work on the house but Karen noticed an uneasiness between them after that as Ben was ever watchful of the space between them.

'The house is looking good; do you like it?' he questioned at one point.

'It is looking great; I told you it didn't need a lot of work. The garden just needs a little colour to make it perfect,' Karen replied, wrapping an arm around him as they stood back and looked at their handiwork.

'You are too easily pleased, I think,' he said.

'Oh, you don't know me that well yet.' She smiled, teasing him.

'We are in for some interesting times, I think.'

'Oh, you'd better believe it,' Karen replied, enjoying the banter then she wrapped her arms round him and when she felt him pull away, she held on tighter. 'Trust me,' she told him and waited for him to relax a little before she let him go.

# CHAPTER TWENTY-ONE

## *The wedding*

The next great challenge was to organise their wedding and take Ben shopping for clothes. Looking into his wardrobe was a change for both of them because it was only the second time she had visited his room the other being with Helen. Ben owned a wardrobe full of the most practical clothing she'd seen. The best clothes he owned were a couple of pairs of moleskin jeans and a couple of cotton shirts worn over a better pair of elastic-sided boots. His only dress jacket had been picked from a second's outlet in town and it was beginning to tell with frayed cuffs beginning and a worn collar.

Shopping was always going to be a challenge knowing how much he loathed it but Karen knew they would have to be good results quickly or he would be gone. Trousers, a white dress shirt, leather vest and a bow tie were among the items. He had the gentleman farmer look down pretty well.

For the first time, Karen saw Ben stand in front of a mirror and looked at himself whereas the house was all but void of mirrors, stating he never had need of them. She believed that he looked at himself differently that day.

'Have you any idea how good you look?' she said as Ben blushed and became very self-conscious. 'Ben, I didn't say it to embarrass you, only to tell you I like what I see when I look at you,' she told him and encouraged him to try on a few more items gently to add to his wardrobe until it became too much. 'It's okay, Ben, we'll call it a day but you do look good in those things.'

'I have some decent clothes and these are more clothes than I have ever owned in my life before,' he told her, concerned about the cost.

'That is why you need to get them now so that you have a few things to wear. Ben, this is not an extravagance, you need clothes for when we go away. I want you to look and feel your best. I'm not trying to make you what you are not but enhance who you are.'

'Okay, you win.'

'It's not about me winning anything, Ben; it's about you looking and feeling as good as you can be,' Karen told him but knew he was having a real struggle. She wrapped her arms around him and held him for a moment. 'You really are a good-looking man. I want you to look your best for you so that you can see the person I see.'

'Thank you,' he stammered, visibly trembling.

'You're going to be okay,' she assured him.

'I know.'

'Do you?' Karen questioned but Ben did not reply.

They walked down the street hand in hand and Karen could feel the tension release from his hand. Karen could still feel the tension in his body as they walked together.

Sitting together in the main street with a coffee, Karen looked at Ben.

'What?' he asked.

'You. You are the man I'm going to marry and I want the whole world to know it. I'm so glad I decided to take a risk and ask you to go out with me.'

'So am I,' Ben replied after thinking for a moment.

'And now we are going to get married a couple of weeks,' Karen replied and looked at him. 'It doesn't seem real just yet, does it?' she asked.

'No, I would never have believed you would move into my place,' Ben admitted.

'But I'm not about to going to just move into your place. I'm moving in with you. I'm looking forward to sharing a life with you,' Karen told him.

Ben just looked at her, not certain how to reply.

'Are you looking forward to us, to being with me?' she asked but Ben seemed unwilling or unable to answer.

'Ben, I need to know what you are feeling. Are you looking forward to it or are you having second thoughts?' Karen asked, looking directly at him.

'No, I'm not having second thoughts, not at all.'

'Are you looking forward to living with me?'

'I am, more than you can know.'

'Tell me,' Karen said.

'I hoped once that just maybe you would but I never believed it until now.'

*

Karen spent her last night in her old room after a quiet night with her mother, Tracy and Gayle. For all of them, it was an opportunity to hear Karen's journey, who finally admitted to them the story of Ben finding her in the mountains and how she had never quite got him out of her system.

'I always wondered after that night when he turned up during the floods. You were most adamant that we should follow his advice,' Gayle said.

'That was because he was right and I knew to trust him.'

'That much was obvious; I just wondered how you learnt that trust and now I know. So, you had kept in touch with him to that point?'

'No, to that point I had not seen him since secondary college.'

'You kept in touch with him after that though?' Gayle questioned.

'Yes, I worked for him that one summer.'

'I remember when you got back you were never quite the same after that,' Tracy told her.

'How do you mean?' Karen questioned.

'The way you talked about him more than the work you did for him. I wondered then if you would end up with him. It just took a lot longer than I ever expected it to.'

'What was Mark then?' Gayle asked.

'Mark was the city guy I thought I should be dating but Ben already had hold of my heart.'

'I knew that you were never going to marry Mark, it just took you a few years to figure it out,' Tracy said.

'Yes, it did,' Karen admitted.

'So, what changed?' Gayle asked.

'One day I saw him differently and I knew then I wanted him as much as I needed him,' Karen replied.

'And now you are going to marry him.' Tracy smiled.

'Yes, I am. I'm going to marry that man who rode down out of the hills,' Karen replied.

They had a fun breakfast, got their hair done and then went for a quick walk around the rose garden. Karen was amazingly calm, so much so that it even. All morning the girls reminisced and told stories, occasionally shed tears of laughter and joy.

\*

Ben spent the night at Michael's, enjoying a few light beers over a barbeque, which Ian and Brendan joined them for – one of the rare times they were all together. They cooked and talked about anything but the wedding. Afterwards, they sat around and talked, with Brendan being full of stories from his travels up north and Ben telling a few of his own about his long walk north with the pack horses. Ian learned a lot about Ben that night as he spoke openly for the first time about those years walking north. Tough and resourceful, he had turned a life time of negativity into a journey of a life time living as many of the pioneers had done, traversing much of the same country with much of the same resources. After listening to Michael, he understood why they had such respect for each other having met each other after traveling not so different experiences.

'I've got to tell you, Ben, how proud I am of you. You have had a tough life but you've held it together and really made something of yourself and your place,' Ian told Ben in a quiet moment.

'Thank you. It's a bit of a work in progress still though.'

'Ben, we are all still a work in progress. You started a lot further behind than most. There are people around here who started off with twice as much as you and haven't done half the job. Some of the young blokes could learn a lot from you as it is. I know of at least two blokes of your age who won't be on the land much longer.'

'We can only work with what we have, I guess. I've got know where to go so I have to make a go of it.'

'Some of them are in the same boat; it's just that you have tenacity that they lack. You have a good business mind and you know what you want. You've gone out after what you want and the great thing is that you are taking others with you rather than brushing you aside. I'm proud to have you as a son in law.'

'Thanks, Ian, I appreciate it and everything you have done for me over the years.'

'I just wish I had done more. You deserved better than the hand you were dealt.'

'You weren't to know that at the time and besides, I'm not sure you could have done much more if you did know.'

'Thanks, Ben,' Ian replied as Brendan walked up.

'Hey, this conversation looks serious; how are you travelling, Ben?'

'Okay, I think.'

'You're going to be fine. You know I've heard this girl you are going to marry is one of the good ones.'

'She is and so is her brother,' Ben replied, shaking Brendan's hand.

The boys finished the night with a bottle of fine port, toasting Ben and Karen and their life together. Ben went to bed but couldn't sleep, sitting up thinking a lot of the night and wondering at what brought him to this point. He wondered how it was that Karen had worked his way into his life after all the barriers he had put over the years yet somehow, she got through and he had connected with her. The future was so unknown for him that he could not get his head around his expectation for the following day. At one point, he got up and went outside, sitting on a deck chair and looking up at the stars. A few minutes later, he heard the screen door open and Brendan stepped out of the house.

'How are you doing, bro? Can't sleep?' Brendan asked.

'No.'

'Got a lot on your mind, hey?'

'Yeah, you could say that. What I can't figure out is what on Earth made Karen want to marry me of all people.'

'You did. You were there for her when she was battling the bottle. You were straight with her and held her accountable for her drinking and she admired that. You have been a closed book for most of your life but you let in when you going through some really tough stuff. She loves you, man.'

'I love her too more than I could dare imagine.'

'Then don't sweat on it. Try and get some sleep, man. You have a wedding and a honeymoon to go to.'

'I will; I just need to look at the stars for a while longer.'

'I hear you; I'll stay if you want some company?'

'No, you're right. Thanks, Brendan. I just want to sit for a while.'

'Not a problem, see you in a couple of hours.'

'Yeah, see you then,' Ben replied before looking back up at the stars and remembering all those nights alone. He also remembered that night lying under the stars with Karen being on the other side of the fire and wanting just so much to just hold her. He hoped that one day he would be able to do that and perhaps now he may have that chance.

\*

Fiona and the girls were up early to decorate the rose garden with ribbons and bows exactly as Karen wanted. Ian helped to set up the tables and chairs ahead of the arrival of the caterers. Most of the setting up was done the night before so it did not take long. Ian seemed more nervous than Karen as he laid out the chairs for the musicians.

'Are you okay?' Fiona asked.

'I'm fine – it's just that Karen is getting married. I have long thought about this day but now that it is here, it seems like yesterday. She was this little girl crawling around this same garden. Now our little girl is getting married. Where did the years go?'

'I know but Karen is not a teenage girl. You must remember that we had three children at school by the time I was her age?'

'Yes, but it was a different age then?'

'Not really. Now your little girl is going to be Ben's wife and one day another little one will be crawling around this garden. A grandchild.'

'I suppose there will,' Ian replied.

'And you will enjoy that little one just as you enjoyed watching Karen crawl around here.'

'Grandkids, hey?'

'Yes, it is Karen's turn now. I will go and give her a hand and when she is ready, I will call you,' Fiona assured him.

\*

Karen got dressed in front of the mirror she had prepared for other special occasions but they all palled in comparison this moment. Fiona and Tracy were there to give her a hand to share the moment while Gayle ensured then that everything was ready in the rose garden before the first guests arrived. Her classic feminine white dress had been cut to fit her perfectly with her long dark hair covered in a simple veil. Fiona knew that Karen had always had a great sense of style and her wedding dress was a classic and very much Karen. Tracy assisted her with the dress, making sure it was all in place and sitting as it should.

'Thank you,' Karen said after Tracy had ensured the last fold in her skirt hung just right.

'I appreciated everything you did for me when I got married. It has been a pleasure to be able to return the favour.'

'So how do I look?' Karen asked as she slowly turned for her.

'Ben will love it.'

'I hope so.'

'I don't think you will have any worries on that score,' Tracy replied as she admired the dress.

'Thank you,' Karen said as the two of them embraced.

*

Ben changed into dark trousers, a shirt, a jacket and a bow tie. Not only did he look good in it but he felt comfortable in it and could wear it again for other functions. Karen had taken him shopping using the experience she had gained in Melbourne. It had been an uncomfortable and challenging experience for Ben but with Karen at his side and preparing for their wedding, he had gone with the occasion. Ben had always been a reluctant shopper so it was a challenge to buy clothes not only for their wedding but also their honeymoon. As stood in front of the mirror and looked at his own reflection, he could not believe that this was his wedding day and that he was about to meet Karen as his bride.

'You look good,' Michael assured him.

'Thank you, this feels good,' Ben replied as he adjusted his tie.

'How are the nerves holding up?' Michael asked with a smile.

'Not too bad for the moment. I suspect it will be different once we get there.'

'You're doing alright. I was a lot more nervous at my wedding but you helped me get through that. I married a great girl and you are marrying a good one as well. We are lucky men,' Michael told him.

'Yes, we are indeed very lucky,' Ben replied before walking to the car.

Neil and Fiona had the gardens looking wonderful and the girls spent time decorating the area with potted flowers and white ribbons. Karen had arranged for caterers she had met through work so that her parents would not have to worry about the food. She had deliberately kept the menu simple but with plenty of it also ensuring that any leftovers could be used to feed the handful of guests staying over the following day. Music came from a local violin group who worked gallery openings and the like, whom Karen had met at the opening of a new tourist centre in Lakes Entrance. They were just as happy to perform for Karen's small intermit wedding as they were for larger functions. A temporary floor was brought in from the local square dance group and used to cover the stones of the verandah between the pillars as a dance floor for the bridal waltz.

*

Ben arrived with Michael at the decorated side gate. Gayle was there to meet them and lead them through the gardens to the chairs at the front of the garden close to the columns under which they were to be married.

'Is there anything I can get you? I've been assured that your bride will arrive on time.' Gayle smiled.

'I'm fine for the moment but thank you,' Ben replied.

'You look really great and I can promise you so does Karen.'

'Thanks, Gayle.'

Ben was amazed as he walked into the garden and saw how good it looked. He could now see why Karen wanted to get married here and was not just being polite to him.

As expected, Ben looked nervous while Brendan and Gayle did their best to get him to relax. Ian met them, assuring Ben that all was well and offered a small flask of rum to settle the nerves, which was greatly appreciated. Others stepped up to wish him well, including Helen.

'I just wanted to wish you all the best for today and to thank you for inviting me to your wedding and for never giving up on me.' She smiled with a tear in her eyes.

'Thank you. Even if I had not found you there would have been an invitation for you and a place at the table,' Ben replied.

'I know; thank you. Karen truly is a lucky lady to have you,' Helen replied before kissing him on the cheek and then the two of them embraced.

*

Ian knocked gently on the door of Karen's bedroom. Fiona opened the door to him to see Karen waiting for him. Tracy slipped quietly out the side door into the verandah to give them a few minutes alone.

'Our daughter doesn't scrub up too bad, does she?' Fiona said as she took Ian's arm.

'You look radiant, my dear, just as your mother did when she came to me. It is a fortunate man who gets to see such beauty,' he told her, bringing a tear of joy to Karen's eyes.

'Thank you, thank you for everything; I have appreciated every opportunity that you have given me and especially all the love. I always wanted to spend my last night here and not some hotel and to married in the rose garden. It is just perfect. Thank you,' she told them.

'It has been our joy and pleasure,' Fiona replied.

'Shall we or do you want to keep the young man waiting awhile longer?'

'I don't want this man to wait – he's waited long enough,' Karen replied.

Karen linked arms with them and walked between her parents from her room around the verandah to meet Ben and the minister as the orchestra played Here Comes the Bride to announce her arrival.

Ben waited for Karen between the pillars in the rose garden. His first glimpse of her got the look Karen was hoping for; he could not take his eyes off her as she took his breath away. They walked Karen to Ben and the ceremony began. When asked, 'Who gives this bride to be wed?', Fiona and Ian said they did and in unison took Karen's hand and placed it in Ben's.

The ceremony was not a long one, apart from a short testimonial about Ben and Karen as a couple, followed by a short sermon about enduring love before they said their vows. Karen recited her vows with surety and confidence so that everyone could hear her. Ben was nervous but held her eyes as he recited his vows to her.

To everyone watching, there was no doubt at all that they meant every word to each other. The minister then announced them man and wife.

'Ben, you may kiss your bride,' the minister told him. Ben looked into her eyes and Karen expected a polite quick kiss on the mouth; instead, it was lingering, loving kiss. When some of the guests began to wolf whistle, Karen waved them away, causing everyone to laugh.

They signed the register and marriage certificate in the lounge room, which everyone could see through the main doors. Ben watched Karen sign her name as Karen Templeton for the first time, which she did without hesitation in her pen stroke. It was then more than at any other time that he knew that Karen was his. Tracy signed as Karen's witness and Michael as Ben's then everyone took a moment to embrace and the minister took a minute.

'Ben and Karen, can I say it has been my great pleasure and privilege being your minister at your wedding? Thank you for that privilege. I have one more duty to perform and that is to announce to your family and friends as you take your first steps together. May your life together be filled with all of God's blessings and joy,' he said as he held his hands over them. 'Are you ready?'

'Yes,' they replied in unison.

Pastor Tony stepped into the doorway looking out onto the verandah and the family and friends waiting for them.

'Ladies and gentlemen, after some delay, it is my great pleasure, I present to you Mr and Mrs Ben and Karen Templeton.'

Karen and Ben stepped into the rose garden to the cheers and applause of everyone. Karen glowed while Ben smiled that lost smile of his, looking to Karen to ensure it was as she had hoped. A reassuring kiss on the cheek caused him to relax a little and accept the embraces of the guests.

Tracy made a point of giving him a hug. 'There has never really been anyone but you since I first saw you in the city all those years ago. You should know that,' she told her.

'Thank you – that's nice of you to say.'

'I'm not just saying it, it is the truth; she's yours now,' she added.

'Thank you,' he replied and kissed her on the cheek to her delight and Karen gave his arm a gentle squeeze of approval.

Everyone was quick to embrace them and shower them with their love. As a concession to her sister, she attended the ceremony but then left before the reception. While her sister congratulated her, the politeness was forced and Karen was glad she was not staying for the reception. She left, unsure if they would see much of her during the years ahead, such was the distance between them.

It was different with Brendan whose congratulations was sincere and most welcomed. When he shook hands with Ben, the two men greeted each other as friends and Karen had no doubt that their friendship would only grow in the years ahead.

The quartet played as the caterers made the last preparations. Karen dragged Ben onto the small dance floor that was laid down for the occasion. They danced to I Really Got the Feeling by Dolly Parton, a song Karen had a recording of as everyone applauded but Fiona would recall later that the rest of them may as well have not have been there. For a few short moments, they were lost in each other's eyes.

Everyone knew then that they were more in love than they ever showed to the outside world to that point. Ben stood tall and strong as he waltzed and whirled Karen around the small dance floor, his eyes on no one but her. They were joined by other couples including her parents and Tracy and her husband. Brendan grabbed Gayle and waltzed her around the floor much to Karen's delight.

Everyone sat at a single table in the garden, which made for such a great occasion. Jack and Maureen were there and Maureen could not be happier for both of them. Helen was there with Martin, the two men shaking hands with genuine warmth as they got to talk briefly between courses. All the time they talked, Helen and Martin held hands and Martin constantly looked to Helen.

Ben got to dance with Helen, wishing that he had got to dance with her at her wedding.

'You did not get to dance my wedding but we get to dance at yours. I told you that the best was ahead of you and still is,' Helen told him.

'Thank you, you were right.'

'You didn't think Karen would marry you, did you?'

'No, not really,' Ben replied.

'Well, I did. I've known for some time. She did say anything; she didn't have to. Women just know these things sometimes. Karen is an amazing person; she knew we had to work through some things and then it was going to be your turn. Now Karen is your wife and I could not be happier for both of you.'

'Thank you, Helen, for everything.'

'Thank you for never giving up on me because when I found out you were alive, I so much wanted to share this day with you. Meeting you again has given Martin a new lease of life; we are happier now because I have my brother back.'

'Thanks, Helen, I appreciate it.'

Karen danced with her new brother-in-law.

'Thank you for coming today. I know Ben appreciates it,' Karen told Martin.

'Thank you inviting us. It means a great deal to both of us. I have liked Ben from the moment I met him and not just because he is Helen's brother. I hope that our families can get to know each other in the years ahead.'

'You are all welcome to come and stay any time.'

'Thank you, I think Helen needs some time to visit and catch up. Finding Ben has filled a hole in her life that can only be filled by family.'

'I know what you mean.'

'I know you do, that's why I wanted to thank you for helping them get together and filling in the pieces. Helen and Joel are the world to me; you have helped bring us closer together. Thank you,' Martin told her.

'You are most welcome. Now, I think I would like to dance with my husband.'

'Yes, I think Helen and Ben have had a chance to catch up,' Martin agreed and went to leave when Karen held his arm.

'If Ben hasn't already offered, we would love to have the three of you to come and stay.'

'We would like that very much, thank you,' Martin replied before heading to Helen. 'I think your wife would like a dance and I would love a dance with my wife,' Martin told Ben who stepped back and Martin stepped into Helen's arms and they began to waltz as young lovers holding each other close and looking into each other eyes.

Karen stepped up to Ben's side.

'Ben, you didn't miss out on witnessing your sister fall in love because those two are falling in love all over again. Your sister has found her missing brother and can now truly move on and begin to love her family anew,' Karen told him and Ben turned away. Karen held and they danced with tears in Ben's eyes.

Helen looked across the table at them and then turned to Martin and whispered quietly to him.

'I think it is time to make another baby tonight; what do you think?' Helen asked as they held each other close.

'I wanted you to say that for some time. I don't want Joel to miss the family you missed.'

'He won't. Not now,' Helen told him and they held each other close and danced to a lovely old tune that Karen loved.

Close by, Fiona and Ian danced together and looked at Karen and Ben.

'I think our little girl is all grown up, don't you?' Fiona said.

'Yes, and a finer man she could not have found to marry,' Ian replied.

'I couldn't agree more. I think she has always loved him,' Fiona said.

＊

At one point, Ben was sitting at the table looking lost as Karen was talking with Tracy and Gayle.

'How are you coping, Ben?' Fiona asked, sitting down beside him.

'Right at this moment, all this doesn't seem real. I keep thinking that in the morning, I'm going to wake up put my overalls on and go to work as if it just another day and all this will be over and it will be just another day.'

'I can assure you that this moment has not even begun yet. Tomorrow, you will wake up next to your wife. You are at the start of an amazing journey that if you work at it, it will last a life time. Right now, you enjoy this moment because life as you know it is about to change forever.'

'Thank you, I will,' he replied and Fiona patted the back of his hand.

Karen walked up to him after Fiona had a quiet word in her ear and sat beside him. She took his hand. 'How are you, my husband?'

'I'm good. You look just completely amazing,' he told her.

'Thank you. I hoped you would like it.'

'I love it and I love you,' he said and kissed her.

'I love you too,' Karen said as she held him.

'Is this what you hoped your wedding day would be?'

'Yes, and every bit more.'

'It's been quite a day, hasn't it?' He sighed.

'Yes, it has. Are you tired?'

'A little. I didn't sleep much last night,' he admitted.

'Then we should go home,' Karen said, standing up.

'We don't have to leave yet if you don't want to. The night is still relatively young,' Ben offered.

'We have a honeymoon to go to and I don't know about you but I am quite looking forward to that,' Karen told him, taking hand and Ben stood up with her.

Fiona picked up straight away that they were leaving. She realised that their moment had come and walked the few steps to them.

'We are going to head off now. We have an early start in the morning,' Karen said, holding Ben close.

'I know. You two have a great time and we'll see you when you get back. You are neighbours now, so don't be strangers and drop over any time.'

'We will. Thanks for everything, Mum, it has been a wonderful. I could not have asked for better.'

'You are most welcome,' Fiona replied before hugging both of them.

But that stage everyone else realised what was happening and formed a line so that they could all say goodbye. Ian shook Ben's hand then the two men embraced and Ian wished them well. Gayle was in tears, crying on Karen's shoulders while the two of them embraced. Ben received an embrace from her despite his own discomfort. Jack and Maureen embraced them both and invited them home when they returned, an invitation Karen was sure they would accept. Tracy and Karen embraced as only friends could, both pleased to be able share such great occasion with each other. Helen hugged Ben and cried a little, telling him how great it was to share the occasion and to know that he had his own family now. Martin and Ben shook hands and embraced, much to Helen's delight.

With the final embraces over, they the stood at the arched side gate to wave to everyone and for that final photograph. Karen gave a contented sighed and turned to Ben.

'That was perfect. Now, Mr Templeton, please take me home.'

That was when Michael opened the gate for them.

'Mr and Mrs Templeton, your carriage awaits,' he said with a sweeping arm, directing their attention to an open black carriage team that was used for shows and trials events. The carriage was decorated in the same while ribbon used in the garden. Karen was delighted by the surprise. 'This is my wedding present to both of you,' he said.

'Oh, Michael, this is a wonderful surprise, thank you,' Karen replied with a weepy embrace.

'Thanks, mate,' Ben replied, the two friends embracing.

'The pleasure has been mine. Thank you for everything.'

Kevin Barry, their driver, assisted Karen into the carriage and took them on the same farm lanes Karen had taken on her discrete visits to see Ben just as the evening shadows were beginning to lengthen, out of the eyes of most people in town who knew little of the occasion. They were driven up to the cottage gate, which had been decorated with a white bow. Looking at the cottage, Karen saw her home for the first time as Ben's wife.

Ben assisted Karen down from the carriage and Kevin waved them farewell. Ben then handed Karen a pair of scissors to cut the ribbon across the gate to the cottage before walking hand in hand into the house.

'Welcome home, Mrs Templeton,' Ben said, squeezing her hand.

'And a happy home it is going to be, Mr Templeton,' Karen replied, imagining her children playing in the garden.

They were delighted to find that the girls had done their work decorating the house for them laying out lace and ribbon as well as champagne and chocolates. There were little gifts left for them from locals who wanted to wish them well. Karen opened the bottle of champagne and poured a glass.

'Do you want some to celebrate?' she asked.

'No, thanks. I really don't like it. A port would be nice though.'

'It's a good thing I bought this then.' Karen smiled, holding up a bottle of the finest Australian port she had the girls leave on one of the side benches.

'Thank you,' Ben replied, looking at her in wonderment.

'Here's to us,' Karen said, the two of them toasting each other.

Ben sat on the seat beneath the kitchen window, taking in the breeze that was teasing the curtains as Karen began to look at the small gifts that were on the kitchen table.

They opened some of the small gifts, which included some ornate salt and pepper shakers, a butter dish and some delightful small figurines. Karen was delighted by the gifts and the cards that went with them. They read the cards and laughed at some of the notes that went with them.

Ben made some coffee in a new plunger that was part of a coffee kit that someone had left them. They sat together on the bench seat and sipped their coffee. Karen turned to Ben. 'I love you so much,' Karen said and then kissed him passionately.

'What did I ever do to deserve you?' he asked.

'You have loved me and have been there for me when I needed someone to be straight with me. I love you and we are good for each other. Together, we are what the other needs and I have always enjoyed your company. Right now, I want to enjoy it even more,' Karen told him. 'I'm going to have a shower and then we can spend some time getting to know each other in a whole new way,' she told him.

Ben woke with a start during the night when he felt someone in the bed beside him. He sat up and looked down at Karen asleep beside him and wondered why she ever came to sleep in his bed. She rolled over and looked up at him.

'I'm here and I'm not going anywhere,' she told him and pulled him to herself and then stretched across his chest, Ben again feeling her nakedness against his skin.

\*

In the morning, Karen woke to find the bed empty beside her and smelt the aroma of fresh coffee and breakfast cooking in the kitchen. She got out of bed and stood briefly in front of the mirror to brush her hair. She was Mrs Templeton now, she thought, and a smile came across her face before she put on a dressing gown tying it around her waist and then headed to the kitchen.

'Good morning, my husband,' Karen said when she entered the kitchen, noticing that Ben was fully dressed and ready for the day.

'Good morning,' Ben said, turning to meet her with hesitation in his eyes.

Karen walked up to him and wrapped her arms around him. 'How are you this morning?'

'I'm good,' Ben replied and kissed her on the forehead.

'Well, I'm better than good because I'm here with you and last night was great and I can't wait to do that again with you,' Karen told him, hoping it would take some of the hesitation from his eyes.

Ben did not say anything but held her close.

'I'm really glad that I married you and know that we are going to be good together,' she said softly and it was then that she felt the tension ease a little from Ben's shoulders. 'Now, how are you?' she asked.

'I'm the better for seeing you,' Ben replied.

'That's good because you look good,' Karen told him.

'Hungry?' he asked.

'Famished.'

'Sit down. Breakfast will be ready in a minute,' Ben told her as he returned to the stove.

'This is nice,' Karen said as she sat at the table.

'It does smell good, doesn't it?' Ben admitted to himself.

'I wasn't talking about the food; I was talking about having breakfast made for me by my husband. Life is good,' Karen told Ben who blushed. 'I didn't say it to embarrass you. I'm telling you because I love you and I love being with you,' Karen told him.

Ben looked at her and Karen loved the way he looked at her at that moment. She stood up, wrapped her arms around him and kissed him.

'You are a beautiful man, Ben Templeton,' Karen told him and kissed him again.

'You are a beautiful woman, Karen Templeton,' Ben replied as he held her close.

'I'm going to have a quick shower. Have we got time?'

'Yes, you go ahead,' Ben replied.

Karen returned wrapped in a warm dressing gown and drying her hair. 'Where were you? I was waiting for you.'

'What for?'

'Ben, I was waiting for you to join me.'

'You want to shower with me?'

'Yes, that's why I asked,' Karen replied but Ben didn't respond.

'Ben?'

'I would find you, um, too attractive.' He blushed, looking for words and could not make eye contact with her.

'Ben, I know that you have been teased mercilessly by women in the past but I am your wife. I love you and I love your body. I want to satisfy you and I will not reject you,' she replied, sitting on his knee and kissing him. She could feel his embarrassment. 'It's okay. You will get used to me because who I am and what I do with you is for your eyes only and I want you to know me as only a lover can,' she told him.

Ben served breakfast in silence before sitting opposite her at the table where he looked up at her. 'You are an amazing and beautiful woman,' he said and she knew he meant it with all his heart.

✻

Karen called her mother before they drove to an airfield near Bairnsdale where a local airline ran flights to Launceston via King Island. Fiona was delighted to hear from her.

'Thanks again for everything, Mum.'

'You are welcome. Did you like the way they did the house up for you both? I hope there wasn't anything too tacky, given that Gayle can forget herself at times?'

'They did a great job. The place is wonderful.'

'Good, how is Ben?'

'He's good; he's loading the car right now.'

'And things went well between you two last night?'

'Yes, very good thank you,' Karen replied, not quite believing she had said that to her mother.

'I am pleased for both of you; I thought Ben may have been a bit hesitant.'

'He was but we overcame that. I have married a good man, Mum.'

'Yes, you have. Have a great trip and we'll catch up when you get back.'

'We will,' Karen replied.

\*

As part of their trip to Tasmania, they hired a car to cruise the wineries, staying at a couple of them before traveling down to Hobart for a couple of days. Karen was a little concerned at how Ben would enjoy the wineries but he took it all in, enjoying tasting the wines and food. He showed considerable interest in the wineries and as always, she was fascinated by the depth of his knowledge of the industry. They relaxed as they sat on the balcony of one of the winery cafes, enjoying the view of Tamar River.

'Haven't you been the surprise? You seem to be really enjoying yourself.'

'Why wouldn't I be enjoying my honeymoon?' He winked at her.

'I'm not talking about that.' Karen blushed, secretly delighted that Ben would flirt with her. 'I mean the wineries; you seem to have a very good understanding of the industry.'

'It's one of those industries that have done really well around the entrance but there is opportunity for cold weather varieties in our area. There are a couple small wineries north of us that could come down here and really learn from these cold weather wineries.'

'You're always thinking, aren't you? You are enjoying the wineries though, aren't you? The food and wine as well as these views?'

'It's great, it really is. The wines are good and the food is amazing – having you to share them with is sensational.'

'Thank you,' Karen replied, reaching for his hand.

They stayed the night at a cottage above the river where they could sit on the verandah. From their bedroom they were able to look over the river and the vineyards of the Tamar. Karen walked out of the bathroom after having a shower, wearing nothing but a sheer shirt as she dried her hair. Ben looked up at and Karen loved the way he was looking at her and made no attempt to cover herself.

'What are you thinking right now?' she asked him.

'In my wildest dreams, I never thought I would live to see you as you are now.'

'And do you like what you see?' she asked as she looked at him.

'Very much,' Ben replied as his eyes took her in.

'Good. I'm glad you like what you see,' Karen told him throwing her towel onto the bed and opening her shirt. 'I love you so much. I want you,' she told him.

*

On the drive south, they stopped at Ross where they walked the town and took photographs. Ben appreciated the architecture of the town, taking photographs of the bridge. They stopped for a picnic beside the river with views of the famous bridge. On a clear sunny day, it was nice to take the time stop and take in their surrounds. It was the most relaxed Karen had ever seen him and was delighted. After lunch, they continued on to Hobart where they moved into an apartment close to the city. Karen loved shopping and while Ben looked interested, he struggled with the crowds in Salamanca Place. Later, they both enjoyed walking around battery point.

While waiting for tea one night in the city, they began talking to another couple who were waiting to be seated. After exchanging niceties, the old couple realised where Ben and Karen were from.

'Our daughter was rescued from some atrocious weather from the mountains in that part of Victoria some years back. You may have heard of it?' David told them.

'How long ago?' Karen questioned.

'Coming up seven years, I think,' he replied, looking to his wife, Joan, for confirmation.

'Yes, it was the winter she did year twelve. She is about your age,' Joan replied.

'I remember it; Ben was on the rescue team and I was in support with the auxiliary providing meals and some communications,' Karen told them.

'Really?' Joan questioned.

'Yes, Ben directed them to where he thought they may be after most other leads were exhausted.'

'We were told that one of the team had found them on a hunch.'

'When Ben gets a hunch, people listen. When people can't be found,

Ben is their best shot. Jack Carmodia, the old hand of Mountain Rescue, says Ben is the next generation.'

'Karen, please?' Ben said, looking uncomfortable and trying to get her to change the subject.

'I can understand you don't like the attention, Ben, but our daughter Talia said that one of the men gave her an old teddy bear filled with hot rocks to hold and keep her warm. That wasn't you, was it?' David asked.

'That's Ben's rescue bear. He heats the rock and gives it to his patients to warm them up.'

'You were the rescuer who gave Talia the bear?' Joan questioned.

'Yes,' Ben replied almost apologetically.

'Talia will want to meet you,' Joan said, looking to David for confirmation.

'Absolutely. She would not forgive us if we met with you and did not give her the opportunity to thank you.'

'That is not necessary; I was only doing my job.'

'But it's not your job, it's a volunteer position,' Karen reminded him.

'That's what I thought,' David told them before making a call on his mobile phone. It was obvious he was on the phone with Talia.

'You are not going believe who we are sitting with at the moment; the man who gave you the warm bear in the mountains all those years ago.'

'You're kidding?' They heard the scream.

'No, his name is Ben and he is with his wife, Karen. They are here on their honeymoon.'

'What? Hold them there, please. I'm on my way,' they heard an excited voice reply.

David closed the phone. 'You will please be our guests for dinner tonight; Talia really wants to meet you to thank you,' David asked them.

'Please, it is not necessary. Talia did thank me at the time,' Ben replied.

'But we would like to thank you as a family. Had you not found Talia that night, she would not have been alive in the morning. I don't know if you appreciate what it means to be told that but without you, our lives would have changed dramatically. Please let us do this?' Joan told him.

'Okay, thank you. We will,' Karen replied.

'It was a tough night. We only just made it ourselves.'

'You were struggling yourselves?' Joan questioned.

'They were at the limit of their resources; in fact, they were going to be pulled out within the next few hours if they had not found them. A team had already been organised to assist in getting Ben and the others out; it was that team that met them at the road junction,' Karen told them.

'There was only an hour or two in it?' the woman asked.

'Yes, another two hours and Mountain Rescue would have had pulled out or to be rescued themselves as it was weeks before they were ready to carry out any further work.'

'Yes, I am sorry but we were only going to get one chance at it. We got lucky. It was extremely cold and there was no room for niceties so I didn't really get to know your daughter at all other than as one of a number of people in need of critical care,' Ben apologised.

'I don't doubt you but I can assure you Talia remembers you,' David told her.

*

Talia was in tears when she saw Ben.

'Karen, would you mind if I give your husband a hug?' Talia questioned.

'You'll have to ask Ben that.'

Ben reluctantly accepted her embrace.

'Thank you so much; I would not be alive today if it hadn't been for you. Thank you for giving me a second chance at life.'

'You are welcome but it's what Mountain Rescue were formed to do. We were just doing our job.'

'But that night was more than a job. The conditions could not have been much worse than that and we were nowhere near where we told you we were; how did you ever find us?'

'We got lucky; that's all.'

'Ben, I've been told that had it not been for you, we would not have been found; that you have a rare gift for finding people in the most terrible conditions. The luck was that you were around that day. There is something that I want to give you and Karen,' Talia said and stepped aside to pick up a parcel, which she handed to Ben, encouraging him to open it straight away.

Ben pulled the paper away to reveal a large toy bear with a bravery medal pinned to the bright blue vest the bear was dressed in.

'It is something to give your children to remind them what a remarkable person their daddy is,' Talia told them.

Ben was speechless and suddenly choked as he held the bear.

'Thank you so much. We will treasure it,' Karen told her.

Ben shook his head, unable to respond, offering only a softly spoken apology.

'Please understand that Ben is very grateful but he finds praise, especially of such magnitude very difficult to accept,' Karen told them and gave Ben a hug as he turned away to hide tears.

David sensed then that Ben had not had an easy life.

Talia knelt down in front of him and placed a hand gently on his knee.

'I know that you did not remember what I looked like but I remembered you. I know how close I was to dying that day. We had run out of everything and we just weren't going to be alive in the morning but then I remember your exhausted face looking down at me and knew then that I was going to make it. I thought you were one of those old guys from the mountains and had no idea that you were my age – that's how cold wet and exhausted we were. You said to me you are safe now we are going to get you out and I knew then that I was going to make it home. You were not giving up on me and you would not let me give up. You gave me that bear and told me to hold it close and I did. Thank you,' she told him.

'Thank you,' Ben replied without making eye contact with her. 'Thank you for remembering me.'

'I will never forget you, Ben Templeton,' she told him and then embraced him once more.

'You are most welcome,' Ben replied but still looked embarrassed when he then looked at her parents.

'How long did it take you to recover afterwards?' Karen asked Talia.

'I spent three days in hospital in Melbourne and then a few more in hospital in Hobart and I returned to school a week after that. What about you, Ben, how did you recover?'

'I went to school the next morning,' Ben replied.

'Really?' Talia questioned.

'Yes, but he fell asleep in class and was sent home. It took weeks for Ben to recover fully. The Rescue Auxiliary supplied him with hot meals for nearly a month to assist with his recovery.'

'Your family would have been grateful for the help,' Mary said and Ben turned away and looked almost ashamed. Karen went to respond but Ben tried to stop her.

'Karen, please. They don't need to know,' he pleaded as he turned his head away.

'Know what?' David questioned.

'Ben was living alone; he had no family at that time. The meals and other assistance he received from the auxiliary were his benefit alone,' Karen told them as she held Ben's hand.

'And yet you still went out and risked your life for others?' Talia questioned but Ben did not answer.

'Yes, he did. Like I said, you got lucky that night,' Karen replied, uncertain if she had said the right thing.

'It was a long time ago,' Ben said with a smile, which failed to hide so much.

'In some ways, it was but for me, it was only yesterday because I have never taken a single day for granted since,' Talia told him.

Ben did not reply but offered her a weak smile instead.

It took a while for Ben to join in the conversation after that to explain who Mountain Rescue were and how they operated. Karen explained a little of what Mountain Rescue did, about Jack Carmodia, how membership was by invitation only and Ben's place in the team. They talked too about the tourist industry of Victoria and Tasmania, where they all learned just how much knowledge and understanding Ben had of the industry, how important some of the specialised support services like Mountain Rescue were to ensure the safety of people and the long-term viability of the industry.

At the end of the evening, David stood up to shake Ben's hand.

'Can I say, Ben, what an amazing person you are. I knew you were some kind of mountain man with great bush skills but I must say, your knowledge of the wider world is impressive. I can see that you have not had an easy life; your community is doubly fortunate to have you.'

'Thank you,' Ben replied, shaking David's hand.

Karen picked up the bear, ensuring that they did not leave it behind. Talia embraced both of them.

'Thank you for allowing me to meet you both. I really do wish both of you all the happiness in the world.'

'Thank you. We will treasure the bear and tell our children where it came from,' Karen replied, believing it would be the last time they would ever see each other again.

They did not speak about the meeting until they were at Stanley a couple of days later after Ben had had a restless night. Ben was sitting on rocks close to their cabin above the beach at the caravan park.

'What were you dreaming about last night? You were very restless,' Karen asked.

'Talia. I'd forgotten her name and for the life of me, I could not remember what she looked like nor any of the others for that matter. I could have passed her in the street and not recognised her. I have only these vague images of who those people were.'

'That's understandable given everything that was going on; you didn't have time for niceties. It took everything you had to get in there, get the job done and get everyone out. You were all exhausted when you came in I doubt any of you could have spent another night out there.'

'No, we were about done. It was time to start rotating teams until the weather cleared. It was not a good time for any of us. All I can remember about that rescue was the weather. When those snow showers came in there were beginning to think we might not be able to make the road group. We were in real trouble. It was a very near thing.'

'I heard that. It was a very near thing for Talia because she knew there was probably only an hour in it. After that, you would have had to wait till the morning and she simply didn't have that long.'

'They didn't and neither did we. I've never been that cold before or since. All I could remember was how tired I was afterwards. It took me weeks to recover. I'd forgotten that.'

'I remember you at school the next day – you looked wasted. You were tired for weeks after that but then you were always good at forgetting the tough times.'

Years later, they were surprised to receive an invitation to Talia's wedding and after talking with David on the phone, they decided to go. They were met by Joan and David at the airport and treated as their guests driving them to their hotel where a hire car awaited them. Ben and Karen joined David and Joan at their table where they caught up with each other's families.

Talia's new husband made a point of thanking Ben publicly for saving her from the cold, promising to keep her warm at night in future, which caused a wave of delightful laughter. As they left, they gave a card with a photograph of their daughter Abby hugging the bear that Talia had given them. Talia was delighted by the gift and thanked them both.

# CHAPTER TWENTY-TWO

*Settling in*

Returning home, they gave themselves a few days before returning to work. For Karen, it was an opportunity to move the majority of her things into the house, merging her life with Ben's. Standing on the verandah with a cup of coffee, she breathed in the air – the smell of the place she now called home. There was something she wanted to do, making sure that they finished up early. That night, Karen made love to Ben as his wife in their home and in the morning, shared breakfast with him.

Ben returned to work, catching up with Michael and supervising the work of a number of new horses. For Karen, it was the first real-time to see how Ben lived and worked. Sitting down to breakfast with him, Karen came to the realisation of just how hard Ben worked, having been at work for two hours before she woke up.

The one thing the place lacked was colour. It was not a case of repainting the house but adding life and colour to the small things such as cutting back a few trees and installing a couple of skylights. She organised some tradesmen to install the skylights while Ben and Ian cut the trees back, turning much of the timber into firewood. Ian and Ben had become friends once they returned home, both often stopping for a cuppa and a chat as well as giving each other a hand. It was nice for Karen as she had hoped the two had connected but their genuine friendship was very pleasing.

Her parents were among the first people they had for dinner. They had done a great deal with the house in the short time they had been together. Fiona was delighted with how things had changed as Karen showed her around. She saw too the changes in Karen, enjoying being married to Ben who clearly loved her.

'You're making quite a home of this place, you bringing back the colour that was here when Ben's mother was still alive,' Fiona told her.

'What was she like? Can you remember?' Karen asked.

'I can't say I knew her because as a family, they kept to themselves a lot, feeling like outsiders, I guess, given that neither of them had family in the area. What I do remember of her was that she was rather a shy person like Ben but she loved her kids. She attended all the kids' things at school and worked around the school but it was hard to get to know her. I think she lived in the shadow of Ben's dad. I don't think he was cruel or anything, it's just that he was: always very wary of people and didn't like having people in the house. She used to have a lot of simple flower beds around the front of the house that were lovely in the spring and summer.'

'I remember that; I am going to plant flowers in the front to give the place a real cottage feel,' Karen told them.

'It should look beautiful,' Fiona told her.

'I hope so. I want it to be a happy place to live, not based on the past but what we have now.'

'It's the only way to have it,' Fiona agreed.

Karen was welcomed back to work as Mrs Templeton. Everyone was delighted for her. Her network of professional women became even more important as they discussed careers and family. For the first time, Karen could talk about starting a family with real credibility within the group. It excited her but made her realise also that her life really had changed because she was married to a man who would be the father of her children. Some of them had met Ben and got to know him a little since some of the walls had come down since they were engaged. Ben went with her to one of her partners' dinners in town, which was a great success, given that Ben was able to meet new people and talk with them across the table. Karen could see him struggling at times but knew he was staying in it to support her and she appreciated it.

Eighteen months later, Karen was approached to take of an employment secretarial services agency as CEO and financial partner. It took Karen some time to consider the proposal, having used the company to provide staff for her own office on a number of occasions. After several months of researching the position, she decided that she would take a long-term view of the position, believing that she could make a long-term business, which would give her flexibility to raise a family. One of the first things she did was set up a duplicate office at home so that she could do as much work from home as possible for when they had children.

# Chapter Twenty-Three

*Memories of old and new*

A few months later, Ben took Karen riding up into the high country proper to see the final snows of the winter being replaced by the beautiful native flowers and grasses. They were soon past much of the country that Karen knew until they reached a short plateau, which Karen thought she recognised.

'There is something familiar about this place,' Karen told Ben as they rode through the mountain ash.

'It should be. This was where I found you that time.'

'When we were at school?'

'Yes. The cave is just of there at the base of those rocks,' Ben replied, indicating a steep section of the mountains which near vertical for two-hundred meters.

'Can we go there?'

'Yes, if you want,' Ben replied.

As they rode up to the entrance to the cave, the memories of that night came flooding back. Karen stepped down off her horse and looked at the shallow cave with wonderment.

'Who could have imagined that the two people who once spent the night in this cave to escape the cold would return here one day as a married couple?' Karen told him.

'It was a long time ago,' Ben told her.

'It was but also seems like yesterday; I can almost see us sitting in the dark talking. I was terrible to you that night – it's a wonder you ever spoke to me again,' Karen said as she turned to him.

'You were a little lost and scared and you didn't know me that well – it was fine.'

'No, it wasn't because you were true to every word and told no one about that night that I know of.'

'It was nobody's business but ours so why tell anyone?'

'Yes, but I was lost and you saved me. Didn't that mean something?'

'Yes, I saved you a night in the cold and got you home the next morning, which was a reward in itself, I guess.'

'Can we spend the night here and sleep under the blankets together? I would like to replace those memories with better ones.'

'Sure, we can stay the night but I don't have bad memories of this place or that night. I asked you to trust me that night and you have ever since.'

'Yes, but I was still an ungrateful bitch if I remember correctly.'

'Well, you and I must have different memories then because you have treated me with respect ever since.'

'We both know that's not true.'

'That was then, this is now; I'll get a fire going if you want to set up our swags in the cave,' Ben told her.

That night, they slept in each other's arms after talking half the night away. Karen could not remember feeling so safe, warm and loved as she did that night. In the morning, Ben made them breakfast over the fire as Karen slept. She woke to see Ben just as he had been all those years before. She watched him for a few minutes before speaking to him.

'How are you this morning?'

'Good. How did you sleep?' Ben asked in reply.

'Good but more importantly, how did you sleep?'

'Yeah, fine. Why do you ask?'

'Because I slept very well knowing you were beside me. I can't imagine what you must have been thinking last time.'

*

They rode down to the edge of the state forest where Ben led Karen towards a cabin on the edge of the park. Hans' cabin was on private land on the edge of the snow line. It was empty now as Hans had died some years ago. Karen remembered reading about him in the paper.

'This is where I came after my shoulder was broken.'

'I remember you telling me. How long did you stay here?'

'Just under five weeks. Then I had to get back to school.'

'Tough days?'

'They were among the toughest I could ever remember.'

'So, what happens to it now? Doesn't he have family?'

'No, he had no family. He left to me.'

'Really? What are you going to do with it?' Karen asked in surprise.

'I'm going to rent it out to people with very specific needs for solitude.'

'It's a little basic?' she questioned.

'It's rented as is because I want it to remain as it is and those who rent it understand that.'

'You don't advertise it then?'

'No, not at all. Most come to me as a referral from people I trust and respect. They are heavily vetted before they even hear of the place.'

'How does that work?'

'I worked with a rehab unit who look for solitary places for people who need a little time out. I meet with the client and guide them in on horseback and they stay one or two nights on their own or with someone and I then come and collect them and take them out via a different route so they are unlikely to find their way back.'

'Doesn't this place have main road access?'

'It does but the vehicle park is some distance away from the cottage. If anything does happen, the local SES and ambulance can get to the house via an unmarked track that select individuals within those organisations know well.'

'It's all very secretive.'

'No, just solitary. There is a difference.'

'And you need that at times, too, don't you?'

'Yes.'

'And that's when you come here?'

'Yes.'

'Then it is an asset to be treasured,' Karen assured him.

*

That evening, Karen stood on the edge of the verandah dressed in those knee-high riding boots of hers and riding trousers and tweed jacket. Ben had always admired her sense of style.

'What are you looking at?' Karen asked with a smile.

'You should be on the cover of one of those fancy country clothing catalogues.'

'Flattery will get you everywhere.' Karen smiled.

'I'm not just saying it; you look incredible for someone who has spent four days on horseback, living rough.'

'I'm pleased that you noticed.'

'What's not to notice? You're beautiful,' Ben told her.

# CHAPTER TWENTY-FOUR

*New traditions*

Karen was really looking forward to their first Christmas with Ben and her parents and Ted, who usually made it. Work was frantic but she still found the time to work her on her favourite time of the year. Ben appeared to be busier than ever, working his horses and getting the last of grass hay in. When not working on his own place, he was helping others with theirs as if trying to make himself busy, working longer and longer hours.

'What's going on, Ben?'

'How do you mean? I'm busy, the same as you are?'

'No, you are almost inventing work and you're never home.'

'What do you know about what I do? You're not out in the paddocks with me,' he snapped.

'No, I don't. Do you want me to be?'

'No,' he snapped. 'No, I don't,' he replied, softening his voice.

'Do you need to hire some people? There are plenty looking for work.'

'No.'

'Then what is it?'

'I'm busy, that's all.'

'It's more than that. What's going on? You have never spoken to me like that before and you are as tight as a bear trap and just may snap.'

'I'm sorry.'

'I'm looking for answers, not apologies; why are you like this lately? Don't you want to be with me anymore?'

'No, it's not like that at all. You know I love you.'

'Then what is going on? Are there financial issues you're not telling me about? What is it?'

'Christmas is a mad time of year, you know that. Michael needs to get away and orders and accounts to be finalised; it's just busy.'

'Yes, we all are but we are also getting together with my family and there is my work break up. Are you too busy for those things too?'

'I don't have time; I have to get away,' Ben replied, his face suddenly looking trapped.

'You're not going anywhere,' Karen said, standing in front of him, her hand against his chest. 'It's none of those things, is it? It's Christmas, isn't it? You can't cope with Christmas, can you?'

'Everyone loves Christmas.'

'That's not what I said. When was the last time you spent Christmas with people? When was the last good Christmas that you can remember?'

'A while ago.'

'When?' Karen snapped.

'When I was thirteen,' Ben replied, bowing his head.

'Then this Christmas will be different because you will be spending it with me. Now, if that is here, at my parents' place or by a campfire in the mountains, I don't care but you will not spend another Christmas alone.'

'But you have your family.'

'You are my family. Ben, we will do as much or as little as you like but we will spend it together. Please don't make me spend Christmas alone,' she pleaded.

'Life is so unfair burdening you with me like this at Christmas. You should have had someone who could embrace the things you love.'

'You are who I love and you are not a burden. I did not draw any short straw when I married you and don't you ever say that I did,' Karen snapped. She then held his arms and looked at him.

'I am going to show you what Christmas with family and friends can be like. You go about your work and I'll organise everything I promise I will not embarrass you,' Karen told him in a softer voice.

*

At the end of the week, Karen arrived early to see to the arrangements for a barbeque for Michael and the others who helped out throughout the year. Tom from the local butcher shop was more than willing to help out. They had a small gathering down by the river where they shared a few beers, enjoyed a spit roast and sat around the campfire. For the handful of people, which included her father, it was a great opportunity to catch up with everyone.

'Now, this is more like it, isn't?' Karen asked in a quiet moment.

'Yes, it is, thank you. I had no idea what to do.'

'Yes, you did. You were just afraid it would not be good enough,' Karen replied and saw straight away that she had found the answer to the problems beneath.

\*

'Michael, I wanted to thank you for sticking around. It's been a big year and now that you are working your own horses. We can look at delivering a decent income for you in the New Year,' Ben told him.

'Thanks. We're doing okay I knew it would take some time. I know I've said before but you know thanks for giving me a start. You took a chance on me. I appreciate it.'

'You have been a huge asset to me and the town. I appreciate that but I still thought you may have moved on; not that I'm trying to get rid of you or anything, it's just that you seem capable of much more.'

'I still see growth here for both of us. Your quarter horses are doing really well and with the stock horses and feed, the business is growing. There are other things keeping me here though. I have something else to ask. Would you mind if I married Melanie Robins?'

'Why would I mind? Of course. No, that would be great news – that is, if you've asked her yet?'

'No, I want to return straight after Christmas and propose over New Year's.'

'Go for it. Is there anything I can do? Not that you need my help with the asking.'

'Actually, there is. I have a huge favour to ask.'

'Ask away.'

'My offer at Herman's Cottage has been just accepted. It's going to need some serious work if I'm going to have it ready for Melanie after a spring wedding. I was wondering if you would give me a hand to do it up.'

'Of course. We'll have a look at it and see what you need.'

'It will mean a lot of work,' Michael warned.

'It doesn't matter. You know I'll help you in any way I can. We get some other guys to help and who knows, we'll get the job the job done between us.'

'Thanks, Ben, I really appreciate it; you have become like a brother,' Michael replied, shaking his hand in thanks.

'It's okay. You're among family here,' Ben told him.

'I appreciate that. That's why I would like to make Herman's Cottage our home.'

'Then a home we'll make it. You have a great Christmas and we'll get into in the New Year.'

'Thanks, Ben,' Michael replied, the two shaking hands once more.

*

That Christmas proved a challenge as they attended a midnight service and then spent Christmas tea with her parents. At the service, they met everyone who was delighted to see them there. Ben was terribly ill at ease as he met everyone as the service got underway late. At the end of the service, everyone gathered for a late supper.

'Ben, welcome. It is good to see you at Christmas service again. It has been a long time but I hope is not the last,' the minister told him.

'Thank you,' Ben replied, attempting eye contact.

Others greeted them with equal warmth, welcoming him and wishing him well for Christmas and the New Year. Karen got to see how much he was respected by everyone. Their words were very genuine and heartfelt. She realised that night that there were few families that had not been affected by Ben's generosity It was time for him to join the world he so passionately served.

*

Ben sweated, hiding away through Christmas Day, trying desperately not to show the tension that exuded from every inch of his body. Karen tried to reassure him and Fiona welcomed him warmly with a kiss. Ian and Brendan welcomed him and sensing his discomfort, gave him space.

Ben could not help but warm to Fiona as he found a quiet moment to sit alone out on the verandah.

'How are you going?' she asked.

'I'm sorry to spoil your Christmas.'

'You have not spoilt my Christmas; it is you I am concerned about.'

'I'm doing okay,' Ben replied.

'I wish I could believe you. Ben, this is your first real Christmas in many years, isn't it?'

'Yes, but that doesn't excuse my behaviour, I should be better for you and your family.'

'You are family now and you don't have to apologise because we understand that this is very difficult for you.'

'I'm sorry,' Ben apologised, fighting back tears.

'Don't be. It's okay, Ben. You stay out here as long as you need to, we understand,' Fiona told him as Karen approached them. She pulled up a chair beside him and then began to cry silent tears. 'I think these tears are a long time overdue,' Fiona told him. They sat with him for some time and then slept in the chair.

He was better later in the afternoon when he was able to sit with them and they talked over an early tea before heading home.

Ben looked exhausted when they got home but then he went into the spare room and brought out a present for her.

He smiled with tired eyes he said as he handed a small gift-wrapped box.

'What's this?' she asked.

'Something I got for you a long time ago,' Ben replied as Karen carefully opened unwrapped the box and opened it. Karen opened the box to find a thin necklace made by a jeweller who used to live in the area and worked in the area but sold most of his pieces into Melbourne and Sydney.

'Oh, Ben, it is beautiful. Thank you,' she said and kissed him.

Ben took it from her and placed it around her neck.

'How long have you had this?'

'A long time.'

'You are full of the most wonderful secrets,' Karen told him as she looked at herself in the mirror.

'You are my most wonderful secret,' Ben told her and Karen wrapped her arms around him and just held him, grateful for him and wanting for him to enjoy family so much more.

*

Karen worked for some time planning a special meal for Ben's birthday but he was not back from his trip when she got back from work. She called him, concerned by his whereabouts.

'Ben, where are you?'

'I'm still a couple of days away. I got tied up with Fenton's horses and now giving a crew a hand with some wild horse on the edge of Kosciusko.'

'Why aren't you home? I have everything ready for your birthday.'

'My birthday? I wouldn't be worried about that. I haven't done anything about that for years. To be honest, I had forgotten all about it.'

'But we talked about it before you left; you promised you'd be home for your birthday.'

'I really don't remember. I tend to switch off when anyone talks about it; birthdays just aren't my thing.'

'Well, it's my thing, okay? I want to celebrate your birthday with you. Now, please come as you said you would.'

'Okay, I'll be home in a couple of days but I really don't see what the issue is.'

'The issue is that you don't like yourself very much and I know you don't like celebrating your birthday but I do. I want to celebrate your birthday. Now, please come home.'

'Okay, I'm on my way.'

Karen was almost frantic when Ben arrived home a couple of days later, rushing out to meet him when he pulled up in the yard. She wrapped her arms around him as soon as she got out of the truck.

'Hey, hey, what is the panic about?' he asked when he saw her.

'You. You give so much to others but when anyone else wants to give something back, you run off. You make such an effort for my birthday; don't you think I want to do the same for yours? Ben, I am not just anyone I am your wife and I am grateful that you were born. Now, please, let me have your birthday. Let me show you that I love you and let me celebrate your birthday,' Karen pleaded.

'Okay, Karen, I hear you,' Ben replied as he held her close.

'Don't just hear me, Ben. Be here,' Karen told him as she held him. She took him into the house where she served up a roast dinner with all the blessings and then presented him with a new Akubra hat. Ben loved the hat and was equally delighted by the effort she had put in for the meal.

'Next year I would like us to go out for tea to celebrate; can you be here for that?'

'Do we have to?'

'No, but it would be nice; my family want to come too.'

'Why would they?'

'Because they want to celebrate your birthday. Ben, I'm not the only person in the world that loves you – they do too and Brendan really does enjoy your company,' Karen told him.

'Okay, I'll think about it,' Ben replied, being the best he could agree to at the time.

Later that night, Karen lay beside him in bed.

'I need you to know how much I love you. I love being able to cook you a special meal, sharing a bed with you and waking up beside you. I married you so that we do this. Ben, I can't do that if you're not here.'

'I know that now and I am sorry. It just hasn't been of any significance to me but it's important to you so I will do it for you.'

'I just wish you could do for you. I wish you could say, "Hey everyone, I'm turning thirty and want you to come and share my birthday with me".'

'Well, I think you will be waiting a lot longer than my thirtieth for that to happen.'

'I know but it's one of my dreams for you.'

# CHAPTER TWENTY-FIVE

## *Melanie and Michael*

Melanie accepted Michael's proposal in the New Year and everyone was delighted. Up that point, Karen knew Melanie to say hello to but had never really got to know her and Melanie turned to Karen in the hope of finding a friend despite the age difference. Karen willingly invited her into her home.

'I hope you don't mind me calling in but there are so few young couples around to talk to about setting up a house and things. I really hope you don't mind?'

'Not at all. You can call in any time.'

'The men are going to start work on the house soon and I don't know the first thing about building and timber; I'm afraid I'm feeling a bit useless at the moment.'

'But you know about colours and curtains and things, don't you?'

'Of course,' Melanie replied.

'Well, there you go. You decide the colours in the house and what fabrics will work in what rooms. I'll give you a hand if you like?'

'Would you? I would love to have someone apart from Mum. She's great in the kitchen and all that but there isn't a lot of colour in our place, probably because she has always worked.'

'We'll work on the garden too if you like and turn it into one of those old English cottage gardens?'

'I was thinking that same thing; you've done such a great job with your place. It used to look such a sad place. Since you married Ben, it has come to life and so has Ben.' She smiled.

'Thank you. That is a lovely thing to say.'

'It's true; Mum always said that Ben was a man growing old before his time. I saw the two of you kiss one day down the street before anyone knew you two were going out together and remember thinking how much he had already changed. It's good to see him happy,' she said, Karen suspecting that she had a soft spot for Ben.

'So are you looking forward to the wedding?'

'Yes, very much. I think it will be wonderful,' Melanie replied but with a tinge of apprehension in her voice.

'But you're worried about something?'

Melanie was reluctant to speak and took a few breaths.

'I'm not like a lot of the other girls around here; I've never been with a man and I don't know a lot about that sort of things. Of course, I know where babies come from and all that, I'm not a child; it's just that...' Melanie cut short then looked at her. 'Mum won't talk about it and I know it's a private thing but I don't know much.'

'And you want someone to talk to?'

'Yes, I know it is a terrible thing to ask and I know that we hardly know each other but I am certainly not going to talk to the other girls around town. Before I know it, I will be known as the virgin queen and will be laughed until we're married and after, probably, as well.'

'Melanie, it's fine – we'll talk. I was a virgin on my wedding night too.'

'And you weren't worried about what might happen?'

'No because I knew that Ben was too and he loves me. It was something that I was really looking forward too because it can be very good.'

'And you enjoyed it?'

'Yes, I still do and so will you. Sex is not something to be afraid of. Michael loves you.'

'But he's been with other girls.'

'Yes, he may have but he has not had a wife or a wedding night before – only you get to be part of that; that is yours. He will not do anything to hurt or embarrass you; he loves you.'

'You think that is how Michael thinks of it?'

'Michael doesn't say much but I know that he thinks the world of you and is very much looking forward to making a home with you in the cottage. Closer to the day, you should talk with him when you do the pre-marriage course. You will find that it helps.'

'Thank you, Karen, talking with you helps more than you know.'

'I'm glad I can help.'

'Thanks for being a friend.'

'Of course; I'll make a cuppa and we can look at some colours, unless you want to talk more about it?' Karen said.

'No, I'm fine. I can ask more questions later though without causing embarrassment, can I?'

'Of course. Melanie, I have been fortunate in that I have mother who I have been able to share everything with and Mum and I were able to talk about sex and family. I'm not your mother but I am a friend if that helps?'

'It does, thank you,' Melanie said before accepting the magazines Karen offered from a side table.

It proved to be the beginning for Karen and Melanie after that as Karen watched Melanie blossom into a woman in love. She walked with a new spring in her step and people in town treated her differently after that. While she was only twenty, she seemed to grow up overnight. Karen even went lingerie shopping with her closer to the wedding, which they both enjoyed especially when Karen was able to pick up some pieces for herself as well.

'Michael is not going to think I'm slutty wearing this, will he?'

'No, he won't. Not when he realises it is just for him.'

'Thank you. I'm beginning feel like a woman now.'

'But you are a woman and being engaged does not make you more so or less so because you're not. You are the equal of any woman in this town; don't let anyone tell you otherwise.'

'Thank you,' Melanie replied.

*

In the New Year, they began work on the house. They recycled a lot of timber from one of the yards and a couple of homes under demolition. Taking the best of the timber and sanding them down, they found some cleaned up really well. Among the timber were mountain ash and blackwood and some pieces of oak, which they used in prominent places for strength but also to make a feature of them.

Slowly, the cottage was extended and transformed. Other men in the town dropped in to give a hand without being asked, offering their time and tools to the project. Michael was a little surprised that people who he knew only from a distance would drop in and give a hand for a couple of hours. They began to dig the holes for the front fence when one of the local tradesmen pulled up with a post hole digger.

'Want a hand, boys?' Jim asked from the back of his ute.

'We could, yes,' Michael replied.

'You're in luck. The digger could do with a run,' Jim said as he pulled the rope from the digger.

'Thanks, I really appreciate this. It will save us a lot of time.'

'It's pleasure; you two blokes are the first to give others a hand. It's about time to give you a hand.'

The holes were dug in no time and they soon had the posts in and lined up.

'Thanks, Jim. The girls will be over with lunch shortly. You are welcome to join us,' Ben offered.

'Thanks, but I have a job to do this afternoon. I'll drop back later and see how you are getting on.'

'There will be a barbie on for you and whoever wants to drop in.'

'I'll do that. Thanks, boys. I'll see you later.'

*

That first barbeque was a great success, welcoming anyone who turned up. For Melanie, it was a big event as she welcomed people to her future home. Having worked for many years in her parent's bakery, she was used to being the anonymous face behind the counter. For many of those who came to help out and enjoy the barbeque, it was an opportunity to meet them and congratulate them on their engagement. Karen gave her a hand with the cooking and lent a bit of moral support to Melanie who seemed overwhelmed at times.

'That was a really good day,' Karen said to her as they were washing the dishes after the barbeque.

'It was – everyone has been so kind. I can't believe the amount of time Ben is putting in. I know he's Michael's boss but he does so much more than provide a wage for Michael.'

'That is because they are friends. They come from tough places and they have a lot of respect for each other. You know you and I are lucky women to have two good men like we have.'

'Yes, we are both going to be married to good men.'

'Yes, we are.'

*

Michael and Melanie were married at the local Uniting Church by the minister who had served the community for over thirty years. Having christened Melanie, he was now delighted to be able to marry her. There were not a lot of weddings in town anymore as most of the younger people moved on after leaving school. A few returned to get married in their old hometown to please their parents but most had lost any real connection to the town by that stage as they married people from other places. Because Melanie and Michael were locals, the whole town turned out to watch them. Melanie was both delighted and a little embarrassed at the attention.

Ben was Michael's best man and took the role very seriously to ensure that everything was done and that the day was as good as it could be for both of them. He had organised the buck's night where the local men could meet and have a few drinks and wish Michael well. It had not been dissimilar to Ben's buck night, ensuring that Michael had no regrets and was ready for the wedding a week later. Ben also worked with Melanie and Karen to make sure the church and small reception in the hall next door was right on the day.

Michael's parents had relented and attended the wedding. He was not overjoyed at their support, meeting with them the night before being very formal, the damage done between Michael and his father on display as the two of them could not make eye contact and their handshake being very formal the two not embracing at all. Ben felt the tension and understood where Michael was coming from the two, having talked at length about his family.

Melanie and Michael emerged from the church to a huge cheer from those waiting outside. They threw flowers and many of the girls Melanie had barely known at school rushed up to congratulate her and wish them both well for the future. The reception was held in a back room of the hotel with a few family friends.

Michael took advantage of his family assets for the first time and took them to the family holiday house down on the coast. He treated her like royalty as they honeymooned on the coast taking her to the places of his youth before he went off the rails. Melanie was treated like royalty and she felt very much like Michael's queen.

# CHAPTER TWENTY-SIX

## *Working with family*

Ben was working with Ian to repair a stock yard damaged when hit by a stock truck. The job wasn't going as well as they had hoped and was taking a lot longer than they hoped. Fiona rang Karen at work to let her know where Ben was and she should join them for tea. Karen stopped at home on the way to collect some clothes for them as Fiona had suggested they may as well stay the night.

'I'm sorry that this has turned into such a bugger of job; I just didn't expect that pole to fragment like that. You have always been a good neighbour so I really appreciate this but had I known it was going to be this big, I would have hired someone to do it,' Ian apologised.

'I wouldn't worry about it, these things happen. The job takes as long as it takes.'

'Thank you but you have your own place to run.'

'Michael has got it covered for the moment and he understands. In fact, he'll be over tomorrow to give us a hand if we still need it.'

'Hopefully it won't come to that but I really appreciate it.'

'Not a problem, we're neighbours,' Ben replied simply.

Ben was not happy about staying despite the lateness of the hour but

Ian insisted and it gave Fiona and Karen an opportunity to catch up. Karen helped Fiona make tea while they talked.

'It's good to see Dad and Ben working together again. I always hoped that they would get along once we got married,' Karen said.

'You seem to forget that Ben and your father were working together a long time before you two got together and I think that would have continued even if you hadn't got together because Ben is that kind of neighbour. You're right though, it is good to see them together.'

'Yeah, he's always there for others. I just wish he could as generous to himself at times. You know our honeymoon is the only real holiday he's had since he got back from his trip north.'

'Well then, you are going to have to decide that you are going to get away for a couple of weeks each year. It will have to come from you though because I doubt Ben will get around to it if left up to him. Your father is the same way; he didn't think he needed a break until we got that cottage on the coast. The first time we went there he slept away the best part of the first couple of days.'

'That's what I think Ben needs too. I think he needs to just stop at some point and just recharge himself.'

'He probably does, I'll give you the details and I suggest that you do not give him a choice.'

'I don't intend to.'

*

Neil and Ben only quit for the day when Fiona called them in for tea. Removing dirty overalls, they washed up in the old laundry before they entered the house, still talking about the job. Ben greeted Karen with the briefest kiss after greeting Fiona.

After tea, Ben excused himself so he could shower and change as he did not want to sit around their house in the clothes he'd been working in all day. He was under the shower when Karen stepped into the shower with him.

'What are you doing?'

'Having a shower with my husband. What does it look like?'

'Not here.'

'Why not here? Are you expecting someone else?'

'No, no, I'm not. I don't want to do this – not in your mother's house.'

'Why not? We'll be sharing a bed later or don't you want to do that either?'

'No – I mean, yes. Karen, they might know you're in here.'

'Ben, I suspect Mum already knows we take showers together. You're my husband not some not boy I've snuck in from high school.'

'I know but this is still their house. Now please,' Ben pleaded.

'Have it your way,' Karen snapped and left him.

Later, Ben sat in the lounge and picked one of Ian's agricultural machinery books to read, showing no interest in the television, which suited everyone. Fiona noticed a tension between Karen and Ben after they had their showers. Ben had changed into jeans and shirt but Karen had dressed for bed.

Karen went to bed after saying good night and getting the briefest kiss from Ben who was almost asleep in the chair. Fiona waited a few minutes before waking Ben.

'Ben, you can't sleep here. Go to bed – with your wife,' Fiona told him.

Ben reluctantly got up and headed to bed where Karen was awake and waiting for him. He changed and climbed into to bed to find her naked.

'Karen, what are you doing? Where are your pyjamas?'

'Since when have you objected to me being naked in bed with you?'

'Since we're in your mother's house.'

'And again, I think she already knows.'

'They may hear us,' Ben insisted.

'Dad's hearing is not what it was so he won't hear us at the other end of the house.'

'And your mother? Her hearing is fine?'

'And she will think we have a normal, happy, healthy sex life,' Karen assured him.

'Why is having sex in your parents place so important?' Ben questioned.

'This was my old room.'

'I figured that much out; it still doesn't answer my question.'

'This was where I came after you saved me that night.'

'I assumed that too.'

'Didn't you think about what it would be like here with me; after the rescue, I mean?'

'No,' Ben replied immediately.

'Come on – you're a guy. Didn't you think about where I'd be that night? In this room, in my bed?'

'Yes, but not in the way you think. I thought about you being at home here, feeling safe in your own bed and that I helped to get you back here. I never thought beyond that.'

'But why not? Surely you were curious at least?'

'I didn't let me myself be curious. What would you have said if I said I did imagine you lying naked in your bed? It would have grossed you out at the time.'

'Well, that's where you would have been wrong. I thought about you as I was lying in my bed that night. I remember thinking about you and wondering where you were sleeping that night. Where did you sleep that night?'

'Just behind Watkins Dam. It has good shelter there and close to home.'

'Better than home?'

'Much.'

'I dreamed about you that night. Did you dream about me?'

'Not that I can remember.'

'Or will admit to.'

'I really don't remember,' Ben replied.

Karen shifted so she was leaning across his chest. 'I remember my dream about you as though it was last night. It was like I had woken up and you were making love to me. I was shocked at first but then I realised I was enjoying it, really enjoying you,' she teased. 'I dreamed that you came inside me and you weren't wearing a condom. Instead of being shocked, I was okay with it for some reason. That was when I woke up. I was so turned on and so embarrassed. I have never had that dream about anyone else. I must have known something,' she told him.

'And you want me to make love to you right now?'

'No, I want to make love to you,' Karen replied as she began caressing him.

*

Karen showered, dressed for work and headed for the kitchen to have breakfast with Fiona before heading off to work.

'Morning. The boys back on the job already?'

'Yes, about an hour ago. I take it you and Ben got over whatever it was you between you last night?'

'Yes, we made up,' Karen replied.

'I know. I heard you.'

'Did Dad?'

'No, your father was asleep at the other end of the house.'

'Good. We... I didn't do it to impress anyone. Ben and I are working through some things.'

'I am concerned about the tension between you two, not your love making afterwards.'

'We're okay, Mum, really. Ben still has a lot of issues but we are working through it.'

'I can see that, but just be careful that you don't push him too far; he may back away.'

'I can see that now. I made some assumptions about him that I had no right to make.'

'I'm glad you understand. Ben may be your husband but he still has his troubles from the past. Marrying you has helped but it has not made them right. It may take him a life time to get over them. Don't keep pushing, not so hard, at least,' Fiona told him.

'Thanks, Mum.'

# CHAPTER TWENTY-SEVEN

*Babies*

Melanie and Michael had a son eighteen months after they were married. For Melanie, it was dream come true as she nursed her son. Ben and Karen went to see them at the hospital. Michael was ten-foot tall and a prouder dad could not be found.

Karen held their son in her arms and smiled at Melanie.

'So, what do you think?'

'He is beautiful, Melanie. Congratulations.'

'Thank you. Do you think Ben would like a nurse?' Melanie questioned.

'I don't know. Ask him?'

Karen handed Travis to Ben who held him without fuss.

'Hello, little man. I'm your uncle Ben. Your parents come to our house because they are our friends and so will you. We have a sand pit you are going to love,' Ben told him as if he was already a little boy.

'Ben is good with him,' Melanie said.

'He is, isn't he?' Karen replied looking at Ben and feeling strangely jealous then shook off the feeling. 'You must bring him around to the house.'

'Are you sure?' Melanie questioned.

'Of course, we would love have the three of you around for tea. I would love to watch him grow.'

'Thanks, Karen. I will let you know once we have him settled.'

'Of course,' Karen replied.

They took their little family home, where they had many visitors offering their support. Melanie seemed to thrive as a mum, returning to her parent's bakery a few months after Travis was born. Her mother was delighted to be able to look after her grandson while Melanie worked and Michael was a regular visitor, finding his in-laws to be really good people whose company he enjoyed. Their first family Christmas was a great occasion for all concerned and while Travis was too young to know what was going on, it was still a great time as they watched him light up when a new play thing was put in his cot.

Travis proved to be a happy baby who embraced everything and seemed to love it most when with Michael who often walked and played with him after work. Karen often dropped in on the way home to catch up Melanie and Travis and was delighted as Travis began to recognise her and give her a smile.

*

Tracy was one of the visitors to their place over the next few years. She arrived with her baby and Karen was a little worried but Ben picked up Tracy's little girl and walked the garden with her when he was unsettled. Karen was amazed at how Ben was with her.

'I don't think you will have any trouble when your own time comes,' Tracy told him.

'I think you're right.'

'Are you planning to have children any time soon?'

'Yes; we've talked about it but we both have a lot on at the moment. I really need to get things tied up with the agency yet.'

'Things are going well at the moment?'

'Yes, they are. The company is expanding and I am able to recruit the right sorts of people at the moment. I've got some good people on our books so we are meeting our client's requirements for the moment. I want to be in the position where I can work from home and have someone run the office on a daily basis before we start a family.'

'Sounds like you have it all worked out.'

'I really wish that were true. It's a plan and we all know about the plans of mice and men.' Karen shrugged.

Several weeks later, Tracy was back on another visit when Ben was away delivering and training horses in Queensland.

'Are you okay? You seem a little distracted.'

'I'm fairly sure. I have some news.'

'Yeah, what sort of news?' Tracy asked.

'This time next year, Stacy may have a little playmate.'

'Really? You're pregnant?' Tracy questioned.

'I think so. I'm very late and I feel terrible every morning.'

'Does Ben know?'

'No. Not until I'm sure. I've got a doctor's appointment at the clinic this morning I should know in a couple of hours. You will be the first to know, apart from the doctor, of course.'

*

'Good news?' Tracy asked when Karen walked into the kitchen a few hours later.

'I think so, yes.'

'Call him.'

'I can't. I have to be there to see the look on his face when he finds out he's going to become a dad. Can you believe it? Ben is going to be a dad and it is me who is going to give him a child,' Karen said through a teary smile.

'Yes, you are. You are going to be a mum.'

'Yes, I am. Can you believe it?'

'I can actually. You are going to be a great mum.'

'Thanks.'

*

She went to see her mother, needing to share the news with her. Walking into the house, she took one look at her mother and burst into tears. Fiona sat her down and Karen told her the news.

'I take it the timing is not great?'

'It could be better; it's not like we were really trying or anything. I so much want this baby but I'm not sure we are ready.'

'You'll be fine, both of you will. Have you told Ben yet?'

'No, I want to be with him when I tell him.'

Stephen Brown

'Good idea. It is not something to be shared over the phone.'

'This makes you a grandmother. It doesn't make you feel old, does it?'

'I thought I would be a grandmother a few times over by this stage but your brother hasn't found anyone and your sister is showing no interest at all in having children. I had two school-aged children and you were about to go to kinder when I was your age.'

'I think I'm young to be having a baby but I forget you had your family so advanced by the same age.'

'We had different expectations back then. I had the family I wanted and most people my age had their families at the same age. I'm really looking forward to being a grandma and being just over the hill from you. You remember I am always here, especially when things aren't perfect and bub is screaming and you're exhausted. My mum did it for me I will be there for you.'

'I still miss her,' Karen told her.

'We both do.'

*

Karen chose a room and began renovating it; it would be for their first child.

Ben arrived home to the smell of fresh paint and a room clearly renovated.

'Are we doing the room up for anyone in particular?'

'Yes, our baby.'

'You're jumping the gun a bit, aren't you? We're not expecting one for another year or two, are we?'

'No. It's about six and half months, actually,' Karen replied, waiting for Ben to do the math and watching his eyes widen.

'Do you mean?' he questioned.

'Yes, Ben, I'm pregnant. We're going to have a baby,' Karen replied, holding his gaze.

'Really?'

'Yes.'

'Wow,' Ben replied, trying to take it in. 'I thought we were still talking about it.'

'We did a little more than talk, if I remember correctly,' Karen said, unsure where the conversation was going.

'Yes, we did,' Ben agreed.

188

'Yes, and you're going to be around to help, aren't you?' Karen asked but was not sure why.

'Hey, yes, of course. You have and are giving me things that I thought I would never have and had no right to. My world turned upside down the day you kissed me on my front verandah and told me you wanted to go out with me. To that point, I thought I knew what direction my life and yours were going and suddenly they had collided and my life has never been the same since. Now you are carrying our baby, our child. You have given me so much. You are amazing,' Ben replied, wrapping his arms around her.

'Thank you,' Karen replied, crying in his arms.

Melanie was around as soon as she heard the news.

'Congratulations, Karen. You must be so pleased,' Melanie said as she joined her in the kitchen.

'I am finally. I didn't realise how much I wanted children until Travis was born. Having him around has made me realise that I want children of my own.'

'Karen, I may not be the most experienced mother in the world but if you ever want a break or just someone to talk to, day or night, please don't hesitate to call me.'

'I appreciate that, Melanie. You are so good with Travis. I would like our kids to grow up together.'

'Thank you – that is a great compliment because I would really like that too,' Melanie said and the two women embraced. 'Now, tell me, how is the nursery going?' Melanie asked.

'Come on, I'll show you,' Karen told her as she led her to the room she had been renovating. Karen enjoyed sharing the joy of her pregnancy with another woman and young mother. Melanie was blossoming as a mother and as a woman and Karen loved her for it, their friendship growing with each passing day. She admired Melanie and that admiration and respect was reciprocated.

*

Gayle arrived in town a couple of weeks later.

'Don't you look all glowing and pregnant? Why is that? You are so good at everything, even when you're pregnant you look great.'

'Thank you, I think.'

'No, really, you look great. Is Ben excited?'

'It's bit of mix between excitement and fear I think.'

'I think that's about normal for most expectant parents. He'll be fine; he adores you and he'll adore your kids.'

'Thanks. How are things in Sydney?'

'Good.'

'Just good?'

'It's going really well; I'm in charge of Client Services.'

'You're the Director of Client Services?' Karen questioned.

'Yes,' Gayle replied, looking a little embarrassed.

'Since when?'

'A couple of months.'

'So, you're traveling to all the offices?'

'Yes, I've spent some time in Brisbane and Melbourne, of course, and setting up the new one in Darwin. I'm off to Perth for a week on Sunday.'

'Good for you, I am happy for you; you've worked hard, you deserve it.'

'I'm not entirely sure I have. I have been in the right place at the right time. I go in, set the processes and the quality measures and then get the consultants to send me the details. I then follow up with all the clients.'

'You seem to have it all sorted.'

'Not really. It's bit of a no brainer.'

'What's going on? What aren't you telling me? I thought you would be jumping through hoops. This is what you've been working for. What else is going on in your life?'

'Not a lot. I've got a nice unit on the north shore, compliments of the company. It has a great view of the ocean and close to the shops.'

'You're not sharing with anyone?'

'It's a bit impractical, really. I work all kinds of hours and I'm away at least a couple of days a fortnight.'

'Not much of social life then?'

'I'm involved in a businesswomen's network, which keeps me busy with speaking engagements and mentoring other young businesswomen. A group of us meet regularly in the city for drinks and a meal.'

'You sound surprisingly self-contained. No lover at the moment, I take it?'

'Not at the moment,' Gayle replied, sounding a little deflated.

'Is it that important to you?'

'I wasn't meant to be single; I realise that now but most of the good ones are taken,' Gayle reflected.

'There will be someone out there for you, Gayle. Maybe you are looking in the wrong places?'

'That could be part of it.'

\*

As Karen's pregnancy advanced, Ben was more apprehensive with each passing day. He appeared to avoid his mother-in-law until she met him out by the river, working the horses.

'Hello, Ben. How are you going? We haven't seen a lot of you lately.'

'No, I've been busy.'

'I know you are and I know you're also scared. Ben, we are proud of you and what you have achieved. You and Karen have something special and we want to part of that. We are looking forward to being grandparents and we want to share that with you. I have no doubt that you will be good parents so don't you believe anything else. Let us be part of your life again.'

'I'm sorry; I have been afraid of what you would think of me. I don't have good experiences with family. I'm not sure how I am going to be as a parent.'

'Tell me something thing, Ben. Do you love Karen?' Fiona questioned.

'You know I do,' Ben replied, sounding hurt.

'Then you will love your children every bit as much; they will know they are loved and you will work it out from there. Ben, I know that you can do this. I have no doubt whatsoever. You need to believe in you as much as we do,' Fiona told him.

'Thank you,' Ben replied after thinking about it for a moment.

Their baby, Abby, appeared in a hurry, arriving a week early while Ben was away. Fiona rang Ben to tell him that Karen was in labour but to also to ensure that he returned home safely and not take risks returning home. Ben quickly finalised his business and began the long drive home, stopping for fuel and a few hours' sleep along the way. It was tough going with truck and trailer and it was hard not to panic but a call to Fiona assured him that everything was going well and that he needed to be safe above everything so that he could make it home to meet his new baby. With that, Ben pulled into a roadside stop and slept for a couple of hours before continuing.

He arrived at the hospital late the following day after driving most of the night. He was met by Fiona and Ian in reception.

'How is Karen? Is everything okay?' he asked desperately.

'They're fine. Karen is resting but you go in. She'll want to see you,' Fiona assured him.

Ben quickly turned to a nurse who escorted him to room where Karen was recovering. He stepped quickly to her side as she opened her eyes to him. He immediately sat in the chair beside the bed and took her hand.

'Are you okay? I should never have left you,' he pleaded.

'I'm fine; we both are. Someone was in a bit of hurry to join us, that's all,' Karen assured him and then lifted a little bundle at her side. 'There is someone I would like you to meet,' she said, holding the little bundle and tucking the top of the blanket aside. 'Ben, I would like you to meet Abby Templeton. Abby, this is your daddy,' Karen said, holding her daughter so that she could see him.

Ben's eye's widened. 'Oh, she's beautiful. Can I hold her?'

'Of course, you can; she's your daughter,' Karen replied, passing Abby to him who took her in his arms and sat back in the chair beside the bed, tears rolling down his cheeks.

'She is so beautiful. You are beautiful. I love you so much,' he said through his tears.

'You once said that no one would love you. Now I know two people who love you: me and Abby.'

There was a gentle tap on the door and Fiona stuck her head around. 'Can we come in?' she asked.

Karen waved them in.

Ben looked at them. 'You have a granddaughter,' he told them.

Fiona wrapped her arms around them both. 'Yes, we do and she is beautiful; much like her mother, I think.' Fiona smiled.

The nurse was there to teach and assist Ben to feed and change her.

'How is he doing?' Karen asked the nurse later after Ben left to pick up some things from home.

'He's a natural. He's nervous like most new dads but he'll be fine – you both will. He loves you both very much; it's the reason I do this job.' The nurse smiled.

'Thank you,' Karen replied.

'You are most welcome.'

*

Taking Abby home was the beginning of a new phase of their lives. Ben was very attentive to his girls, as he called them, ensuring that Karen had as much time to recover as possible, making breakfast for her and feeding and changing Abby before heading to work for a few hours.

Melanie, Michael and Travis were among the first visitors to see Abby at home. Naturally, Melanie was delighted and hugged Karen.

'She is beautiful, Karen. Congratulations,' Melanie told her.

'Thank you, we think so,' Karen replied.

Michael was really happy for Ben, knowing how much she wanted a family. The two shook hands. 'Well done, mate. A daughter.' He smiled.

'Yes, I can hardly believe it.'

'Believe it, man. She is right there,' Michael said as he placed a reassuring hand on his shoulder.

*

Abby was a very happy and alert baby. She very quickly knew who Mum and Dad were and seemed to shine for Ben whenever he spoke to her. At the end of each day, Ben spent time with Abby, not just feeding and assisting with her bath but walking with her in the garden and introducing her to the horses and other animals. Abby seemed to love it and Karen often joined them on their walks, watching Abby respond to everything, noticing she seemed to take a delight in the horses and loving it when Ben walked with her on the horses. They would walk by the river and she loved to sit in the shallow water and splash about, giggling with delight. It was times like that that would sit and look at her in awe.

'She is a pretty little thing, isn't she?' Karen said.

'Just like her mother,' Ben replied and kissed her cheek and looked back at Abby. 'As long as I live, I will never get sick of her giggle.'

'She won't giggle like that forever,' Karen told him.

'But I will remember it forever,' Ben replied.

'We both will,' Karen replied.

Abby was very aware of Ben and loved to see him each day. She always had a smile for Ben and when she began to crawl, she would up to Ben with a big smile at how clever she was and Ben loved it.

Jesse was getting old and tired and did not go out with Ben too often but remained about the house. She took one look at Abby and seemed to know who she was and took on a role of protecting the house yard.

When Abby played on her blanket, Jesse would sit on the edge and watch, not Abby but everyone and everything that passed. The working dogs were kept well at bay and strays were not tolerated. When Abby began to crawl, Jesse let her crawl all over her and when Jesse had enough, she would simply move away and if Abby pursued her, Jesse would either join in or climb out of the way.

Ben took Abby into town in her pram one morning to give Karen a sleep in. He bought a paper and went to the bakery for a coffee. Abby was awake and loved watching people go by as long as she could see Ben as well. The people at the bakery were always happy to see Ben because of their association with Michael. They were delighted to see Abby and welcomed Ben with open arms. Melanie brought Travis out to see her.

Ben was sitting at table when two of the town's older women came to admire Abby. Both women were known to Ben and had in the past been outspoken critics of Ben and his family before he married Karen but Ben was happy enough for them to admire Abby who delighted in them as she did with most people.

'Ben, you have a beautiful little girl.'

'Thank you.'

'She is a lucky little girl, this one, because she will always know who her daddy is and will grow up knowing she has a dad her loves her,' one of the women told him.

'Thank you. I appreciate that.'

'You are most welcome, dear,' they told him. Ben had noticed a change in people after Abby was born, most being more receptive somehow.

✳

Karen's parents were great, often dropping in and more than happy to have Abby when both were busy. Fiona often made meals for them, which she dropped over to them, staying to bathe Abby and get her ready for bed. Fiona could not have been happier because Abby was always happy to go to grandma and loved being walked around the garden once she had taken her first steps. Fiona had been with Karen when Abby took her first steps at eleven months.

Travis and Abby took to each other straight away, being just a few months apart the two of them delighted in each other. Travel would walk and crawl about her and Abby delighted in crawling after him.

The first time Ben saw her walk, which was later that day, Abby had a smile of delight as she took the handful of steps from the edge of the couch to the door way to meet him.

'Aren't you the cleverest girl?' Ben said as she picked her up and she squealed with delight.

'How long has she been walking?' he asked.

'Just this afternoon and she thinks she's pretty clever too.'

'And she is, aren't you, baby?' Ben replied as he bounced her in his arms and laughed with delight. 'I never thought that having a child could be like this.'

'It's moments like this you remember forever, no matter how old they get,' Karen told him.

*

Just before Abby's first birthday, they were sitting in the garden one evening just before they got Abby ready for bed.

'What do you think of having another child; a brother or sister for Abby?'

'Now, you mean?'

'Yes. Let's make another baby.'

'That's not an offer I have had before.' Ben smiled.

'Do you want to? I don't want Abby to be an only child.'

'Yes, I'd love to have another baby with you.'

'We'd better start practicing tonight.'

*

Karen found out she was pregnant a few weeks later in time for Abby's first birthday. She was delighted. Ben was concerned for her but she had a good pregnancy and was looking forward to the birth of their second child. Every time Ben looked at her, she appeared to be glowing, which he could only admire as she seemed so happy.

'You're really looking forward to having another baby in the house, aren't you?' he said as he looked at her across the table one tea time.

'Of course, I'm having the family I was looking forward to having with you. You don't know what it means to me to be doing this.'

'I wish I knew why.'

'Because you are the best thing to happen to me; having a family with you is just one way of showing you just how much I love you,' Karen told him.

'I love you too; more now than when I married you,' Ben replied looking at her.

Lisa arrived precisely on time a smaller baby than Abby but no less healthy. For Ben, the birth was in shock as he realised what Karen had to go through to give birth to the girls. Having missed Abby's birth, it was hard to be at Karen's' side during the birth. When they he held Lisa in his arms Karen assured him that she was okay and he could only admire her all the more.

Holding little Lisa in his arms, Ben saw a smaller version of Karen with her fine features and jet-black hair and his heart glowed her.

'This is just how I imagined you would have looked when you were born.'

Abby was brought in to admire her little sister by her grandparents who were delighted to have another granddaughter. She was delighted to have a little sister.

Less inquisitive than Abby, she clung to Karen and Ben but more so to Karen, needing constant reassurance and so much less sure of herself than the very independent Abby. Wary of strangers, she was easily upset if she could not see Karen or Ben and did not like being picked up by anyone else apart from her grandparents although she did display a preference for her grandmother.

Abby would bounce about any time Ben arrived home and was happy to give him a kiss and say goodbye when he went away. Lisa would always standoff and wait for Ben to leave and follow him. She could barely walk when she would make her way down the back steps to the back gate where she would stand by the gate and look up between the palings to see Ben. Inevitably, he would stop, get out of the truck, lean over the gate, pick her up and give her a cuddle then put her down. She would then stand up and wave to him.

When Ben returned, Abby would run to him, yelling 'Daddy, Daddy!' as she ran outside to meet him. Lisa would look up and then stand by the door; she would point to the door and say, 'Dad.' Abby would bounce around him and tell him about everything in her life. Lisa would wait her turn for Ben to finish with Abby then she would pat him on the side of the leg and look up him with big expectant eyes. Ben would pick her up and say hello to her. Lisa would look at him, always a little unsure about him.

One time, when Ben returned from a week away, he picked Lisa and walked with her. She returned with a fluffy dog. When Karen asked her about it, Lisa held it up to her. 'Dad give it me,' she said and from then on it was always with her, well into her teens even though she had forgotten then why it was one of favourite things.

Ben knew she was different to Abby and when he spent time with her, it was doing things she liked. He would walk in the garden with her or sit down by the river and watch her explore the wild flowers. When she showed fear instead of interest in horses, he did not push her but looked for other interest to engage her.

Jesse was a good guardian for the girls but especially for Lisa, who would hide behind him whenever she was afraid. Many a time they found Lisa asleep on blanket beside Jesse who was ever alert and watching over her while she slept.

People often saw her with the dog and asked her if she loved the dog.

'Dad give it me,' was how she always answered. All that mattered was that Ben had given it to her. Someone said they always knew when Ben was away because she would carry the dog around with her. When Ben was home, she put the dog away till he left again.

Once, when Ben had been away for almost a fortnight, Karen was with Lisa in the kitchen when she sat.

'Will Daddy remember me when he gets home?' she asked with sad eyes.

'Of course he will, sweetie. Why would you think he wouldn't?' Karen asked.

'Dad gone a long time. Dad is coming home?'

'Yes, he is. Lisa, your dad loves you very much; you are his special little girl.'

'Abby is Dad's special girl, I'm just Lisa.'

'Both of you are special to your dad; do you hear me? Your dad loves you and he misses you every day that he is away. He spoke to you last night, remember? Didn't he tell you he loved you?'

'Yes,' Lisa replied with her head bowed then looked up at Karen. 'Dad is coming back, isn't he?'

'Yes, Lisa, he is,' Karen replied missing him, all the more. She called him later that day.

'Lisa is really missing you,' Karen told Ben.

'I thought she might. I'll spend some time with her when I get home,' Ben replied.

'When will you be home?'

'For tea tomorrow,' he replied.

'Good because I miss you too.' Karen sniffed.

'Don't worry, I'll be home. I miss all of you. You know how much I hate to leave you.'

'Yes, and I know why but it is never easy.'

'I know that is why I will be home as soon as I can.'

'Drive safe then.'

'I will,' Ben replied.

# Chapter Twenty-Eight

## *Changes for Gayle*

Gayle called in for a couple of days for a short break and clearly had something on her mind. They sat on the verandah watching the girls and began to talk.

'You seem distracted; what's on your mind?' Karen asked after they sat down for coffee.

'I do have a lot on my mind at the moment. I feel I am at some sort of crossroad.'

'In what way? Has work thrown another challenge at you?'

'No, I have about three years to run on my current contract so things are relatively stable at the moment.'

'Don't tell me; are you seeing someone and it's serious?'

'Sort of.'

'How can you be sort of serious?'

'I have lunch with this guy and his little girl from time to time and we go to the park and we've been to the zoo, that sort of thing. We're friends, I guess you could say.'

'That doesn't sound like you at all.'

'It's not or at least, I didn't think it was.'

'So how did this arrangement come about?'

'I met this little girl at a café opposite this bookshop I drop in on from time to time. She came up to me, as bold as you like, when I had stopped for coffee between meetings. Every time I stopped there, she would come over and talk to me. She is the cutest thing and used to tell me about her daddy. I asked her where her mummy was and she told me her mum had gone to heaven. Her father was most embarrassed to be introduced as her friend and naturally, I told him it was okay and he bought me a coffee and we talked.'

'So where is this friendship going, do you think?'

'I have no idea. Todd's little girl, Leah, is the centre of his world, so there are other things to consider this time around, I guess.'

'And you like both of them, I assume?'

'Of course, she is just the greatest kid, with an old head on young shoulders. He is like no one I have ever met. All the single guys I know are single for a reason; great in the sack but not as good as they think they are,' Gayle replied, looking at Karen. 'You don't judge me for that?'

'Gayle, it's not my lifestyle or my life I'm not you but then I have Ben and perhaps he's all I wanted. You have your own life and your own way of doing things that's what makes you, you, I guess.'

'Thank you, you are one of the few people I feel I can be honest with.'

'Todd sounds so different to anyone I've heard you talk about, so what is the attraction?'

'Well, it's not bed because we haven't been there yet and he hasn't asked.'

'That's not what I was implying, I just sense there is a change in you or what you want from life and perhaps career even,' Karen questioned.

'You may be right. I have always wanted to make it into the boys' club and now that I have, that's what it is: a boys' club. Most of the successful women have families and all that stuff. I don't need to tell you that I need people around me and the novelty of sleeping in an empty bed is not that great anymore and I don't just mean for sex. How does the saying go – be careful what you wish for you might just get it?' Gayle said and Karen laughed.

'What?' Gayle snapped, thinking Karen was laughing at her.

'I'm sorry, it's just that once I wished Ben would find someone to love and now look at me, I'm married to him and we have two kids together.' Karen smiled.

'Yes, and look at you, you're glowing and you have a sparkle in your eyes and the way Ben looks at you. I want someone to look at me like that too,' Gayle said, squeezing Karen's hand. Karen could only smile in return, unsure of how to respond for a moment.

'You don't think I've thrown my life away then?'

'I did once but you have your own company, which is growing; you have a lot of experience and you have a guy to share your life with. I was wrong about both of you.'

'Thank you; so why the questioning for you? Is it Todd?'

'No, I thought it was but I've looked at the people around me and my own business and career relationships and few of them are single and of those that are, some are bitter and just as uncompromising if not as ruthless as any of the guys out there. They are single for the same reason some of the guys are. There are some bastards in this world but there are also some bitches as well. They are men in skirts, some of them.

'There is one woman, Colleen, who is single and not like that but she is so self-contained with her career and her business lunches. She had this amazing apartment with this completely private pool in a tiny courtyard. I asked her one day what she did for sex and she said she has never had a great sex drive and doesn't feel the need for it or the complications of relationships that come with it. Some of the other women are not so single but have girlfriends on the side, some are bisexual; a few are willing to admit they are gay but most admit nothing to anyone. I tried that for a while too.'

'You slept with a woman?'

'Yeah, a few times; it was okay but I need a man so you don't have to worry.'

'I'm not worried; it's just that I didn't think you were quite that open.'

'Neither did I but I've tried to make sense of the world I've found myself in. You know, the happiest ones – both male and female – are those who go home to families. I met this amazing woman, Trish, who is just a business genius. We met at this conference a couple of years ago when I first moved to Sydney and we clicked straight away and we've been friends ever since. I met her family in the city one day and spent the weekend with them. She has a teenage daughter she is close to and her husband is great; he's a lawyer specialising in commercial law. Part of me wants that too, I guess.'

'So, what does Todd do?'

'He owns a bookshop. One of the best I've ever come across.'

'Since when were you into books?'

'Since my uni days; it's one of those things you get into when best friends drift apart,' Gayle replied with a wry smile Karen knew she was referring to the two of them.

'I'm sorry,' Karen apologised.

'Don't be. We had to go our own directions or we wouldn't be where we are now. You wouldn't be with Ben had you stayed with me and I wouldn't have met Todd had I stayed with you.'

'Todd's not just a friend with a little girl in town, is he?'

'No. He has one of the best business minds I know. His clients are a lot of the people I know. He provides them with all the latest books and information they want as well as servicing a lot of the academics and students but still has time for the old ladies who are avid readers. It is his shop and his staff are as passionate as he is.'

'And with Leah?'

'He is Leah's dad; he goes to her kinder things with her and finds time to sit with us over a coffee and glass of milk and talk.'

'You're in love with him?'

'I'm trying not to be.'

'Why?'

'Look at me, I've been around and I've slept around. The only woman he's slept with is Leah's mum.'

'He told you that?'

'No.'

'Then how do you know?'

'Because he is a one-woman man; in that, he is so much like Ben.'

'Don't you think you could be faithful to him?'

'Of course, I could.'

'Then what's the problem? Do you think he doesn't feel the same way about you?'

'He does, actually. He wants to marry me and get me pregnant.'

'He's asked you?'

'Yes.'

'I hope he asked you with a better line than I want to get you pregnant?'

'Yes, he did, he was wonderful; he is wonderful.'

'Then what is your problem?'

'I'm afraid that I'm buying into some dream that I will wake up from one day to find that it's over. I'm afraid of being pregnant and bringing a child into this world. What am I going to do with a baby? I'm not exactly the motherly kind. Look at you; you look like you were born to be a mum.'

'It's very different when they are your own. You'll be fine the moment you hold that tiny bundle in your arms and see what you and Todd have produced, you'll be fine. There is nothing in the world like it. You could bring them here and watch them experience life in the country.'

'I would love to do that, I really would. Do you think Ben would mind?'

'Not at all, Ben loves to have people stay and is willing to show people around. In his own way, Ben has been concerned for you too, hoping that you would find someone that you could really be happy with one day.'

'Why would he think that I really need someone?'

'For someone who is so desperate to remain single, you having been chasing a lot of relationships over the years and you haven't exactly been celebrant in that time.'

'No, I haven't; I've just never met the right person.'

'Until now?'

'Yes, until now,' Gayle replied.

'You're going to marry him then?'

'Yes; yes I am.'

'Congratulations, Gayle. I am really happy for you,' Karen said, embracing her.

'Don't congratulate me. Todd may have changed his mind by the time I get back.'

'I don't think so. I'm sure you will be very happy and a great mum.'

'I could always rely on you to lift me up,' Gayle replied.

# CHAPTER TWENTY-NINE

*Reunion*

When word got around about the reunion, Karen was among the first to get on board and assist with the organisation. She knew right off that Ben did not want to know about it so Karen kept the details from him and then encouraged him to look after the girls on the day, which he agreed to do without hesitation.

'Today went well,' Karen said to after they got home and put the girls to bed.

'It was better than I thought.'

'You felt accepted today,' Karen suggested.

'I did actually. It's hard to believe.'

'Not really. They just saw the person I saw many years ago. They saw the man I married and the father of my children for which I am very grateful.'

'Yes, but you were always a bit one-sided towards me.'

'Yes once I got to know you and today they got to know you a little better. You are a really good person and they saw that today.'

After the success of the first day, everyone got together at Karen and Ben's property for day two of the reunion in the town. For most, it was the first time they had seen the house in years and for almost everyone, it was the first time they had ever been on the property itself. It was strange, arriving for a picnic and barbeque at what for a long time was known as the haunted house. The house had lost most of the big trees around it, removing the shadows that made it such a sad-looking place. The fences had been repaired and the driveway and paths cleared. Flowers lined the front garden and a swing adorned the verandah along with a number of potted plants.

Down the side lane to the back of the house, they followed the picket fence to the garden at the rear where a marquee had been set up under the shade of a tall tree. A swing set stood in one corner of the garden and a sand pit filled another corner beside the back verandah. Karen greeted everyone like they all expected Karen would but the sight of Ben walking around with Lisa in his arms took some getting used to. Abby was delighted to have so many people visiting at the one time, making friends with all the kids that had arrived with their parents.

'Who would have ever thought we would have ended up here for our reunion?' Petra questioned.

'Yes, can you believe this place? You and Ben have done a great deal with the place, it looks great.'

'Thank you, it's taken some work but we are getting there,' Karen replied as she directed the women to seats in the backyard beneath a gazebo.

'I guess you never thought you'd be living here either?' Liz questioned with a smile.

'I actually thought about buying the place at one point when I thought Ben had left for good.'

'He did leave for a while then?'

'Yes, he actually walked to Queensland with his horses after we finished school.'

'Do you mean the day he left after our last exam; it must have taken him years?'

'Yes, almost two actually,' Karen replied.

'And he went on his own?'

'Yes, he did. He basically lived off the land for two years as he made his way to Queensland and back,' Karen replied.

'So how did you two go from that to this?' Kay asked.

'By keeping in touch and breaking down the barriers one by one.'

'Did you ever discuss buying or building another place?' Petra questioned.

'We did but the reality is the house works for us and it's better to put the money into the business rather than another house. We have plans to build guest accommodation on the rise at the end of the block.'

'Do you think there is going to be a call for that sort of thing around here?' Diana questioned.

'Ben already gets more people staying than the town has accommodation for so we have to do something. We have spoken to some of the other accommodation houses in town who have plans but nothing that really supports our business. Our only real option for growth is to build the accommodation on site.'

'So, what are you looking at?'

'We have plans approved for three self-contained units at the top of the street. We are having plans drawn up for some mountains hut style accommodation on property we own at the foot of the mountains proper but that is a few years away yet.'

'So, they just stay here as B&B accommodation?'

'We are not really positioned on the main road for that. Those using the accommodation are here for taking the trail rides for the moment. The mountain-style huts will be used as accommodation in their own right but we will also being conducted four-wheel drive tours and some high-season cross-country skiing and adventure hiking.'

'Wow. Ben has proved to be the quiet businessman; I just never thought he'd end up as a full-time tour guide,' Diana said.

'Oh no; the horses are still his main source of work and income.'

'Really?'

'Yes, he still breeds, breaks and sells horses, which are his main business. The tours and accommodation is a profitable sideline.'

'Well, I can only admire both of you.'

'Thank you. We work with what we have.'

'You certainly do and have a really great job doing it.'

Rodney arrived and Ben greeted him warmly, the two men shaking hands.

'I never thought I'd see those two together,' Marie said.

'Neither did I but we all grow up and we all move on.'

'But how did they get together? They were never friends at school.'

'We all change and grow up a little and they have grown to respect each other. Rodney is a cattle buyer and the two of them have met on many occasions at various sales. Ben invited Rodney to drop in one day and it went from there and now he drops in whenever he was on his way through. They have since ridden the mountains together looking at cattle and a friendship has developed out of that.'

'What do you think of Rodney?'

'Yeah, he's okay. He's Ben's friend more than he is our friend, if you know what I mean, but he is always polite and respectful to me and we talk when he comes for dinner but not a lot more. If Ben is not home, he is always quick to keep moving after saying hello.'

'Is he married?'

'He was but his wife left him for another man. I think that had a pretty big impact on him because he has never been the same since. She remarried a couple of years ago but he has been living alone since.'

'Is he seeing anyone now?'

'In recent times he has begun to talk about a woman he has met on a number of occasions at the sales. She owns a cattle property on the New South Wales side. She is nothing like his first wife and certainly is not rushing into anything. I actually hope he makes it this time because he is a nice guy and deserves better than what he's got to this point.'

'Ben is a very different person these days. How did you get close enough to him to have children with him? He was just so distant at school I didn't think anyone would.'

'There are reasons for that. Ben had it tougher than most will ever know. His father used to be away a lot so he basically lived alone in this place most of his secondary school years and he did not find his sister until very recent times.'

'That certainly explains a lot. There was always something about him as if he was hiding some big secret.'

'It's not a secret he wanted to share with anyone at the time.'

'You love him, don't you?' Marie questioned as they watched Ben and Lisa with the horses.

'Yes, I do. He's great with the girls.'

'It's more that though, isn't it? I can see he's good with the girls but he really got to you at some point, didn't he?'

'Yes, that's why I married him.'

'No regrets?'

'Only that I didn't marry him earlier.'

'It's that good, being married to Ben?'

'Yes, it is. He is my best friend in the world. I know it is hard to believe but there really isn't anyone like him. We are the centre of his world, that is something that I have wanted from the person I married and I have that with Ben.'

'He seems to be good with the girls.'

'Yes, he is. Abby idolises him and can't wait to see him after he's been away. She launches herself into his arms and tells him everything she's done that day. Ben is so patient with her and can pull her into line when she goes over the top.'

'Lisa is a sweet thing but she doesn't look like she will be like Abby.'

'No, Lisa is a clingy child who needs to know one of us is around. She is apparently a lot like Ben's mother, who was tall and thin. Lisa loves Ben and her eyes light up whenever she sees him.'

'I noticed that yesterday when he went to pick her up, her eyes lit up and held her arms out to him.'

'Oh, yes, that is Lisa she will go to very few people but she knows who daddy is.' Karen smiled.

'I'm really happy for you, Karen. Ben has surprised everyone.'

Ben joined them for the barbeque, proving as always to be an excellent cook.

Helen gave him a hand. He still looked to Karen for reassurance but continued to engage people, answering their questions as he went.

A little later, as Ben walked around with Lisa asleep in his arms, it was clear that girls knew their dad and delighted in him. He was the most natural dad. The other women loved watching him because it was once so hard to see the softer side of him. They also noticed how Karen looked at him as he walked in the garden with Lisa and realised, they were a special couple which was nice given some of the disasters in their own group, a number having endured failed marriages.

'You really do have something special with Ben. I'm really happy for you and probably more so for Ben. You two are so good together Are you thinking about having any more children?'

'We've talked about it and haven't ruled it out just yet. I know Ben is happy with the two we've got but we still have time to figure it out.'

Ben sat with and fed Lisa with Karen and Abby while they all had lunch and talked with some people. The common link was their children watching them grow and he was happy to talk to them about the house and the girls.

Petra especially liked what she saw and made a point of telling how good he was with the girls.

'Thank you. These are my girls. I love all of them,' Ben replied.

'We can all see that but the great thing is your girls can see that too. I think they are very fortunate to have you for their father,' Petra told him. Ben blushed and thanked her softly.

'Ben is not good at accepting praise, is he?' Petra questioned Karen later on.

'No, he's had a lot of negative people over the years so he finds it very difficult to accept praise.'

'That makes sense.'

Everyone was reluctant to leave and thanked Karen and Ben for a great day. Ben walked with them with Lisa asleep in his arms and a tired Abby following Karen who took her hand as they walked to the gate.

Petra was among the last to leave.

'Thank you both for the last couple of days. It has been great,' she told them.

'It's been our pleasure,' Karen replied.

'Ben, you are a natural. I'm really happy for you.'

'Thanks, Petra.'

'I would love to make a return visit if that's okay with you,' she told them.

'Any time. Just let us know you are coming and we'll make sure there is room for you,' Karen replied.

'I would love to bring my children next time.'

'By all means you can, we'll make one of the cabins available.'

'Thank you. I will be in touch.'

Some kept in contact after that, writing and calling from time to time. For Karen, who had known most of them quite well when they were at school together, it was easy to renew old acquaintances but Ben had known few of them even to say hello to so he had some difficulty relating to some of them. Petra did return with her own children who delighted in the animals as Ben showed them around and they gave him a hand to feed some of them.

'Ben is just so good with the kids; I am truly amazed,' Petra told her. 'He has taken to my two as if they were his own.'

'It's surprised me too. I suspect that he would have been a very different person had his family remained intact,' Karen told her.

'Yes, I think he would have been quite a catch,' Petra added.

'Oh, believe me, he still is.'

'And look at you, still so in love and from what I see, so is he.' Petra smiled.

'How long have you been separated?' Karen questioned when she noticed the tan lines for her wedding band.

'A little over two years and now Ken wants a divorce. I signed the papers a couple of weeks ago so I will be a single woman again soon.'

'I'm so sorry, Petra. I didn't mean to pry,' Karen told her.

'Actually, it's good to be able to talk about it to someone without it turning into a judgment session.'

'Can I ask what happened?'

'Sure, we just drifted apart, I guess. We really tried to make it work but Ken kept taking jobs in the west and I've never wanted to live there. I took the kids over there for a holiday and we tried living together again but we just clashed over everything. By the time the holiday was up, I knew I was coming back alone just as Ken knew he was staying there without us.'

'How are the kids taking it?'

'Better than I am for the most part. Ken has been away so much over the last few years that he's become a stranger. He never writes or hardly ever calls. He's good with the money side of things. I've been very fortunate in that regard because he has not failed to meet a single payment. I suspect that will end one day but in the meantime, the kids don't have a father.'

'It must be hard?'

'It is but you get up each day and do what you have to and then go to bed at night grateful to have survived another day.'

'I can't imagine what that is like; it must be a tough way to live.'

'It is but I'm sure that it will in time improve especially when the kids are a bit older. You are very fortunate with what you have with Ben.'

'Yes, I am.'

'I'm really happy for you.'

Karen was doubly grateful for what she had with Ben after spending time with Petra and could only wish her well.

# CHAPTER THIRTY

*Down*

Karen received the call that Ben had been found after a bank had given way under his horse, resulting in both being thrown into a gully. A local was attracted by the screams of the injured horse that had to be put down as help arrived in the form of SES volunteers, local ambulance paramedics and the police who quickly coordinated his extraction from the gully and transport to the hospital. For Karen, it was a double blow as Lisa had been admitted to hospital the previous day with a chest infection.

Dropping Abby at her parents', she rushed back to the hospital where she was ushered into the emergency department where Ben was supported in an upright position, his arm supported in a brace and being fed oxygen. He was conscious but only just. They were attempting to stabilise him while awaiting the outcome of his x-rays.

Ben blinked at her in recognition but it was obvious that he was in a lot of pain. Shocked by the state he was in, she composed herself and reached for his free hand, which she held and he responded by squeezing her hand. As he looked at her, she could see him fighting for every breath, his ribs cracked and broken in a number of places.

When the medical team arrived, it was not with good news. Ben's injuries were extensive and he needed to be transported to Bairnsdale to receive the right range of care. An ambulance had been ordered and they were trying to make him as comfortable as possible in preparation for the trip. When Karen rang her mother, she was frantic.

'Mum, this could cost us everything. Ben has so much on at the moment and may not be able to work for months; everything he has worked for may be gone.'

'Karen, Michael already has things under control, his father-in-law is already around there and your father has already got some of the locals organised. Michael can take the horses to Dubbo as planned and your father will cut the hay in the north paddock.'

'Mum, we can't expect people to do those things.'

'No, but they will be done just the same. Now, you concentrate on Ben and Lisa and let me worry about everything else.'

Karen returned to be with Ben, who was heavily strapped and being checked by one of the doctors. As much as she tried, Karen could not help feeling that her world was falling apart. She waited with him until the ambulance arrived and then rushed off to check on Lisa. She stayed with Lisa until she was asleep and then drove to Bairnsdale to check on Ben. Karen was frantic when she arrived, looking for Ben who had been admitted and was awaiting surgery on his shoulder.

The surgery took hours and it was well after midnight before the surgeon returned to talk to her.

'Your husband's injuries are extensive but we have been able to stabilise him. We have stopped all the internal bleeding and I can only tell you that he was a very lucky man. Had things been much worse, we may not have been able to save him. We had to reconstruct his shoulder because of his old shoulder injury, which had not healed properly and should have been pinned years ago, which is why the surgery took so long.'

'He's going to be okay, though, isn't he?'

'Yes, but it is going to take time.'

'Can I see him?'

'Yes, but I must warn you he's not looking too good at the moment because of the surgery. His face is swollen but that should reduce in the next few days.'

Karen was horrified at Ben's swollen and bruised face. It looked a lot worse than when she had last seen him and he was clearly in a lot more pain. She tried to be strong but the tears flowed.

'Oh, Ben, I love you so much I can't stand to see you in so much pain.' She cried as she took his hand. Ben blinked at her, squeezed her hand and then closed his eyes. Karen stayed at his bedside for a few more hours before driving back to check on Lisa.

She arrived in the early hours of the morning. The hospital staff were very concerned about her and called the consulting physician who ordered her into a private room in the nursing quarters. Karen only complied after being escorted by two nurses to the room and stayed until she was in bed. Despite her deep concern for Lisa and Ben, she collapsed into a deep sleep.

Waking in a panic, she was going to get dressed straight away and rushed across to the hospital but found her clothes missing.

'What's going on? I have to get to the hospital,' she asked a nurse whom she met in the corridor.

'Your mother has got some clothes for you from home; you go and have a shower while I get your clothes and then I'll take you to breakfast,' the nurse told her calmly.

'I don't have time; I have a sick child and husband to look after. Give me my clothes,' Karen snapped.

'After you have had a shower. Both your husband and daughter are receiving the best care possible; it is you who needs looking after.'

'How could you possibly know what I need?'

'Because your doctor has told me that you are my priority for the moment. You have a shower and I'll have an update of Lisa and call the Bairnsdale hospital about your husband by the time you are ready for breakfast,' the nurse told her.

As angry as she was at being stopped from rushing to the hospital, she was grateful to have showered changed and had breakfast before seeing Lisa who was making good progress. She called Fiona to check on Abby after talking with Ben's doctor. She stayed with Lisa until she went to sleep after spending a couple of hours with her.

It was on the road to Bairnsdale that the last few days caught up with her as she struggled to concentrate on the windy roads. She felt the pressure of being away from the girls but knew Abby would cope; she was just that type of child but Lisa would be frantic if she was away too long.

Sitting with Ben, Karen could feel his pain from the operations as he drifted in and out of consciousness. For someone who was always so physically strong, Karen found it very hard to see Ben in so much pain.

Fiona and Ian arrived at the hospital with Abby to see how Ben was and offer support to Karen. Karen left Abby with them and went back to spend time with Lisa. As expected, Lisa was frantic, calling for her and Ben. Karen sat with her with tears rolling down her cheeks as Lisa slept in her arms. At one point, she fell asleep and woke to find Lisa back in her bed, a pillow behind her own head and draped in a blanket. Karen gathered her things, left Lisa and went back to visit Ben who was still asleep.

'Go home, Karen, there is nothing you can do here. Ben is going to be out of it for the next few days at least, so go home and get some rest.'

Karen arrived home to find the gardens tidied and food in the freezer. The fridge was stocked with all kinds of meals and the table set was ready to sit at. The response from the town was humbling for Karen, who was overwhelmed by the generosity poured out to them as a family. Clothes were washed, lawns cut and hay carted. All Karen had to do was tend to Ben. Michael called in to update her on the business activities that had been attended to.

'Michael, I cannot thank you and Melanie enough for what you have done for us. I am very grateful, thank you.'

'It's our pleasure, you have both done a lot for both of us over the years; hey, I doubt I would still be alive if Ben had not given me a break.'

'Still, you have gone above and beyond.'

'It's not just our work. Once word got out, people came running.'

'Really?'

'Yes; you and Ben have the love and respect of this town and everyone wants to help. You let me know what you need and someone will be able to help. I will be able to get those horses up to Griffith next week because Max and Richard Haines have agreed to cover me here.'

'Thanks, Michael. I thought we were going lose a lot of business as a result of this.'

'There are too many people in this town who want you to succeed to allow that to happen.'

'I can't tell you how much I appreciate that.'

'It's fine. Melanie will be around later to give you a hand with the girls.'

'That's fine; I'll be fine.'

'Please. She wants to help – it will mean a lot to her.'

'In that case, yes. Thank you. I could do with a hand. I'm sorry, I don't mean to sound ungrateful. I'm very tired at the moment.'

'We know. That is why Melanie will be around later to give you a hand until the girls are in bed.'

'I don't know what I'd do without you and Melanie. I know you work for Ben but I consider you both as very good friends.'

'We feel the same, thank you,' Michael replied before he left.

*

Lisa was released from hospital two days later but Karen continued to travel to Bairnsdale on a daily basis to visit Ben who was making a slow recovery and was expected to require additional surgery. The girls were becoming frantic when Karen relented and took them to see him. Lisa took one look at him and rushed to get her dog from Karen's bag, which she then placed in Ben's hand and looked up at him wide-eyed. Ben placed one hand on the toy dog, raised his other hand and touched her cheek, tears rolling down his face.

A week later, Ben was transferred back to the local bush nursing hospital so he could rehabilitate closer to home. Ben began to receive a constant stream of visitors after that as many of the locals dropped in to offer their support. Karen was able to return to work as Ian and Michael continued to run things on the property. It was a humbling time for Karen as she could hardly believe the support she was receiving from many of the locals she had only known from a distance at that point.

Melanie was a regular visitor, giving Karen a hand while Ben recovered, the two of them taking a break with a cup of tea in the kitchen after hanging the washing out.

'Melanie, I cannot thank you and Michael enough for your help. I could not have done it without you.'

'I doubt that very much – you seem to have things under control.'

'Appearance can be deceptive. I may look calm but believe what you can't see is that I'm swimming frantically just to stay afloat. How is Travis going anyway?'

'He's fine; he loves school and is pretty excited to know that Abby will be at the same school next year.'

'Abby is really looking forward to it too; she's become a real tomboy and will probably be joining him in the sand pit.'

'Oh, I don't doubt that.' Melanie smiled.

'Can I say, you seem very content with your little family. I know you were devastated when you found out that you could not have any more children but you're okay now though, aren't you?'

'Yes, I am, thank you for asking. I'm lucky I have Michael and I know he wanted more as well but we have Travis and we are really enjoying watching him grow.'

'He is a great kid; the girls love him.'

'Yes, it's like they are cousins.'

'Yes, they are. It will be good to see them grow up together.'

Ben's recovery was slow but everything was done when required by an army of volunteers who came each day to offer their help. As Ben recovered, he walked or drove around in a side-by-side with his shoulder strapped, overseeing the various tasks. While recovering from his injuries, Ben worked at a financial partnership deal to ensure that Michael was not only a wage but had a share of the profits from training the horses.

When Ben was fully recovered a couple of months later, Ben and Karen held a community barbeque at the reserve to thank everyone for keeping everything going while he was ill. Most of the town turned up and turned it into a real party. At one point, he stopped everyone to thank them collectively for their assistance.

'Thank you everyone for coming today and sharing this with us. You have all assisted us tremendously these last few weeks; we would not have made it without your very generous help. On behalf of Karen, the girls and I, thank you,' he told them, which drew a huge applause because they knew how hard it was for him to speak out that way, especially after making a determined effort to thank each one personally.

*

When everything settled and was back on track, they took the girls to the beach when they were young. It was a time for them all to recover from the last few months. Abby ran around, exploring the beach and playing at the edge of the water. She ran back and forth, showing them each new thing she found and later, Ben went for a walk with her to explore some of the rock pools. Lisa stayed close, showing no interest in the water but reluctantly joined Ben and Abby to explore the rock pools while Karen made lunch. Abby was ever fascinated by the colour and movement of what she found whereas Lisa wanted to know more and wanted to know about each thing she found.

Later, they sat in the shade of a tree on the edge of the sand and ate lunch. The girls slept, Abby on the ground at their feet and Lisa lying with her head on Karen's lap.

Karen reached for Ben's hand. 'This is good.'

'It is.'

'This is just how I imagined it would be with our kids. This is one of my dreams that you have made come true. Thank you.' She smiled.

'You are most welcome. What we have here is beyond anything I could have dreamed of. I know we have been through some tough times but I am so grateful that you've stayed so that we can share things.'

'Let me tell you something, Ben; yes, we have been through some times but all they have done is make the good times better and the good times have far outweighed the bad. It's the tough times that have helped me appreciate you more. You are the way you are with the girls because you don't take a day with them for granted. You didn't learn that from the good times but from the bad when you never thought you would have them and when you didn't think you'd be around to see them. It's the same with me, Ben.'

# CHAPTER THIRTY-ONE

*Gayle's wedding*

Gayle was married in Sydney. Ben and Karen flew up to Sydney for the weekend for the wedding, leaving the girls with their grandparents. Karen was always wary about leaving the girls with anyone but her mother assured her that they would be fine. Todd was delighted to meet them and told Ben that he was a bit intimidated to meet him, given how much Gayle had spoken of them both.

It was strange to see how nervous Gayle was as she stood in the corner of the gardens where the ceremony took place. As her matron of honour, Karen stepped in to reassure her until the ceremony began and then she settled speaking her words with growing confidence. After the ceremony, she looked truly happy.

Karen was among the first to embrace them. 'Welcome to the old wives club.' She smiled.

'Yes, I finally found someone to tie me down, so to speak.' Gayle smiled as Todd's daughter raced up to her and wrapped her arms around her. Gayle lifted her onto her hip.

'This is my new mummy,' she announced with great delight.

'Yes, I am, sweetheart.' Gayle smiled as she embraced her.

*

Within the year, Gayle gave birth to a baby boy. Karen went up to visit her in hospital, sitting up in bed with her son in a baby trolley beside the bed.

'Look at you; you look great,' Karen said, greeting her with a kiss.

'I have a baby boy.'

'I know, congratulations. How is he going?'

'Good. How am I going to raise a little boy?' Gayle said with tears in her eyes.

'You'll be fine. He is going to grow up to love his mother and you will love him.'

'But I don't know what to do.'

'You'll be fine and you can call me night or day.'

'Thanks. You were always such a natural mother.'

'Hey, don't put me on any pedestal. There have been days when I've not known what to do and gone home to my mother and just cried.'

'Yes, but for the most part, you have thrived.'

'As you will too. Gayle, you will be fine, Todd knows what to do and so will you. You have a baby boy and he is beautiful. When you are ready, you should come and visit and let him see the horses and we can talk about old times.'

'I would love that.'

*

Gayle did visit with her son and Gayle had changed so much. Instead of being the helpless mother running after her little boy, trying to stay in control, she was a confident mother who delighted in her son.

'It is so good to see you. You look great with Dillon. I told you it was different with your own.'

'It took some time, believe me, but being able to ring you day and night was a real help.'

'Yes, it's nice to hear from you a bit more than in the past. Children are a great leveller, don't you think?'

'They certainly are. I had no idea just how much work they took up. I seriously wonder what I did with my time before Dillon came along.'

'It's good that the three of them get along,' Karen said.

'The girls loved him and he seemed to really take to Abby,' Gayle added.

'That's because Abby has more testosterone than most boys.' Karen laughed. 'I can never figure out where that comes from but I've learnt to accept that that is Abby and I love her for it.'

'She is going to break some hearts, that one. One day she will bloom into something really beautiful and no one will be able to take their eyes off her,' Gayle told her.

'That's what worries me,' Karen replied.

'I wouldn't be too concerned, by that stage she will have the guys sussed and they won't stand a chance.' Gayle smiled.

For reasons unbeknown to them, Abby took to Gayle becoming her favourite aunt. Karen's sister seldom visited and had little contact with the girls over the years.

Her sister had become a stranger to all of them, with little more than a card or a quick call for birthdays and Christmas. Part of it was that she was wary of Ben but that did not account for distance from the other members of the family. The girls hardly knew her and Karen was grateful that she did not try to bribe the girls with gifts so that they would remember her.

# Chapter Thirty-Two

*Changes and growing up*

Brendan was always a welcome uncle who was happy to hear how the girls were going. When he married and had his own children, Ryes and Loran, they became welcome younger cousins who loved to visit and the girls sometimes stayed with them. Brendan's wife, Lucy, and Karen became friends and kept in touch on a regular basis, either ringing or writing. When Brendan took over the land from his father, the two families became very close as Ben and Brendan had always got along and in time, he warmed to Lucy, who was prone to be as shy as Ben was. With their parents around for birthdays, they completed the cabins at the end of the street, which eased the chronic shortage of accommodation in town. Ben employed local builders to construct the cabins, which was a boost to the town. The cabins were constantly booked so Karen employed contractors to service the cabins on a daily basis after trying to attend to it for a while with Abby. It had been a financial risk at the time but the cabins were soon paying for themselves.

The mountain cabins took longer to get up because of the significant planning issues around their intended use and the disposal of wastewater and sewerage but Ben worked with the planners and designers to come up with solutions that satisfied all parties without compromising his vision for the cabins and their use. Once under construction, Ben kept a close eye on the work, ensuring that there were no shortcuts and that they were finished to his exacting standards. He took Ian along to look over the cabins and explain how he intended to use them. Each was well-sited with excellent views but also sheltered from the worst of the weather.

Karen and the girls were the first people to stay with Ben in the cabins to ensure they knew what their guests would be getting for their money. Karen loved the ideas because they gave a good insight into the cabins and how to personalise each one. The girls loved the adventure of staying in each new cabin and exploring the new surroundings. It all assisted Karen to put the best services to the cabins, which the local business community was willing to bid for.

As each cabin came online, the effect was noticed in the local community as people shopped locally and came into town to dine at the hotel or the bakery, which had expanded its menu and seating capacity. The numbers were small but it was a step forward, adding a little more outside money to the community and getting the area noticed in the eastern part of the state. For Karen, it was not only a boost to the tourist industry but also to the family business. While the cabins produced an income, it was modest as most of it went to paying off the loans but formed the cornerstone of their growing business.

Lisa took up the violin at an early age and quickly showed a lot of promise. Ben listened to her every practice when Karen thought he would find it irritating. It was not long before she was performing in school musicals. As she grew in confidence and technical ability, she began to perform at a variety of events and venues.

The girls could not have been more different. Abby was a complete tomboy who did not appear to have a feminine bone in her body. She was never happier when outside, working the horses with Ben preferring jeans, shirts and working boots over dresses or skirts. Lisa was a lady and always tried to look her best. Tall and lean, she modelled herself on Karen but only more so, preferring full-length skirts and blouses. While she wore jeans when working around the house, she even managed to add a real feminine touch to her clothes with a soft scarf or shirt.

Hoping the girls would grow up together, they had, in fact, little in common and it was rare to see them together away from home. Lisa's friends were all town girls who could not wait to get away from the small town and country life to careers in the city. In that respect, Karen could understand Lisa but Karen never really left the country whereas Karen knew that Lisa would not return.

Karen and Abby seemed to clash a lot as Karen tried in vain to get her to dress in something remotely feminine. Even when they went to church, Abby would wear polished R.M. Williams boots and pressed white jeans all year round whereas Lisa would not be seen in less than a full-length skirt in winter and a freshly ironed dress in summer with slip-on low-heeled shoes.

As much as she tried, Karen seemed unable to get close to her firstborn whereas she found Lisa tiring at times. Lisa could not understand why Karen sometimes needed space from her even in her teens and insisted she be more independent to the point that she lashed out one day.

'For someone who is keen to leave, why are you always at my feet? When you leave do realise that I won't be coming with you? You are always under my feet yet you don't like being held, why is that?' Karen snapped.

'Fine,' Lisa snapped, stormed out of the kitchen and sat on the end of the verandah. Karen finished preparing dinner, made two cups of tea and went out to sit with her.

'Lisa, I'm sorry. I could have handled that better.'

'Why do want to get rid of me so quickly?' Lisa sniffed.

'I don't ever want to get rid of you. You are just in such a hurry to leave as I was at your age but I have to admit that I was a lot more independent than you are.'

'Did you ever think that I am just making the most of our time together because once I leave for uni, I won't be home much?'

'Yes, and I am happy that you see it that way but the reality is, Lisa, you are going to have to do things for yourself. If you want to cook then wait till I'm at work then it is all yours. I just wish you were a little more independent like Abby and that Abby was more feminine like you.' Karen smiled.

Lisa did not reply for a while then turned to look at her mother. 'You know that Abby is really beautiful under all that drab?'

'Yes, I know I see it every now and then, I just wish she would show once in a while.'

'She will one day, Mum, and she will outshine the lot of us,' Lisa replied.

'What about you, Lisa? What makes you so insecure? You have so much going for you,' Karen asked.

'Because I know that one day, I am leaving here but unlike Abby, I won't be back. There is never going to be my kind of work here for me.'

'I know but you will have a life of your own making that, I'm sure, will shine.'

\*

'How on Earth did we end up with two girls so opposite?' Karen lamented one day.

'I have no idea,' Ben replied as they watched the girls tend the horses.

Karen's parents had only laughed at such comparisons and both girls were close to their grandparents. They loved Helen and Martin and their cousin, Joel all of whom were regular visitors over the years. Joel had often stayed for the summer working with the horses and cattle. The girls loved him and the three of them often went riding together, being the few times that the girls seemed to get on really well together.

Helen and Karen had become close friends, often ringing each other just to catch up. Martin and Ben talked but there remained a distance between them as often Ben had to go off to do his work when Martin stayed. Sometimes they rode together but Martin was never at ease on the horses.

As they entered their mid-teens, Karen was always concerned about how the girls would react to their own growing awareness of boys. Abby seemed to have a number of males in her circle of friends, which was large because Abby had that ability to talk to anyone. Lisa was considered to be a snob because she kept to herself, having few friends and would have nothing to do with any of the local boys to the point of rudeness. Abby would often have friends around, which included some of the boys in the group but Lisa wanted little to do with them. One thing Karen did notice with Abby was that while she enjoyed male company, there was never one guy and little, if any, physical contact between them. Abby also never dressed up for the boys, always wearing loose-fitting jeans and tops as if trying to hide the true shape of her body. Lisa was attractive and Abby's mates were attracted to her but she stayed away and never made eye contact with any of them if they stayed for meals.

One day when Ben arrived home from a couple of days away working the cattle in the high country, Karen picked up a towel and told the girls to stay at the house. When she arrived back at the house forty-five minutes later, her hair was ringing wet and her clothes clung to her damp body.

'Have fun, did we?' Abby asked with a smile.

'Yes, we did, thank you. I enjoy being with your father,' Karen replied, looking at both of them.

'Oh, Mum, how could you? That is disgusting,' Lisa snapped and went to leave the kitchen.

'No, Lisa, you do not leave. That man, your father, is the love of my life and both of you are a result of that love. There has never been anything disgusting about our love-making; it is one of the great joys and privileges of being married. Now, all three of us have discussed this and I thought you understood that it is a part of life.'

'Well, it's not going to be part of my life,' Lisa snapped.

'Well, I certainly intend it to be part of mine. I want that to be part of my life when I grow up,' Abby snapped at Lisa.

'And that's it; it is supposed to be part of married life. It is what two people who love each other and are committed to each other share.'

'Oh, great, so if some guy tells me he loves me and, for some reason, I cannot fathom at this point, persuades or bullies me into marrying him. I don't think so and you two are just disgusting. I don't want anything to do with sex or either of you,' Lisa snapped at them and headed for the door but Karen beat her to it.

'Stop right there. What has happened to you? Has someone molested you? Has someone touched you in a way that has made you feel uncomfortable or violated?'

'No.'

'Then why? For someone who is so clingy, why is it now that you can't stand to be touched by anyone? You used to so much need Ben's attention that you would wait up till all hours to get a cuddle off him but now you won't let him near you and it breaks his heart. All he wants is to embrace you, to hold his daughter. You are his daughter and he loves you, surely a gentle hug across your shoulders is not all that bad.'

Lisa did not answer for a while. 'It's not Dad. I just don't like to be touched by anyone, that's all,' Lisa replied and walked out of the room.

'It's okay, Mum. She is just going through a phase,' Abby said as she wrapped her arms around her mother. 'Lisa is very insecure about her looks and hides it by keeping everyone at bay.'

'Are you sure that's all? You two share a room – you would know if she had been interfered with, wouldn't you?'

'Mum, she hasn't been molested. We've talked. You see her. She has a great body and the boys have noticed and try to ask her out and she hates the attention. She thinks they are only after one thing and in some cases, she is right but not all of them. There are some nice blokes about among them but Lisa can't see the good from the bad and has become very cold as a result.'

'Are you sure that's all?'

'Yes, you know she has always been insecure, now it's about boys. She is frightened by what you and Dad have. She thinks it's something you have to do because you're Dad's wife,' Abby replied.

'You don't believe that, do you?'

'No, Mum, I think that what you have with Dad is great. I hope I'm as fortunate one day,' she added and the two of them became close again after that.

Lisa remained distant from everyone after that but that did not stop Ben from listening to her practice night after night. He was unaware of their conversation but felt Lisa becoming more distant from him.

'What can I do, Karen? She won't even accept a hug from me anymore,' Ben lamented.

'Hopefully, it's just a phase she is going through but I think it's her way of hiding her insecurities about the opposite sex,' Karen replied.

'But she will be married one day, surely she knows that.'

'Part of me does but at the moment, she is too insecure to think about that and has her mind set on staying single for a very long time,' Karen told him.

# Chapter Thirty-Three

## Horse training

There were many visitors to the property during those days and Ben was a guide and mentor to many of them. As a horse trainer, he was one of the most sought-after in the state. Given the unwanted title of horse whisperer, he was courted by many to train or heal their horses. Among the unwanted attention was that of one of the local churches who were determined to expose him as some form of animal worshiper who spoke satanic chants to them.

To end the speculation, he conducted a number of sessions with horses of choosing others. Wearing a microphone, he spoke soothing words always with a calm voice as he worked with the horses. Hating such scrutiny, he felt trapped and inhibited at first but found that others were very interested so instead of justifying himself he found himself educating more people than just the church people. Everyone stayed for each of the sessions during which he explained the history and systems presented by each case and then went through a series of exercises with each horse. In the end, the sessions lasted all day with lunch served in a large marquee. By that time, the doubters were few in number. Karen had dropped in to see how it was going and decided to stay for lunch.

'It appears to be going well; you appear to be convincing the doubters.'

'I'm no longer interested in the doubters; they are here to learn like everyone else or they can leave,' Ben told her.

'Good for you.' She smiled, enjoying the new decisiveness.

\*

At that time, the town had established an annual equestrian event so they were seldom empty. Ben conducted a number of sessions that were sold out where he explained his horse-handling techniques following on from his session with the church people. It had been a painful period in his life, which he had turned into a real positive.

Karen loved watching him grow as an educator to the point where he gained accreditation to teach bovine studies under the supervision of a local TAFE teacher. He worked with students who wanted to learn and was blunt with anyone who didn't.

'Do not ever come here to waste my time or that of other students on this course. I, for one, will not tolerate it. If you step out of line, you are back on the bus, no questions asked. There is one boss on this course and it is me. Remember that after you go home, this is still someone's home and business, just as the animals are. Now, we shall commence,' he told them.

After going through his demands, he worked well with those who did want to learn. His trail rides were very popular as he taught them the basics of riding trails in preparation for the more challenging cross-country and ridge rides. Most who came to the course had some experience with horses but some had little or none. He tailored the course to meet everyone's requirements.

Abby was on one of the courses and hid in the background for most of it but was given away when on the trails, which she already knew very well. She was very comfortable in the bush on a horse and she had trained her own horse from a foal. It was in the bush that they knew that she was Ben's daughter and he didn't mind others knowing it as he watched her lead the less experienced and used her to demonstrate some of the skillsets he was imparting during the lesson.

'She is her father's daughter; she could ride through here in the dark,' Karla Berryman, the principal instructor, said as they watched her descend a steep wooded section of slope.

'She already has,' Ben replied.

'I don't doubt you. I have to wonder then what's she doing on this course – she should be given credits for it.'

'Perhaps, but others need to see her and learn from her just as she needs to learn from them. It will be that way every time she is in the bush.'

'Does that mean you still learn from others each time you go into the bush?' Karla questioned with a smile.

'Of course, I learn how each student takes in the information that has been presented to them and I learn how they then translate that learning into practice as they descend their slope. I can critique them from what I observe and assist them to do it better.'

'In this situation, I appreciate that but what about in your work with the cattle or with Mountain Rescue?'

'With the cattle, there are different styles among the cattleman and women, some of who are a little better here or there even though they are as at a group at a very high level. I continue to learn from them and watch what I do and change small things if I think they will help. With Mountain Rescue, we often have different people operating with us with a range of skills. Sometimes I need everything we have to keep them up with Mountain Rescue or even change routes in order to get the group through.'

'Now, that is why I ask you to lead this course because you are a student as well as an instructor. The industry needs you.'

'Thank you; to be honest, I really enjoy doing this – it looks like some of them need it and the more competent ones seemed to be enjoying it as well.'

'You have summed that up very well. I have been getting very feedback from all the students and the school. I would like to talk to you at some stage about how to turn this from an experiment to part of the college curriculum if you are interested.'

'I am but as you can appreciate, I have a lot on my plate with the horses so we will have to sit down with my diary and see how we can do this with everything else I have on.'

'Of course, that is why I am sounding you out now so that you can come to the meeting with your requirements as well as ours. We want you to conduct the course but we appreciate it's not a simple case of dropping everything to run this course, you would not be who you are if it was not for those other commitments. It's not just how to handle horses that we want you to teach but the business of horses from breeding to running the tours.'

'Okay, I will need a bit of a hand from Karen and the girls but I will have a look at it.'

'Don't hesitate to call if you need help; please remember this is a negotiated deal we may be able to help with ideas as well.'

'I appreciate it.'

*

Both girls were excelling with their horses in their own fields. Abby was a natural on a horse in the bush, working with cattle in any kind of weather. She loved the bush and she loved horses, especially the bush horses. Lisa developed a love for horses and show jumpers for which she had a real flare. She seemed to understand at a young age what it took to be a good jumper. She knew how to get a horse to jump but she also knew when a horse was not going to be a good jumper. She trained her own horses and began placing in a number of shows and began to give some of the other local girls a hand to train their jumpers as well. Some believed that Lisa had a real shot at the Olympics if she kept progressing and even Karen agreed but Ben saw it differently.

'Sure, she enjoys show jumping but her passion is music. Her future is not with show jumpers but playing in the theatres of England and Europe,' Ben told Michael and Melanie as they watched her complete her final round which not only got their attention but Karen's as well.

'Do you really think so?'

'Absolutely, she enjoys the jumping, don't get me wrong, but it is only for a time. Music has got hold of her and I don't think that she will be at all happy until she has performed in London professionally.'

'That's ambitious,' Michael said.

'It is and she knows she will have to give up the horses to do it but she will get there or, at the very least, do everything she can do to get there.'

'She could be the same way with show jumping,' Melanie suggested.

'She could be but I doubt that very much. There is no question that she has the talent and the money for her to do would be found, so don't get me wrong on that score, but talent and money, as we all know, are never enough. Without a real drive and passion, it just isn't there. When we get home tomorrow night and the horses and her kit are squared away, she will go to the shed and practice for two hours, then and only then will she consider TV or bed.'

Later, Karen sat with him in front of the campfire.

'Do you really think that Lisa will follow music instead of the horses? Do you want her to be a musician?'

'Yes, I believe she will follow music. I want her to follow her dreams and music is her greatest dream.'

'It's just that she is right into show jumping at the moment.'

'Yes, and that's because she knows that it's only for now and she is trying to enjoy every minute of it.'

Lisa loved dressing the part every bit as much as the jumping whereas Abby hated dressing for anything. There were few photographs of the girls in their riding gear; probably one of the best was a bush carnival with both girls in the riding gear they loved most. Lisa always seemed to have the capacity to make any outfit look feminine. She would add a silk scarf to her jeans, always wore polished shoes and had her hair made up. Everyone made a comment about how much she had Karen's sense of style, which Lisa did not mind at all.

At another weekend gymkhana, Lisa slipped away to practice while Karen and Abby were making tea. Abby was as good at cooking over a campfire as she was over a stove. Karen liked cooking with Abby because she enjoyed it so much and was never afraid to experiment and usually got it right producing some wonderful flavour. It was something that Ben also loved and the three of them shared. While they were cooking, they could hear Lisa practising as the sound drifted across the valley. The sound was captivating; Abby and Karen stopped to listen then realised that so had most people at the park. For the next twenty minutes, the valley was silent except for the echo of Lisa's violin. When she walked back down to their camp after her practice, the whole valley applauded her. Lisa was embarrassed that people were listening but now she found the whole valley calling for more so that after tea, she found herself at the main campfire with some of the other people who were playing guitars. Lisa was clearly outside her comfort zone but Ben told her she was a musician and told her to embrace the moment. She did and it became a great night as let her musical inhibitions go.

'So, the girl can play country; I'm impressed,' Abby said to no one in particular.

'Of course, she can. She is a musician, and it's all music.'

# CHAPTER THIRTY-FOUR

*The passing of Jack*

A major blow to Ben at that time was the passing of Jack Carmodia, who died of heart failure at home. While not unexpected, it was still a blow because Jack had been a mentor and father figure to Ben for many years. While Jack was still the official leader of Mountain Rescue, Ben had taken over in recent years but Ben kept Jack very much in the loop, briefing him after every meeting and exercise. Ben withdrew into himself as Karen expected but she was not ready for the extent of his withdrawal.

They went to the remote cemetery in the hills above the valley. A large crowd had gathered at the cemetery to pay their respects. It was so different to Ben's father's funeral where there was only half a dozen to see him off. People came from all over the district because if he was not liked for his directness, he was still very well respected. A lot of the cattlemen came on horseback with the men from Mountain Rescue leading the horse up the lane to the cemetery. Ben rode in the front line of the group as they wheeled around in front of the main part of the cemetery which stood at the top of the rise. The horses were tied up on a line set between two trees at the edge of the cemetery.

The funeral was conducted by the local minister who knew most of the locals by name. His words were few and well-chosen before Jack's neighbour and district Mayor spoke about Jack and his long involvement with the district. It was through his words that Karen learnt so much more about Jack and understood a little more about the person he was. The local men and women stood in silence while his eulogy was given and then one of Jack's sons, Peter, spoke about Jack as a father to his brothers and to Ben who was by that time considered family.

When it was over, he joined a group of men on a tribute ride to one of the huts from where Ben intended to ride home but then stayed in the high country.

Karen could only sit on the back verandah and wait for Ben each night. In desperation, she called Maureen.

'I'm sorry to trouble you, Maureen. I'm sure you are missing Jack terribly but Ben has not come home and I'm sure he is living in the high country somewhere.'

'It's no trouble at all, Karen. You should have called me sooner. I do miss Jack and I know this is not how he would have wanted to be remembered. You leave it with me, I'll send the boys out and we'll find him.'

'Thank you, Maureen. I didn't know who else to turn to.'

'It's no trouble at all and you know you only have to call, night or day.'

'Thank you,' Karen replied.

Maureen called her sons and they were soon at the property, saddling horses and setting off into the high country. It took just five days to find him in an isolated cabin in a shallow gulley just below the winter snowline. One of the boys stayed in the trees to keep an eye on the camp while the other went home and collected Maureen.

Maureen left the boys above the camp and went to the camp. She found Ben sitting in front of an open fire, staring into the flames. One look at him told her that he had not washed or changed his clothes in a week or more; his hair was filthy and his face unshaven.

'What are you doing, Ben?' Maureen asked from the top of her horse before climbing down.

'Thinking,' he replied seeming to know she was there and guessed had been there for some time.

'Well, while you were thinking, you have a wife at home who misses you terribly and two girls are frantic thinking that their father might not be coming home.'

'I'm okay. They should know that.'

'You not okay and they need you at home, not sitting here missing Jack. This is not how he would have wanted to be remembered,' Maureen told him and Ben looked up at her for the first time.

'He was the nearest thing to a father that I had.'

'Don't you think I know that? I miss him too and so does Karen but she misses you too, terribly. Don't make a tough situation worse by withdrawing from the people who love you the most. Go home, Ben,' Maureen told him.

'Do you want to join me for a cup of tea?' he offered, holding up a billy to her.

'I'll make the tea while you go and clean yourself up. We'll have a cuppa and then you are going home,' Maureen told him.

'Yeah, sure,' Ben conceded.

'Good; just don't expect a happy reunion. If I was Karen, I would strangle you,' Maureen told him as Ben went behind a tree to take a sponge bath and change his clothes.

'I suspect she will come close,' Ben replied.

'The only reason she won't is because of the girls,' Maureen told him.

'I know that too.'

'Good; let's make this a short cuppa then,' Maureen told him.

'Yes, that may be wise.'

Maureen rang Karen as soon as she got home.

'Karen, we found him. He is on his way home. He should be home in a couple of days.

*

It was just on dusk when Ben rode in the yard. Karen, who was sitting on the verandah, had been waiting for him. She put down the magazine she had been holding in a vain attempt to read any of it and went to him.

'Where have you been? Damn you, Ben Templeton, do you know how many nights I have sat up waiting, hoping you would ride into the yard? I've had no idea where you've been or how you've been. I did not give birth to the girls to raise them on my own. Now, get yourself cleaned up and go and tell the girls you love them,' she screamed at him before she stepped up to him, wrapping her arms around him. 'I love you, Ben, please don't ever do this to me again,' she said softly.

'I'm sorry,' he whispered.

'Sorry doesn't cut it, not this time. Now, I know that Jack was the nearest thing to a father that you had but we're your family now. We've been through tough times before together and it is how we are going to do it now. No more running off; too many people love you and rely on you,' Karen told him.

That was when the girls approached. Abby ran to him and wrapped her arms around him. Lisa stood at a distance with the same big round expectant eyes she had when she was younger.

'You and Mum aren't going to split up over this, are you?' Lisa asked from a short distance away.

'Not if I can help it,' Karen immediately replied as Abby took Ben's horse away to be brushed and fed, leaving Ben to shower and change in the shed while Karen and Lisa went back to the house.

Ben and Karen sat up and talked half the night as he found words to express some of the deep pain he was feeling and began to cry. Karen held him close and later held him in bed where his sleep was plagued with sadness. In the morning, Karen let him sleep while she got up and got the girls off to school and then left for work.

Later that day, Lisa returned home from school and went looking for Ben who was working in his office.

'Are you okay, Dad?' she asked.

'Yes, Lisa, I'm okay. How are you? Listen, I'm sorry to have left you like that,' Ben told her as tears began to roll down Lisa's face.

'Hey, what's the matter?' he asked, standing to comfort her but she took a step backwards.

'I didn't think you were coming back.' She cried.

'I was always coming back; you know I could never leave you, not forever,' Ben told her and went to comfort her but she held out her hand to stop him.

'Then why did you leave us?'

'You know why, I lost the closest thing to a father I ever had and didn't know what to do.'

'But why couldn't you stay?'

'I don't know, Lisa. As parents, we don't always have the answers we would like. It doesn't stop me loving you, Lisa, now or ever,' he told her.

# CHAPTER THIRTY-FIVE

*Wider family*

Joel took up a farming apprenticeship with one of the larger cattle properties in the district as Helen said the country had captivated him as a young boy when he stayed with Ben. While he had grown up in the city, the truth was that his heart was in the country and the apprenticeship was the perfect way for him to live there. He was a regular visitor after that with Abby and Joel remaining close.

Travis had gone on to university to study law but that had not brought him closer to his grandfather because he took up law in spite of him not because of him and dismissed any attempts by his grandfather to talk about it. Travis and Michael remained close with Travis returning home as much as he was determined to be close to him. He decided to return to the country once he qualified taking up a position with a local firm after gaining some experience in the city.

Helen and Kelly stayed with Ben and Karen when they came to visit Joel. Lisa and Abby loved having Kelly stay with them because she seemed to be the bridge between the two girls, the three of them going off together and having a great time.

Lisa found she needed glasses at that point and Karen took her to

Melbourne to ensure that she had a couple of pairs that really suited her and in time came to terms with the new look.

Travis partnered both girls to their end-of-year dances as all three remained close. Of the two of them, Lisa seemed to have more in common with him in the later years of school. They spoke the same language and shared a number of common interests including music with Travis being quite accomplished with the violin himself. There was a time when there was talk that perhaps Lisa and Travis would get together but as Lisa said, he was more like a brother or cousin because she could never remember a time when Travis was not around.

The girls completed year twelve and went on to further study, Abby going to agricultural college and Lisa to Melbourne where she studied music. It was quiet around the place after that but Abby was home as often as she could make it. Lisa excelled at music, receiving a scholarship to study at the Sydney Conservatorium for a year. She then gained a scholarship to further her studies in England. It was a great opportunity for her; Ben and Karen were thrilled with her success, fully expecting her to take up the scholarship without hesitation. Her grandparents were equally excited for her even though they knew that they would miss her as much as she missed them.

'Congratulations. That is such good news; it's just rewards for years of hard work.'

'I'm not sure if I should go,' Lisa replied.

'Why wouldn't you go?' Karen questioned.

'You wouldn't mind?'

'Of course not. This is a great opportunity for you.'

'What about Dad?'

'He is really proud of you and wants you to go and take up every opportunity. He'll be home tomorrow. Why don't you talk to him then?' Karen suggested but she suspected that Lisa wouldn't for whatever reason.

Lisa seemed reluctant to leave even though Karen knew that she was really looking forward to going to England and the opportunities that awaited there. Abby was excited for Lisa, knowing that it had the potential to establish her career as a concert professional.

It was not easy saying goodbye at the airport. Lisa remained physically distant as she prepared to leave, despite knowing how proud Ben was of her.

'Lisa, you can't walk away without giving your father a hug. He loves you very much as he's just so proud of you. Why is it so hard? He just wants to show you how much he loves you.'

'I just don't like being touched; he understands,' Lisa replied.

'That's just it; he doesn't. He respects your need for space and will never do anything that makes you feel uncomfortable. You also need to understand that you used to wait up for all hours to make sure that you got a cuddle off him when he got back from being away. In a lot of ways, you are still his little girl and understands you more than I do at times. You're hurting Ben more than you can know.'

'I don't mean to. I just can't.'

'You're going to have to tell someone why one day,' Karen told her.

*

Lisa accepted only the briefest kiss from Karen when they parted at the gate. Abby would have none of it and wrapped her arms around Lisa and wished her well. She offered Ben only a weak smile and the briefest of embraces before walking away. Karen could feel his pain as could Abby and wrapped her arms around both of them as they watched her leave the departure area. Ben hardly spoke all the way home; all Karen could do was hold his hand when they stopped for a break at one of the roadside cafés. At one stage, he went for a walk in a nearby park and sat on a bench. Karen left Abby in the café and went to him.

'I've lost her, Karen. I would do anything to fix this but I have no idea how.'

'Ben, it is not your problem to fix, I'm afraid. Lisa has let her own insecurities put up barriers between herself and the rest of the world. You were like that too once, remember? And look how long it took for your barriers to come down.'

'But unlike my father, I have always loved her; she is my special little girl.'

'I know she is, Ben, but the problem is she is not a little girl anymore.'

# CHAPTER THIRTY-SIX

*Abby*

With Lisa in England and Abby living full-time in one of the units, the house seemed fairly empty even when Abby dropped in most days. For Karen and Ben, it was a new start for them as they had the house to themselves again. It did not mean they were any less busy though with the country show circuit and horse shows where Ben was a chief judge.

Karen continued her employment and secretarial service, which, at that stage, had two offices providing recruitment and temping staff covering the LaTrobe Valley and the east. Still based in Bairnsdale, she regularly travelled to Sale and Moe.

As they were preparing for the latest show, they were expecting Abby to arrive to give them a hand to load the car and go with them.

She arrived at the house wearing a full-length skirt over the top of low dress boots. She wore a white blouse and silk scarf tied at the neck. Even her hair had a blue bow in it, causing Ben to do a double-take.

'What?' Abby questioned as she saw her parents looking at her.

'What's the occasion?' Ben asked.

'Nothing, it's just another horse show.' Abby shrugged, trying to display disinterest.

'Do you want to try that again? Who are you expecting?'

'No one in particular.'

'Really?' Ben questioned.

'If you must know, I'm meeting David. David Harman. Alan and Judy Harman's son.'

'David? Why David?' Ben questioned but Abby walked away.

'I think she has plans for David,' Karen said, guiding him away.

'What sort of plans?' Ben questioned.

'I think she has Mummy and Daddy plans for that one.'

'What are you talking about?' Ben asked, confused and a little alarmed.

'I think that Abby has plans to marry David.'

'What? She is just a child.'

'Ben, she is twenty-four. I'm afraid to tell you this but she won't be the youngest bride in the district and I wasn't much older when I married you.'

'But she seems so young; besides, I doubt that David will even notice.'

'Oh, believe me, he'll notice alright. Abby has never dressed like that for anyone. When he realises that she has dressed like that for him, I think it will change things between them. Abby is making the first move but I suspect that we'll have a wedding on our hands before the year is out.'

'But why? They have so little in common,' Ben questioned.

'I don't know. They have been seeing a bit of each other lately and when they do, they talk. In a lot of ways, they are a bit like you and me. David is just like you with a family behind him.'

'But he's so quiet and she is so wild. They will drive each other crazy.'

'I doubt that very much. They both love the land and have similar ideas about the cattle industry. I think they have a lot more in common than you think. I think they will be good together.'

'Perhaps but I think we are jumping the gun; David hasn't noticed her yet. We'll see what the day brings first,' Ben told her, trying to assure himself that he had nothing to worry about.

It didn't take long for Abby and David to link up.

'You look great,' he replied, a little distracted by her new look.

'I had hoped you would notice; I didn't dress up for anyone else,' Abby replied.

'Thank you. you look great.'

'You've said that already. Do I look good enough to go out with? To be seen walking around holding hands?'

'You always looked good enough to go out with.'

'We've both been beating around the bush then. Why don't we go to the catering tent and talk it over lunch?'

'Sounds like a good idea. I'll just let my parents know I won't be joining them for lunch.'

David's parents had noticed Abby as well when she arrived.

'Have you seen that Abby Templeton? She looks like she's on a hunting trip. Why dress like that all of a sudden?' David's mother Rose told her husband, Richard.

'Yes, it does. I can't imagine what her parents must think. Dressing like people may suspect she is a woman after all and if that blouse was any more revealing, people may suspect the girl even has breasts.'

'Of course, she has breasts. What is your point?'

'Abby's okay. You just let her be.'

A few minutes later, David arrived, holding hands with Abby, which caused Rose a little concern.

'Hello, you two. What are you up to?' Richard questioned as he put down his paper to look at them.

'Abby and I are going for lunch at the tent. We want to talk.'

'I'm not sure about that. You can both have lunch here with us and talk here if you must.'

'No, Mum. We need to talk alone,' David replied, looking at her.

Rose looked at Abby who met her gaze squarely.

'You can trust me, Mrs Harman,' Abby told her. Rose looked at her for a moment before replying.

'Yes, I can, Abby; you enjoy your lunch and please come back and join us for afternoon tea,' Rose offered.

'Thank you, Mrs Harman,' Abby replied, taking David's arm.

'Abby, please call me Rose.'

'Okay, thank you, Rose, we'll be back later,' Abby replied and the two of them left, leaving Rose to watch them walk to the tent.

'That was some turnaround; I'm impressed. One minute she is a hussy, the next, you are inviting her for tea.'

'Yes, I know but I've just realised that behind that outfit, it's still Abby Templeton.'

'Was she ever anybody else? She only dressed like that to get noticed and not by the rest of the world, just David.'

'Yes, I see that now.'

'She has got a good head on her shoulders, that one.'

'She does; doesn't she?' she agreed.

'There have been a lot of gold diggers chasing David for years but Abby is not one of them. They are mates and that goes a long way towards making for something long-term. She is a good girl. I think they will be fine.'

'Yes, you may be right. When did you become so knowledgeable about affairs of the heart?'

'Just small things that David has said; this is not the first time he's noticed her. He's never been gushy about her, that is not his way but he's said enough.'

Later that afternoon, Abby and David were walking around, very much the couple. Karen decided it would be best if they went and met David's parents, especially after David had made the effort to introduce himself and tell them that he was dating Abby, who seemed very happy with the arrangement.

'It's good to see them together,' Richard told Ben.

'You think so?'

'Yes, Abby is just what he needs. He will always know where he stands with her. She comes from the land and is not looking for something better in the city. I could not think of anyone better.'

'Thank you. That is quite a compliment.'

'No, I mean it. We like Abby. I wouldn't mind at all if they made something long-term of it.'

'Yes, well, maybe. That is up to them.' Ben hesitated.

'Yes, it is. It will be their decision alone to make,' Richard agreed.

\*

A short time later, David's sister Stella arrived back from catching up with friends from her school days.

'How did David end up with Abby?' Stella questioned.

'How do you mean? Why didn't you think they would end up together?' Rose questioned.

'She has always dressed down but behind those rags has been a swan waiting to emerge and nobody would be able to take their eyes off her. We always thought that one day, look out. Look at her now and she has done it for David. That is pretty impressive. It's the last you'll see of those rags.'

'You don't mind them being together then?'

'No, she will be good for him.'

'You don't think she will be too strong for him?'

'No, behind the bad clothes and the hardness is not only a swan but the gentleness of her father.'

'You know him too?'

'Everyone does. He's hard but there is nothing he won't do for someone lost or having a hard time. He doesn't suffer fools and neither does Abby, which is okay by me because you always know where you stand with her. I'm looking forward to getting to know her. They will be good together.'

'Do you think they can make a go of the property?'

'No doubt at all, they are definitely the next generation.'

'We should have Abby over for tea then?' Rose suggested.

'Absolutely,' Stella replied.

Stella was right about Abby as she was never seen in her old clothes again. It was not that she had thrown out her wardrobe but added a feminine touch to her outfits. Soft shirts and dress shoes added to her jeans and jodhpurs. Others noticed it too but the one person that mattered to Abby was David, who delighted knowing that he was the inspiration for her new look. Their relationship became the talk of the town.

*

Karen chose a quiet moment to talk to Abby about David over the inevitable pot of tea. Since Abby completed college both Ben and Karen had found Abby much more approachable and Karen in particular had finally begun to bond with her rather than fight. She found Abby only too willing to talk.

'Can I ask what made up your mind to go out with David?'

'We've been friends for years; he was one of the groups I've hung around with at the shows and things. The group has started to get thin of late as various ones have paired off. It seemed that every time we met, we would end up working and talking together and I really enjoyed his friends. Just recently I began thinking that it is time I went to the next stage of my life and thought that I would like David to be part of it. We talked and I told him that I was only interested in having one boyfriend so he knew that I was serious.'

'How did he react to that?' Karen asked.

'Well, it didn't take him long to agree to go out with me because he had been thinking much the same way.'

'So how is it going with you two? Is this serious you think?'

'I think so far so good. We are still good friends but now we share a kiss and cuddle every now and then but nothing further and he knows that.'

'And he is okay with that?'

'Yes, he is. He is old-fashioned in that way.'

'And you're not?'

'I am as old-fashioned as he is in that regard, I've already told him there will only ever be one man in my bed.'

'I'm glad to hear it. You won't regret waiting nor only ever having one man. I've seen girls live the other way and believe they do have regrets.'

'I know some of my own generations have regrets already. I don't want to be one of them.'

'That is fairly heavy stuff to talk about. How is he about talking so frankly?'

'He's used to me being direct and he responds in kind. It makes for a tense few minutes while we clear the air but then it's done and dealt with so he doesn't mind.'

'Good. Do you think you will marry him?'

'At some point, yes. We are taking things slow at the moment but I can't see why we wouldn't at some point.'

'Has he said anything to you about it?'

'Not directly but about us getting married but when he has conversations about the future of his parents' place, he talks in terms of "us" rather than "I" so that says something.'

'It certainly sounds like it. I'm really happy that it's working out for you, Abby.'

'Thanks, Mum. You know I really hope to have what you and Dad have. I know it hasn't always been easy but I still see you sitting together talking after tea as you have always done as long as I can remember.'

'It was how we started out, sitting on that verandah talking. It was where I first asked Ben to go out with me and where we sat and talked about you after I found out I was pregnant, we even used to include you in the conversation,' Karen said with a smile.

'And you have no regrets, do you?'

'There are times I would not repeat but marrying Ben, living here and

244

having you and Lisa, I would not change for anything,' Karen replied and Abby knew she meant it.

Abby and David dated regularly after that and everyone began to see a very feminine side to her as they went to tea in town or closer to David's or when they went dancing at one of the local halls with his parents. Abby would sometimes stay in Stella's room when she stayed for the weekend to a dance close by or have tea with his family. David always stayed in the bungalow out the back a place that she never went further than the back verandah even as their relationship extended into months.

One night, Abby looked particularly stunning as they prepared to go to one of the biggest balls in the district. Even then, Rose began to think it was only a matter of time before Abby joined them permanently. With her hair brushed from her face and a long sky-blue gown, she looked stunning, as did David in his three-piece suit and bow tie. Rose took a photograph of the two of them together before they left, both beaming at the camera.

Rose was a little surprised to receive a phone call from David a hour later, asking where his father was but Richard had gone down the road to catch up with neighbours.

'Is there something wrong?' Rose asked with a little apprehension.

'Nothing we can't handle. We'll see you later, Mum,' David replied before hanging up.

Rose went to ask about what was happening with the dance and what Abby was doing but he had already hung up and did not answer when she called back and did not answer the radio so all she could do was wait.

Several hours later, Rose was a little surprised to see David's ute pulling up the driveway. She had not expected them back until the early hours of the morning so went out to meet to see if there had been trouble. One look at David as he stepped out of the car and went to open the door for Abby who appeared to be gathering an old coat about, she could see that David's suit was ruined.

'What on Earth happened?' Rose asked as she rushed to the car to assist Abby out of the ute only to see that her gown was ruined.

'The fence was down on junction with Dudley's Creek. A couple of Ted's cattle were tangled in the wire and his cattle were across the road. We called him but couldn't get an answer. We couldn't leave them so instead of having a ball we had a right old dirty time of it,' David told her. Abby looked at Rose for a moment and then roared with laughter as David blushed brightly as he realised what he just said.

'That last bit did not come out right, did it?' he questioned as Abby laughed.

'No, it did not.' Abby laughed and then Rose joined.

'Well, I can see it hasn't ruined your sense of humour then,' Rose said.

'There will be other dances.' Abby shrugged.

'Not in that dress, there won't.'

'No but I can always buy another dress,' Abby said as Rose led her into the house.

By mid-morning the following day, Ted and his wife Irene arrived to thank them for taking care of the fence.

'We wanted to thank you not just for stopping last night but giving up your night for us.'

'It was nothing, it's what anyone would do.'

'Not everyone, people who know what it means to live and work on the land. Can I have a look at the dress you wore to the ball last night?' Irene asked.

'It's unfortunately ruined.'

'Then we need to replace it. If you don't have to be home tomorrow, Rose and I would like to take you shopping to replace your dress.'

'That is completely not necessary – it was just a dress, and there will be other dances, other dresses.'

'Perhaps but this is a special time in your life and the least we can do is replace your dress. Please, let Rose and I do this for you.'

'Okay, I don't have to be anywhere tomorrow but I can assure you that it is not necessary,' Abby told them.

Abby rang Karen to let her know she would not be home that night, telling her that she was going shopping with Rose but did not tell her why but Karen had already heard from Richard who had sung her praises to them.

'She is a great girl is your Abby, her heart's in the land and she keeps an eye out for people. She did not hesitate to climb into the mud last night to get those cattle out. I'm proud of her and David – they did a really good job last night.'

'Thank you for ringing and saying so. We appreciate that.'

'They're both good kids.'

'They are and I would love to have her as part of our family if things continue the way they are with David.'

'We'll have to wait and see what they think about the idea; we are rather fond of David ourselves.'

'Thank you, folks. We'll talk soon,' Richard told them.

David was delighted to have her stay for Sunday tea and could not stop smiling. He saw it as a turning point but it was like any other evening in most ways. In the morning, David was up early and out on the tractor. Abby had a brief breakfast and fed the calves near the house paddock before Rose called her for a pot of tea.

'You shouldn't be out there doing that; you are a guest,' Rose told her.

'Yes, but if there is something that needs doing–' Abby began but did not finish.

'I know, Abby, it is one of the many things I love about you,' Rose told her and Abby looked at her and Abby realised that Rose meant it.

'I'm not sure what to say other than thank you; I was hoping that one day you would approve of me.'

'Abby, we have got to know each other and I have learnt to love you. I will be proud to call you my daughter-in-law if it comes to that but whatever happens between the two of you, you should know that I love and respect you,' Rose said and offered Abby a hug, which she accepted.

After breakfast, Abby changed and joined Irene and Rose for the drive into town. The three women spent the day in town. Abby was a reluctant shopper but found a dress that she and Irene and Rose loved. When she went to look at the price, they took it from her.

'The price is not your concern today,' Irene told her and had it wrapped. Abby never did learn the price of that dress.

The three of them then went to lunch and had an enjoyable time. The women talked as equals Abby loved the conversation and the laughter of that afternoon, especially when they went looking for another place to have afternoon tea. After eating too much and drinking too much tea, she was delighted with the day. When they got back to the house, Abby thanked them both and they thanked her in turn, Abby feeling really acceptance from them, which was a delight.

'Abby, please don't hesitate to drop in at any time. You will be a welcome guest at my table any time for tea and chat, night or day.'

'Thank you, Irene.'

'Do you want to stay for tea?' Rose offered.

'Thank you but I really do need to get going. I have an early start tomorrow. I promised Dad that I would cut one of the paddocks,' Abby replied.

'I would not expect anything less. Thank you for sharing today with us. We must do it again sometime.'

'I would like that, thank you,' Abby replied before going to see David. She told him she was heading home and they quickly planned another night to go out for tea and onto a dance.

*

A few weeks later, David called Ben and asked to meet with him and Karen, arriving a few hours later looking very nervous. Karen told Ben of her suspicions to prepare him for what David may be about to ask.

'Hello, David. What's on your mind?

'I have come to ask your permission to ask Abby to marry me.'

'I see. I have to say that we have been expecting something like this. When were you planning to ask her?' Karen questioned him.

'Tonight, at tea if you give me the go-ahead.'

'We cannot speak for Abby so all we can do is say yes and wish you all the very best and hope that she gives you the answer you want,' Ben replied.

'Yes, David, you have our blessing.' Karen smiled.

'Thank you both, Mr and Mrs Templeton. I promise I will take care of Abby.'

'You will take care of each other,' Karen told him.

'We will. Thank you both, very much,' David said, standing up to shake their hands.

'You will call us and tell us the outcome, won't you?' Karen told him.

'Of course, I will call both parents as soon as I have an answer.'

'Your parents know you are about to ask her then?' Karen questioned.

'Yes, I sat down and talked things over with them a couple of days ago.'

'We can appreciate that,' Ben replied.

'Mr and Mrs Templeton, thank you both very much.'

'It's Karen and Ben, please,' Karen told him.

'Sure.'

'All the best, David,' Karen told him as they escorted him to his car.

'Thank you, Karen. Do you think she will say yes?' he asked at the last minute.

'You'll have to ask Abby that,' Karen told him.

Ben let out an audible sigh when he left.

'I've been waiting and dreading this moment since the girls entered their teens,' Ben told her.

'I know but it's just the next stage in their lives. The same stage that we took all those years ago.'

'Yes, but it seems like yesterday it was us and even more recent since we were holding them as babies.'

'I know. It's called growing old.'

❊

Abby dropped in on the way to meet David before dinner and a dance at Bairnsdale. She dropped off some dockets for the feed supplements and to catch up before meeting David.

'Dad, the supplements are locked away in the river shed, ready to be fed out tomorrow. Now, the fencing stakes arrived but they were the wrong size so I sent them straight back. I'm expecting the delivery first thing Monday. If not, they will be hearing from me,' Abby said as she dropped the dockets on the table.

'I don't doubt you for a moment. I must say, you look very smart tonight. Any reason for that?' Ben asked, teasing but it was lost on Abby who was all business. Karen was relieved but gave Ben a stare.

'It's the outfit Rose bought for after I destroyed my other dress. I need to keep going. I'm already late.'

'Okay, sweetheart, have a good night,' Karen told her.

'I will, thank you. I will see you in the morning,' Abby replied. Karen watched her leave, knowing that her life was about to change because she fully believed that Abby would accept David's proposal.

❊

Dinner went well as they sat and talked ahead of the dance. They had finished dessert and had ordered coffee as they had a little time to spare.

'Before we go to the dance, I want to ask, would you like to make tonight's dance last for the rest of our lives?' David asked.

'What do you mean?' Abby asked, unable to decipher the meaning of the question. David opened a ring box and pushed it towards her. Abby held her breath.

'Abby Templeton, would you do me the honour of marrying me?' he asked.

Abby did not need to be asked twice. 'Yes, I would love to marry you to become your wife and raise a family if that is what you're asking?'

'You know I am,' David told her and took the ring from the box.

'Then yes, double yes,' Abby said and held out her hand to him. David slipped the ring on her finger and then held her hand up for her to look at. 'We should tell our families.' She smiled.

'You promised me a dance first,' David told her.

'Yes, I did. Let's go dancing.' Abby smiled.

*

A few hours later, they called Ben and Karen to announce their engagement. Karen was delighted and Ben welcomed David into the family and then joined them in driving to meet with David's parents who were equally delighted with the news. That evening they had an impromptu engagement party as Stella was home. She was delighted to have Abby as her sister-in-law the two of them were becoming friends in the short time they had been going out together. It was good to see them happy and Stella remarked just how much David had grown since he and Abby had been going out. Karen and Ben were welcomed by Rose who was delighted to have them as guests and welcomed them warmly. While Abby, David and Stella talked excitedly in the lounge room, the parents talked over supper of Rose's finest cooking, exchanging stories of their own weddings, Ben realising for the first time that Rose and Richard were actually younger than himself and Karen.

The following morning, Abby rang Lisa in England to tell her the news. Lisa only knew David and his family from a distance as they met up at the horse shows that Lisa seldom attended since leaving for university.

'I am so happy for you, congratulations.'

'Thanks, Liz; are you able to get some time off to come to our wedding? I would really love you to be there but I understand if you can't.'

'I'll make time; Abby, I am not going to miss this. You are getting married; of course I'll be there. I know I can't do much from here but if there is anything I can do or get for you please don't hesitate and I'll make sure I get back a couple of days early to spend some time before the wedding.'

'Thanks, Liz, I really appreciate it.'

'You are most welcome. A wedding, Mum will be pleased; how is Dad taking it?'

'He's a bit shell shocked; his head knows I'm old enough but his heart wants to wait a few more years.'

'I thought that may be the case.'

Karen's parents were delighted to see their granddaughter getting married with the prospect of great grandchildren in the next few years. They still lived on the property but the land itself was managed by Brendan who had brought the place next door. Fiona and Ian had known David's grandparents years ago and were very welcoming of David who delighted to meet them again.

*

They met Lisa at the airport. She looked thinner than when she left but looked confident as she walked out of customs to meet them. She immediately embraced Karen and Abby, greeting Ben with a polite kiss on the cheek and immediately saw Ben's disappointment. Karen gave her the sternest look and then held out her arms to him. Ben embraced her.

'Welcome home, Lisa,' he said.

'Thanks, Dad. It's so good to be home,' Lisa said as she felt his arms around her and remembered just how good it was to be held by him. She returned his embrace and for the first time in a long time Ben felt that he had Lisa back.

'I wouldn't have missed this. I really have missed you,' Abby told her.

'I missed you too and now you are getting married. What I want to know is how did you get David to notice you? He always seemed afraid of most women.'

'We've been friends for a few years and with the help of the right clothes and a few blunt questions, he got the message and has taken it from there.'

'So, he asked you then?'

'Only because he knew I was if he wasn't.'

'Good for you. Can I ask, are you planning to start a family straight away or are you going to wait a couple of years?'

'We are going to give ourselves a year and then yeah, sure, we want a family.'

'Well, hopefully I will back in the country on a more permanent basis by then so I can watch them grow up.'

'That would be great. Are you thinking of coming home then?'

'Yes, there are people in England who are looking for experienced expats with the intention of luring them back to help develop local talent and assist them with touring.'

'Have you spoken with them?'

'I have but there are still some things I want to do first, another year I will look at what offers are around.'

\*

Abby wore a classic gown with all the modesty and glamour of the old world for which she had known since dating David.

Lisa dropped in to see her before heading off to the church.

'Abby, you look fantastic. You are just as beautiful as I imagined you would be. It has been great growing up with you. I wanted to wish you all the happiness for the years ahead. I'm sure David is a wonderful guy and I'm looking forward to getting to know him in the future.'

'Well, you have to at least spend some time in the country to do that,' Abby replied with a sad smile.

'I have some news about that but it's not for now. This is your day; this is your time. My news can wait until you get back from honeymoon then I'll be in touch.'

'You will be in touch?'

'Of course, I will. I promise.'

\*

Ben and Karen walked into the church on either side of Abby and took her hand and placed it in David's before joining David's parents. Lisa played for them as they entered the church and later played a piece she had written for them called Lovers Hearts as they signed the register.

David stood proudly beside her and recited his vows to her with confidence as she looked at him and then recited her own. Abby was full of confidence as she recited her own vows to David in turn. With the announcement of them as man and wife, David was given permission to kiss his bride. The kiss was long and lingering, causing wolf whistles but they both waved everyone away, which caused laughter and applause from everyone in the church. When they finished, Abby turned to the congregation.

'What, you lot still here?' she said and everyone laughed. They then walked slowly out of the church, beaming and greeting everyone as they went.

Abby hugged her parents and her parents-in-law in turn, who were all delighted by how relaxed they were during the ceremony.

One of the locals was getting married and everyone had come out to see them emerge from the church. Abby waved to them and was more than happy to meet them and have her photo taken with David. There were people there she had not seen in years.

Michael, Michelle and Travis were among the guests, having shared families for years.

The reception was at the hall next door which was catered for by the local hotel and the CFA Auxiliary as a fundraiser. They pulled all the stops out, making for a wonderful reception.

Abby was radiant as she danced with David. Travis scored a dance the two of the talking and laughing. Later, she danced with Ben, the two of them enjoying the moment, sharing a few final words before handing her over to David.

'Well, Abby, you are a married woman now and a fine man your husband is too.'

'Thanks, Dad.'

'I loved and dreaded this stage of your life but I know it would come, just like our day came,' Ben told her.

Karen and Ben danced while Karen's parents watched two generations on the dance floor together. Ben had relaxed once the service was over and seemed happy enough to be up on the dance floor.

'It seems like only yesterday since our bridal dance,' Ben told her.

'It does and I remember every minute of it and I remember how lucky I felt for having the good sense to marry you.'

'I was thinking the same thing.'

'You don't have any regrets, do you, Ben?'

'No, only the time I've spent time away from you. We have two wonderful girls who are so much like their mother.'

'And they both have a good dose of you in them two; Abby especially is your daughter,' Karen told him.

*

They went to Melbourne for their honeymoon after spending two nights on the coast. One night, they ate tea where Karen and Ben had got engaged and Abby made sure of telling Karen when they returned home.

David and Abby moved into a property not far from his parents' home from where he could continue his work and study into improvements to the family properties. The house was a modest weatherboard dwelling that they quickly turned into a home. They turned into a place where they entertained and were able relax. Karen and Ben joined them for a barbeque within weeks of them setting up home, being pleased how happy Abby and David were in their own place. David's parents also dropped in, the three families enjoying the afternoon together.

Abby was still a regular visitor home, assisting Ben and Karen with a new business plan with the development of the new accommodation business. The luxury units built on new land they had acquired in the hills above the town were attracting new business to the area. Karen employed cleaners to service the units after purchasing material for units as well as employing local builders. The units soon attracted visitors to the area for extended stays. They found that the longer-term visitors were buying groceries in town and using some of the other local services including visits to some of the new wineries in the region.

It was a busy time for them as Karen assisted Ben to consolidate his tourism activities so that he could optimise his activities. The business plan spelled out what activities he would focus on and what activities would be wound up as they provided little return for the services. Only the longer tours were continued, handing over the day trips to other operators who were more than happy to take up work. He continued to work the overnight and longer tours which went further into the mountains. He preferred these tours as he was able to get to know to people who were on the tours and he got to show them the best of the country. The longer trips meant he only did half a dozen a year through the summer and autumn and was away up to five days but he occasional did longer trips upon request. One ten-day trip across into NSW proved to be a trip he really enjoyed to the point where he hosted reunions for the group each year and a number of them joined him for other tours.

*

Abby and David went on a study tour of the US and Canada, visiting a number of cattle properties in Wyoming, Utah and Colorado before heading to Calgary in Canada for the annual stampede. Both of them were excited about the trip and no one was happier for them than Ben.

'You don't regret having not travelled?' Karen asked after saying goodbye to them at the airport.

'No, I did my travelling on the trip to Queensland; I visited some amazing places on that trip.'

'But wasn't that a sad trip, given what you had left and what you were considering at the time?'

'At first it was but then I began to take in what I was seeing. The depression lifted; I knew I didn't have to be anywhere at any given time so in that sense I was free to experience the trip as I wanted to. There is some beautiful country up in the middle of New South Wales and into Queensland. I met some great people on the road and stayed in some great places.'

'I'm glad because you used to speak of that trip with such sadness.'

'They were sad times but that trip was where I put the plans together for our places. I have no regrets about that trip and some good memories mixed with the sad.'

'That's good; you saw some good places?'

'Yes, travelling that way opened some country to me that few ever see and just occasionally I met some people along the way to share them with.'

'Have you seen any since?'

'Yes, one couple stayed on the way through a year after I got back. They knew my situation and camped down by the river so that they were not drawing on my resources. They used the facilities at the shed cooked over the fire pit down then and I ate with them at the fire instead of them coming to the house. They were great days because they appreciated, I was starting over and had a lot of work to do. Barry gave me a hand fixing fences and cutting timber.'

'Have you seen them since?'

'No but they wrote a couple of times. They travelled for a few years before settling in Western Australia somewhere. I have not heard from them for years but I remember them with great fondness.' He smiled.

Abby and David returned a few months later with great stories of their trip. Karen saw a new glow about Abby and wandered then if she did not have other news to share.

Eighteen months after being married, Abby gave everyone the news that she was pregnant. Everyone was naturally delighted, even if David looked a little shell shocked. Abby was naturally delighted and it brought her and Karen even closer together. Ben embraced Abby and David as they were about to make him a grandfather, which he warmed to once he got used to the idea.

'Congratulations, Abby. How did David accept the news? Was he as happy then as he appears to be now?'

'He was a little shell shocked because we hadn't planned to start a family just yet but it turns out that one or both of us is a little more fertile than we first thought. He quickly embraced the idea and now he could not be happier.'

'And you how are you going?'

'I'm good now that I am over the same shock. It is one of those things you dream about growing up – what it's going to be like to have children of your own – but the reality of it is still a bit of a shock. We realised that hey we are married and we're going to start a family soon anyway so here we are and once I got my head around it, I've been fine. What was it like for you and Dad?'

'Much the same, only we had a little more time together before I fell pregnant with you. Once we got over the shock, we really looked forward to having both of you. It really is a wonderful experience despite the mechanics of feeding and changing a lack of sleep.'

Ben and Karen waited with David's parents for the birth of their collective first grandchild. Abby did well and was sitting up and positively glowing when they entered the room to see her and their grandson for the first time.

Ben took his turn like everyone else to nurse his grandson.

'This brings back memories of the first time I held you and he's just as beautiful,' Ben told her.

'Thanks, Grandpa.' Abby smiled in reply.

'Grandpa? When did I become old enough to become a grandpa? I want my money back.' Ben smiled.

'So do I; I'm way too young to be anybody's grandpa,' Richard said, joining in.

'Of course, you are, dear. We all are but we are not teenagers and neither are these two.'

'No, they're not. All the grandmas and grandpas are here for the three of you, day or night,' Richard replied.

'Of course,' Karen replied.

After the letting Abby and David to settle their son, the four grandparents went out for lunch and to catch up. In the time since David and Abby had been together, the four of them had developed a genuine friendship independent of their children and they enjoyed catching up.

Rose turned to Karen as they walked along the street to the café.

'Abby is glowing and looks so good. I'm really pleased to have her as my daughter-in-law. I know that David could not be happier.'

'Thank you, that is a lovely thing to say. I think we have both been fortunate in that regard.'

'Indeed, we have,' Rose replied as walked behind the men who were already discussing the land.

Stella called in a few days later just before Abby went home with Paul. Having previously called, she was looking forward to meeting her nephew at the first opportunity. Stella had been to their home on a number of occasions and the three of them had become friends with David and Stella becoming closer after a few years of drifting apart. When she held Paul for the first time, she was delighted.

'What a lovely little boy you have here. I am so happy for both of you.'

'Thank you. You now have a little nephew.'

'And intend to spoil him rotten for you.' Stella smiled.

'I think Paul is going to love having an aunty about.'

'I'm an aunty?'

'Yes, and I am a mum. Can you believe it?'

'Yes, and I'm delighted for you.'

'Thanks, Stella.'

*

From the outset, Abby was a natural mother, taking motherhood in her stride and organising her life with her baby. Paul was an alert and happy baby, full of wonder at every new thing. David proved to be great help, taking his turn to care for Paul's needs, day or night. Whenever she had the time, she visited both sets of grandparents who were more than willing to help out so that Abby and David could go out to celebrate on their own.

# CHAPTER THIRTY-SEVEN

*Lisa*

Lisa arrived home after the birth of Abby's baby with a guy she introduced as Patrick. Ben was quick to grab Patrick and take him for a tour of the property.

'So, who is Patrick?' Karen asked as Lisa looked very nervous.

'Mum, can we sit and talk?'

'Of course, what is it?'

'Mum, Patrick is not just a friend.'

'That much I have figured for myself, so what is the issue?'

'Mum, the reason Patrick is here with me is that we are here is to get married.'

'Really?'

'Yes, I know that I haven't told you anything about him but I hope that you don't mind?'

'Why would I mind? This is your future or happiness that you're talking about. Lisa, if your future is with Patrick then let us get to know him and embrace him. Now, tell me, when are you planning to marry? Have you set a date yet?'

'Mum, we are getting married in Sydney next month.'

'Next month?'

'Yes, we had to organise everything from England before we left. Everything is taken care of; all you and Dad have to do is get yourself there.'

'Why the rush and why so soon? What aren't you telling me?' Karen asked in alarm.

'We are about to tour again and this is the only time we have before we leave. We are away for three months then we are moving back here to take up positions in Sydney.'

'Then why the rush?' Karen asked as she pressed her hand.

'Because we are ready to live together and we want to make it right before we leave,' Lisa told her.

'Can I ask what caused such a turnaround? You were certainly not interested in a relationship before you left and you made clear on several occasions that you were never going to have sex with anyone. I take it you do intend to have a honeymoon and not just a holiday with Patrick?'

'Yes, but as you once said, it is different with someone you love. It was not something we planned; it just happened.'

'Are you saying you've slept with him then?'

'Yes, twice,' Lisa admitted, looking for Karen's reaction.

'Why? After all you said after you left?'

'It was a surprise to me as well. Patrick and I were sharing a house with some other musicians and had got to know each other really well. The others headed off on a Scandinavian tour for a couple of months, leaving us alone and things went from there. We shared the house for most of that time and we sat up talking most nights. One night we shared a bed it was not supposed to be more than that. We both wore fleecy pyjamas and laughed about unsexy we both looked but cuddled up under the blankets and then one thing led to another and then we just got caught up in the moment.'

'Sharing a bed? Lisa, I had more sense than that. How did you think it was going to end? What happened?'

'I know; it was not something I put a lot of thought into. In the morning, I woke up half naked so I got dressed under the covers and got out of there as quickly as I could. It was not good over breakfast until we talked. We promised each other that it would not happen again but we knew it was not a one-night stand and it was easier said than done. I made the first move the second time. I thought it was supposed to be a guy thing but it wasn't. It created a tension between us and we didn't do it again but I thought I was pregnant a few weeks later when my period was late.'

'Why did you think you were pregnant? Didn't you take precautions?'

'No, just me.'

'Lisa, I thought you were smarter than that.'

'So, did I. It's just that we both got caught up in the moment and things happened. We were fortunate that I was not pregnant at the end of it.'

'Lisa, the first time I slept with your father I was on my honeymoon. If I had fallen pregnant, it would have just meant you and Abby would have been born a few years earlier. That is what I want for you, Lisa, no regrets and you get to enjoy whatever happens.'

'I know, Mum. We talked and decided to cool things until we are married.'

'Good, you won't regret the decision to wait.'

'I know.'

'Your father doesn't need to know the details though.'

'No, of course not.'

'Good. Your father is not naive to things of the world but there are things about you girls that he doesn't need to know,' Karen told her.

'No, and it's not something that I want to discuss with him either. I'm sorry if I've disappointed you,' Lisa offered.

'I'm not disappointed, just a little concerned. You were never one to rush into anything but you seemed to rush things with Patrick.'

'Like I said, Mum, Patrick and I have known each other for a couple of years. The sex only came after spending a lot of time together.'

'Well, then, I'm happy for you.'

'Really?'

'Of course; your happiness has always been important to us. I know that your father will be delighted that you are getting married.'

'Really?' Lisa questioned with real hesitation in her voice. 'I don't want to disappoint him.'

'What is with you? You always expect Ben to be disappointed but that's not what he thinks of you.'

'Perhaps but I'm a musician, not a farmer and I'm not marrying a farmer.'

'That is not what he wants for you at all. He loves that you are living your dream, that you are a musician. You marrying a musician and setting your life down a path of your own making is going to make him very happy. He has always been happy for you to follow your own dreams and loves to hear you perform, he always has. There is no one prouder than Ben of the path you have taken.'

'Really?'

'Of course; you have no idea just how proud he is of you, we both are,' Karen told her. 'Can you explain something to me; what happened to you to stop receiving even a hug from your father?'

'It's not easy to explain.'

'Try.'

'I saw you and Dad together one day; you were having a coffee together on the verandah. I thought I was never going to have that kind of relationship with anyone.'

'Why did you ever think that?'

'I was always this scrawny ugly kid with no breasts that no one wanted. I didn't think that I could have anyone like that.'

'You thought you were ugly?'

'I know I was. I was this scrawny ugly kid and Abby was always the drop-dead gorgeous blond. I was always in her shadow.'

'That's interesting. She always felt that she was in your shadow. I have to admit you were always this tall elegant beauty who just carried herself with such grace and stature. Abby was never the gorgeous blond because she always tried to hide her figure in baggy jeans and jumpers.'

'Yeah, but you ever see her in a swimsuit?'

'Yes, but then covered in hooded tops and tracksuit pants. I can't believe you thought you were ugly. You were always stunning. The gown you wore to the school formal looked stunning on you. You were this incredibly elegant swan who just appeared to float across the room.'

'I was never like that. You are only saying that to make me feel better.'

'No, I'm saying it because others saw it too. A number of people made those exact comments. I can't think of all the compliments I got about you from that evening. A few people commented that you broke a few hearts that night.'

'I did not. I never danced with anyone and all I wanted was the night to be over.'

'But that was just it; a lot of the boys wanted to dance with you but you stuck with the girls.'

'We had made a pact not to. I didn't like many of the guys we went to school with.'

'We'll all that has changed now. You have someone you are going to marry. I hope you will accept a hug from your dad today because this is a big day for him.'

'I know and I will. I love Dad and I love what you and Dad have done for me over the years.'

'And you have clearly got over your hang-ups about sex, I hope.'

'Yes, as you say, it is different with someone you love. Getting engaged made me realise what you and Dad have.'

'Good, because I can't begin to tell you how happy he will be for you.'

'You think so?'

'Of course, it's always been his hope that you would find someone to share your life with.'

They heard Ben and David arrive a short time later.

*

'I take it you and this fine young man have some news for your dad?' Ben asked when he walked into the kitchen.

'Yes, Dad, we are getting married next month.'

'Perfect, I was afraid I was going to miss this one. Congratulations, sweetheart, I am delighted for you,' Ben said, opening his arms to her and this time she stepped into his arms and accepted his embrace.

'Welcome to the clan, it's good to have you with us,' Ben told Patrick.

'Thank you, Mr Templeton.'

'It's Ben, please, Patrick. Now, if there is anything we can do to help with the wedding, please tell us and we'll do what we can.'

'Dad, all we want is for you to both be there.'

'You know we will. Now, what do we have to do?'

'Nothing, everything has been taken care of. You will be collected from the airport and taken care of from there. There is something we would like though?'

'Name it,' Ben told her.

'We would like to come back here for the last few days of our honeymoon and stay in one of the cabins?'

'Of course, we'll make sure the main cabin is ready for you and you can stay as long as you like.'

'Thank you. We are going to spend a couple of days in Sydney and then we want to head back here for a few days.'

'Good. We'll look forward to seeing a bit of you then.'

That night, they sat down to dinner together where Karen saw the real relationship between Lisa and Patrick, the two of them laughing as they shared their experiences touring and living in London. They held hands under the table and they talked about their experiences, the two of them sharing a special friendship.

'They seem happy together,' Ben told Karen later that night.

'Yes, they seem to be. Lisa is really taken by him. What do you think of him?'

'He seems very genuine and he's a worker, I'll give him that. When he came with me, he picked up what I was doing and gave me a hand without having to ask at all,' Ben replied.

'I remember Lisa saying in her letters a couple of years ago saying he was off a farm in the Queensland Tablelands,' Karen replied.

'They've been friends for a while then?'

'Since first- or second-year uni from what I can gather.'

'Well, they seem to be friends as well as being in love.'

'I can see that,' Karen replied.

*

Patrick stayed in the guest room on the edge of the main property. Karen listened for Lisa leaving her room during the night but Lisa remained in her room all night and Patrick in his.

Karen looked at Lisa when she arrived in the kitchen shortly after Ben headed out to work.

'You were expecting some nocturnal wanderings last night?' Lisa questioned when she slipped the kettle on the stove.

'Should I have been?' Karen asked in reply.

'No, but you did, though, didn't you?' Lisa challenged.

'Yes, I'm a little concerned for you.'

'That we are only about sex?'

'That does worry me a little but then last night I also saw you two together.'

'Mum, I would never embarrass you by doing that in your home. I told you last that we have decided not to sleep together again until we are married, we are keeping to that. There is a lot more to us than sex.

Mind you, we are looking forward to it but we have been friends since we started at uni. The last few weeks we have realised that we still have that and more.'

'Good, I am happy for you, Lisa, because I thought you would only give your heart away once.'

'There has only ever been Patrick and the great thing is that I'm the only girlfriend he has ever had. We are good together, I know that. Mum, we have a lot planned in terms of touring. We'll be back here one day to teach and raise a family but that is a few years away yet.'

'I look forward to that.'

It turned out that Ben had always wanted to see parts of Sydney and Lisa was happy to act as a guide, showing her parents the Sydney she knew a few days before the wedding. Karen was surprised how relaxed Ben was as Lisa showed them around some of the places she knew and loved like her favourite café where she could expect good food and coffee. He seemed to cope with the crowds but she knew it would only be for a short period of time. They visited some of the old defence installations and toured the Rocks area visiting some of the cafés and galleries.

Lisa made sure they had places where they could have space and a bit of privacy. She found them a Bed and Breakfast in a quiet street not far from the university, which opened onto a quiet courtyard where they could sit and have breakfast or coffee as they wished. The owner was a gracious lady who welcomed them and treated them as family, which they appreciated.

On the second night in town, they went out to tea with Patrick's parents. They knew little of his parents and were interested to meet them. All they knew about them was that they were Queensland graziers who owned a number of large cropping and cattle properties around the tablelands. Patrick's older brother Ted was always going to inherit the farm so he had to make his own way in life. It appeared that his parents Joan and Philip did not entirely approve of music as a career but they accepted that it was at least classical music. Patrick had a younger sister who shared his musical talent being a concert pianist but the family expectation was that she would marry into one of the other grazing families and teach her children music. Ted was at home working and would arrive on the morning of the wedding.

The meeting and dinner proved to be a very formal affair, his parents appearing to be kept from more important things and seemed to be indulging Patrick. Karen noticed how ill at ease Patrick was in the presence of his father, sensing that he was a disappointment to his father. She felt sorry for Patrick because she knew that he would never have his approval. The only time that Patrick seemed to be at ease was when he was talking with his sister Katherine. While her parents may have expectations of her, Karen suspected that Katherine was more than happy to be making her own way in the world and had many secrets from them. She would not settle for being a grazer's wife, preferring to live a different life in Sydney where she was making a modest living as a performer and session player. While they presented a very united front, Karen just knew that they were not a close family.

The conversation at the dinner table was stilted and Ben looked increasingly uncomfortable for most of it until he seemed to have reached a point in the evening when he made some sort of decision and began to relax. Joan and Philip showed no interest in Karen and Ben or what they did; they were simply Lisa's parents nothing more.

'I very much doubt we'll ever see these people again after the wedding,' he whispered to Karen at one point.

It was when Lisa, Patrick and Katherine were together that Karen saw three soul mates with Patrick and Katherine being little like their parents having little in common. The three of them had a spark for life that Joan and Philip had lost at some point.

When Joan and Philip stood up to leave at the first opportunity, Philip held out his hand to Ben. 'It was good to meet you, Ben,' Philip said.

Ben kept his hand in his pocket.

'No, it wasn't. I know when I am being tolerated,' Ben told him, meeting his gaze, leaving Philip shocked as clearly by Ben's attitude. Karen was surprised but not shocked at Ben as he did not hold back when he felt he was being snubbed.

'I'm sorry you feel that way, Ben, but you must realise that we are busy people.'

'Busy; we are all busy on the land but these are our children and they are about to get married. There is nothing more important in the world than family. Make time,' Ben told him.

'Yes, well,' Philip said and turned his back on Ben who stood his ground.

Ben turned to see Patrick and Lisa looking at him.

'That went about as well as expected,' Katherine said.

'You got that right,' Patrick said, shrugged his shoulders and turned back to Lisa. The three of them then went back to their conversation.

'I must apologise for Ben's abruptness. He's not good at these things,' Karen offered.

'I wouldn't worry about it; it was actually good to see someone standing up to them. Don't get me wrong, my parents are decent people, they have a good marriage and they are involved all a lot of local community work but it's only ever been the three of them. It's only ever been them, Ted and the land; we often wonder why they even had more children. We've always known from a young age that the farm is Ted's and that we would have to make our own way in life. They expected Patrick to be an army officer or a solicitor, anything but a musician. I've always been expected to be the dutiful daughter who would one day marry some local farm boy and extend both agricultural empires by producing the next generation. I always felt that I was some broodmare being paraded before the stallions waiting to be mounted and bred at the appropriate time and be on call in the kitchen and the bedroom twenty-four-seven. I'm fine making my own way but I'm making my own rules too.'

'They seem almost disappointed with Patrick?' Karen suggested.

'Oh, they are disappointed; they want him to get a real job. Music is a hobby in Mother's eyes. She would much prefer to have a lawyer in the family. Dad thinks it's all drugs, sex and rock and roll but then he's only seen Patrick perform a couple of times and even that was a long time ago.'

'I would hardly call classical music rock and roll?'

'No, but he found Patrick playing an electric guitar once while he was mucking around with some friends. Patrick is far better with a violin than he is with a guitar but he can get a tune out of it. The guitar was all Dad saw and that's all he thinks Patrick is about. I don't know about sex but he has never been into drugs – classical violin is what he gets high on.'

'Marrying another musician wouldn't be helping then?'

'No, they expected him to marry one of the local brood mares and make her what they expect me to be. He doesn't want that and he's not getting that with Lisa, he loves her and he wants to travel the world with her and perform on stages across Europe and America, which they are now doing. I could not be happier for them. I'm sure they will have children one day – not to expand somebody's empire but to have a family that they can embrace and enjoy.'

'You have very strong views and clearly don't mind speaking your mind. You are a lot like Lisa's sister, Abby, in that way.'

'So, I've heard. I can't wait to meet her.'

'You know that she is married to a farmer?'

'She is but she chose him and chose the lifestyle; it was her choice and not an expectation. I don't have a problem with the choice – I have a problem with the expectation.'

'I like you; you are nothing like I expected.'

'Can I ask what you were expecting?' Katherine questioned.

'I expected you to be more like your parents.'

'I was once.'

'Can I ask what changed?'

'I went uni and got a different outlook on life. I realised then that I had choices and I didn't have to be a farmer's wife. With Patrick studying music, I followed and I want to teach once I have finished performing. Unfortunately, my parents still keep introducing me to the sons of local farms. Now most are nice enough and some are really nice but I love living in Sydney and I don't want to give that up besides I am seeing someone and who knows.'

'You know, I'm sure your parents mean well.'

'They do, it's just they have a particular view of how the world operates and they just everyone including their children to conform to that view.'

'Don't be too hard on them. They will come around.'

'I had hoped that they would change when Patrick came to the property with us but as you saw tonight, that hasn't happened yet.'

'How did that go?'

'That was when we all saw Lisa for the country girl behind the city sophistication.'

'How did you mean?'

'We went horse riding.'

'She knows her way around horses because of what Ben does.'

'I actually think she embarrassed my father,' Katherine said.

'I'm sure it was unintentional. What did she do?'

'I know it was unintentional. She was just such a natural with the horses. Dad has this horse he calls Bravado, which has always been strong-headed and he does not let too many ride him. Lisa walked up to him with a saddle and had his measurements right off. She had the saddle on him and was riding around the yard before he knew what was going on. Dad was never as good with him and Lisa, for the life of her, could not see what the big deal was about.'

'I'm not sure Lisa was ever that good with horses,' Karen questioned.

'Come on, I know what Mr Templeton does. She may play a violin but she is still his daughter.'

'That is quite a compliment, thank you.'

'It's true. She rode Bravado all day and she was right on top of him when even looked like playing up. She put him over the jumps course and he went over it better than Dad had ever been able to. Bravado seemed to enjoy having someone who called his bluff and was literally eating out of her hand by the end of the day. Dad could not understand it and asked Lisa if she was interested in training him but she wasn't interested at the time.'

'It's a pity because Lisa has trained a few show jumpers in her time. A downside of it was the last time she competed, she was beaten by a girl on a horse that she had helped train.'

'I thought she may have been good at it.'

'Lisa told us that Abby is better.'

'Not with show jumpers, she's not. Lisa has always had an eye for good show jumpers and had a knack for training them. She could easily make a living out of it.'

'I thought she could. Patrick could not take his eyes off her while she worked Bravado and she was none the wiser to what either of them was thinking.'

'So, they weren't going out together at the time?'

'No, that came later when they were in England but I thought they would get together at some point. Patrick was always interested and told me he wanted to go out with her but they were just friends at that point but good friends. They were always good together.'

'Were they?'

'Oh, yes, they are both serious about their music but they also love life and are just the best company. I think they will be good for each other.'

'Thank you. You have told me so much more about than she has ever told me. She has been reluctant to talk about too much in recent times.'

'I think she still thinks she is letting your family down by pursuing music.'

'That is simply not true. We have always supported her.'

'I can see that. Mr Templeton loves her and what she does, you both do.'

'Thank you, we do actually. Both our daughters and their partners are precious to us,' Karen told her and the two women embraced.

*

Lisa stayed in a rented apartment not far from the college and where Karen and Ben were staying so that they could walk to her apartment on the morning of the wedding. Karen went across early to be with Lisa as she got dressed and Ben was to follow later. Lisa was calm and radiant as she sat down with Lisa and Abby for coffee before lunch. The girls had kept their hair as natural as possible so there was no great rush to the hairdressers; all they needed to do was get dressed after lunch.

Ben met David for lunch at a café not far from the college. The two of them greeted each other with great warmth as Ben had come to know and like David since he got together with Abby.

'This reminds me of your wedding. Abby was quite the bride,' Ben said.

'Yes, she was. I'm the lucky man she asked out at the show that day.'

'You know it was Karen who first asked me out?' Ben told him.

'I didn't know that; we have both been lucky men.'

'How is that little boy of yours?' Ben asked.

'He's good; we'll catch up with you next week.'

'That would be good; you have a fine little boy there.'

'Thank you. We think so.'

'Abby would be pleased to see Lisa married.'

'She is, I just can't believe two sisters could be so different but so close at the same time.'

'Yes, you can say that again but they are great girls in their own ways.'

'They are, indeed. You must be proud of both of them.'

'Yes, I am and I am proud of their partners too; you are both good men.'

'Thank you. I appreciate it.'

Ben changed and walked the few blocks to meet Lisa and Karen. Lisa was dressed and waiting for him with Karen when he arrived. Karen opened the door for him so that he could see Lisa standing at the end of the room. She was as Abby had been and he was reminded of Karen with her long lean body in an elegant gown.

'So, what do you think, Dad? I don't scrub up too bad?'

'You look as you always do; you are my angel,' Ben told her and the two embraced. 'I am so very proud of you and the life you are starting with Patrick.'

'Thanks, Dad, for everything. I am living the dream, a dream that you have always encouraged me to pursue. I have not appreciated your love and support as much as I should have,' Lisa began.

'Now is not the time for regret. The thing is that we have always loved you.'

'I know that now, Dad, and I love you both very much.'

'It has been a pleasure.'

'There is one more thing I would like you to do for me.' Lisa began picking up a colourful bag from a side table. 'Could you take care of this until I have a child for you to give it to?' Lisa told him as she handed him the bag.

Ben opened it to find the dog he had given her all those years ago and attached to its collar was a tag with the words 'Dad give it me' written on it. Tears filled his eyes and Lisa looked at her.

'Thank you, Lisa. This means so much more than you can ever know.'

'Thank you. I remember the day you gave it to me.'

'I remember that every day. He was away that Ben you carried it with you.'

'It took me a long time to appreciate it.'

Lisa wore a simple full-length white gown with a small headpiece rather than a veil on top of her long dark hair. She looked like a leaner version of Karen when she was married. She stood proudly with her parents to be photographed before her wedding. Abby wore a similar dress in royal blue as her matron of honour. Both of them looked stunning. Karen was proud of both of them.

She was married on the grounds of the music academy by the university chaplain. Karen was surprised at how relaxed Ben was in Sydney for the wedding. He looked good in the metallic grey suit she had bought for him. In all the years since they had married, Ben had remained as lean as ever and he looked good in the suit. There was something about him that made her realise that he looked like he was from the country, he looked taller and more confident as he met Patrick's parents who had a change of heart since their last meeting, greeting them warmly.

The reception was in the academy gallery and café, with a small intimate group of people most from the music industry. It was a long way from a local wedding but Lisa had never really returned home once leaving for university having been back to town little since. It gave Ben and Karen an insight into Lisa's new life with people from the academy speaking of these two outstanding artists. The staff that had been invited to the wedding were pleased to meet Ben and Karen. Some showed considerable interest in Ben's work and after taking a while to warm to them he was happy to talk to them.

*

The girls were together with their husbands getting to know each other while Ben nursed his grandson on his knee.

'Look at them, Ben. Our girls have all grown up,' Karen said as she watched them talking while they cooked the meat on the barbeque.

'Yes, and it only seems like yesterday that they were like this little one.'

'Did you ever imagine your life would turn out this way?'

'Not until you came on the scene, no. You not only saved my life; you gave me a life greater than I could have imagined. We have a grandson, can you believe it?'

'I think we saved each other and built a life together in this place of ours under the trees.'

'Yes, we have and for the life of me I don't know how you stuck it out.'

'Because at the end of the day, it was you and I and that has been a pretty good place to be,' Karen told him.

# POSTSCRIPT

Travis kept in touch with the girls but always guarded his heart and would not tell anyone about his love life if he had one. His private life was just that – private, and he talked about it less than he did about his work, which was little indeed.

Stella indicated that she was seeing someone but would not commit herself to naming names or letting anyone meet him until she felt that they were serious. There were signs that things were serious when she invited him to meet her parents, David and Abby.

'Why all the secrecy?' Abby asked Rose.

'I'm really not sure but I suspect she is hooked on this guy or she wouldn't bring near the place,' Rose replied.

'So, what do you know about him?'

'Not a lot, only that he is a solicitor from Melbourne working out of an office in Moe and he owns a bit of land and a couple of horses not far from town,' Rose told her.

'Really, where did say they met?'

'She says she met at your wedding but I'm really not sure because she certainly didn't spend any time with anyone that day,' Rose told her.

'I didn't think so; I can't even remember dancing with anyone.'

'She didn't, which was strange for Stella who always loves a party.'

'Yes, perhaps someone had caught her eye that night.' Abby said.

'Yes, well, I guess we'll find out when they come for tea,' Rose said.

*

Abby could not believe it when Stella got out of the passenger's door and Travis stepped out of the driver's door.

'You have got to be kidding,' Abby said.

'What's wrong?' Rose questioned.

'No wonder they have been so coy about their relationship.'

'Do you know him?'

'Yes, he's almost family; we've known each other our whole lives.'

'Really?' Rose questioned.

'Yes, he's Dad's business partner's son.'

'Michael's son.'

'Yes.'

'That's where I've seen him.'

*

'Hello, you two. Aren't you two a surprise?'

'I'm sorry we've kept this quiet but we had to be sure before we told everyone we are together.'

'Hey, that's fine. Just how together are you two?' Abby questioned with a smile but then saw their reaction. 'It's serious, isn't it?' Abby questioned.

'Sorry, Abby. Mum, we need to talk to you and Dad.'

'Abby and David are family,' Rose told her.

'Of course, Abby, you are welcome to join us,' Stella said and reached for her hand.

'Mum, last night, Travis asked me to marry him.'

'Really?' Rose questioned.

'Yes.'

'And what did you say?' Rose asked her.

'That's what we've come here to ask you.'

'But he didn't ask me – he asked you. You need to give your answer to Travis not me,' Rose told her.

Stella looked at her mother for a moment and then at Abby.

'Would you mind?'

'He didn't ask me either,' Abby replied and then held her breath.

Stella then turned to Travis and held his hands.

'In answer to your question last night, Travis, yes, I will marry you,' she told him.

The two of them kissed.

Rose was delighted to welcome him to the family.

Abby and Travis embraced.

'Congratulations, we are finally going to be officially related.' Abby smiled.

'Yes, we are. I hope you're not disappointed?' Travis questioned.

'Disappointed? I'm over the moon. You two were the last two people I expected to get together, that's why I never tried to set you up on a blind date. So, how did you two get together?'

'We met at a function in Melbourne, mutual friends introduced us. I remembered Travis from the wedding so that gave us a starting point for an awkward conversation, I guess. I soon realised who Travis was and told him I was your sister-in-law, which made things very tentative at first but we soon got past that. We took in very slowly at first but as time went by, we realised we were us and not because of our family connections. With that out of the way, things progressed from there.'

'That's great. I'm really happy for both of you. Lisa is going to love your news,' Abby told her.

'Thank you, I can't wait to catch up with Lisa. Is she coming south any time soon?' Stella asked her.

'She will when she gets your news.'

Shawline Publishing Group Pty Ltd
www.shawlinepublishing.com.au

SHAWLINE
PUBLISHING
GROUP

Milton Keynes UK
Ingram Content Group UK Ltd.
UKHW041047200824
447137UK00010B/143

9 781923 171954